ANOTHER TIME,
ANOTHER PLACE

Recent Titles by Kitty Neale

The Candle Lane Series

A CUCKOO IN CANDLE LANE
ANOTHER TIME, ANOTHER PLACE

OUTCAST CHILD
AN EMPTY HEARTH

ANOTHER TIME, ANOTHER PLACE

Kitty Neale

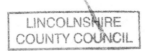
This first world edition published in Great Britain 2006 by
SEVERN HOUSE PUBLISHERS LTD of
9–15 High Street, Sutton, Surrey SM1 1DF.
This first world edition published in the USA 2006 by
SEVERN HOUSE PUBLISHERS INC of
595 Madison Avenue, New York, N.Y. 10022.

British Library Cataloguing in Publication Data

Neale, Kitty
   Another time, another place
   1.   Battersea (London, England) - Fiction
   2.   Domestic fiction
   I.   Title
   823.9'2 [F]

   ISBN-13: 978-0-7278-6381-2
   ISBN-10: 0-7278-6381-9

All Severn House titles are printed on acid-free paper.

Typeset by Palimpsest Book Production Ltd.,
Polmont, Stirlingshire, Scotland.
Printed and bound in Great Britain by
MPG Books Ltd., Bodmin, Cornwall.

This book is dedicated to the memory of my parents, George and Kathleen Underwood.

Sometimes life is like climbing a hill, but when you get to the top the view is wonderful

Anon

Also for Antonio Baidoo: Some people come into your life and touch your heart as this wonderful young man did when he was just ten years old. Recently we found each other again, and I found that despite the many years of separation, he still holds a special place.

Acknowledgements

My heartfelt thanks go to Bill and Dorothy Goodbody. Bill for sharing with me his experiences of being an amputee in the 1960s and Dorothy for patiently answering my many emails and questions. Love you both.

Author's Note

Many place and street names mentioned in the book are real. However, others and some of the topography, along with all of the characters, are just figments of my imagination.

One

Sally Jones sat on the edge of the bath, gently splashing water over her four-year-old daughter. Angela's bright red, curly hair lay in tendrils over her shoulders and she giggled, grey eyes, so like her father's, gazing up at Sally.

Angela's expression suddenly changed and, head cocked to one side, she became strangely still. 'We didn't used to bath like this in the before time.'

'Didn't we, darling? What was different?'

'We used to sit in a tin bath in front of the fire.'

Sally smiled, surprised that Angela was talking about this 'before time' again. When a precocious two-year-old, the remarks had been a common occurrence. There had been one occasion when Angela insisted that washing was done in a big tub with a poss-stick, before being put through a mangle. Another when her daughter said they used to put the iron on to the fire to make it hot. It was almost as though her daughter had lived before and was remembering a previous life, but was that possible?

Gradually though it petered out, and when questioned Angela had no memory of it. Now she was talking about the 'before time' again, and Sally gently asked, 'How do you know about tin baths?'

She picked up a handful of bubbles, gently blowing them before shrugging her shoulders. 'I dunno – I just do. Don't wash my hair, Mummy, it stings my eyes.'

Used to this nightly battle, Sally folded the flannel into a strip. 'Hold this over your eyes to keep the soap out. I'll be very careful.'

'No, Mummy!'

1

'Come on, I'll be as quick as I can,' and pouring water gently over her daughter's head she braced herself for the ensuing screams of protest. For once Angela was surprisingly pliable and, as she gently massaged shampoo into her hair, Sally wondered yet again if Angela had inherited her spiritual gifts. Other than talking about the 'before time' there had been no signs – no imaginary friends, but then again, perhaps it was too early to tell.

Over an hour later, Sally was smiling with relief. Angela was in bed, but would struggle to stay awake until her daddy came home. Arthur's favourite dinner was almost ready, and now she checked her appearance in the mirror. Her own red hair, a slightly darker shade than her daughter's, hung to her shoulders as her husband liked it, and the black dress she only wore on special occasions clung to her hips. Sally frowned. She looked pale, in fact she always looked pale, but her skin, common to redheads, refused to tan. Finding her make-up bag she applied a touch of rouge to her cheeks, and mascara to her lashes, seeing an improvement as her green eyes were emphasized. Just a smear of coral lipstick followed and then she hurried back to the kitchen.

She lifted the lid of a saucepan, stirred the gravy and, opening a bottle of Chianti, she added a dash of the red wine. Everything was ready, and surely Arthur wouldn't be late home tonight. Taking the bottle she went into the living room and after inspecting the specially laid table she poured two glasses, her ears pricked for the sound of her husband's key in the door.

Only moments later she heard the street door open, footsteps on the stairs, and with a flurry Angela ran out of her bedroom. 'Daddy!'

'Hello, sweetheart,' he said, swooping her up into his arms.

'Did you like my present?'

'Yes, it's a lovely painting, and I seem to remember telling you that this morning.'

Sally stood watching the scene, and as usual when she saw her husband, felt a frisson of pleasure. Theirs was a happy marriage, and only the fact that there hadn't been more children caused a ripple in her contentment.

2

As Angela yawned, Arthur said, 'Come on, let's get you into bed.' He threw Sally a smile, 'Back in a minute.'

Sally nodded, kissing Angela before going into the living-cum-dining-room. She checked the table again, moved the vase of flowers a fraction and then wandered over to the window, looking down at the busy road below. Their flat was over a small shop in the Wandsworth Road and, though facing the factories, they had fallen in love with the spacious rooms. It wasn't long before she heard Arthur softly closing Angela's bedroom door so, turning she picked up the glasses, holding them out in a toast as he walked into the room. 'Happy birthday, darling.'

His huge bulk seemed to fill the room and, raising a hand, he raked his fingers through his thick, dark hair before saying, 'Come here, you.'

Sally put the glasses down and flew into his arms, their kiss passionate. For a moment she melted against him. 'I've made your favourite dinner.'

'Sod the dinner,' he growled. 'You look and smell gorgeous and I've got other things on my mind.'

'Later,' she said, running from the room, shrieking with laughter when Arthur chased her.

His nose lifted as they reached the kitchen. 'Do I smell stuffed hearts? Mmm, in that case I can wait.'

'By the time you've washed and changed it'll be ready.'

'Angel fell asleep almost as soon as her head touched the pillow, and thank goodness for that,' he said, winking lewdly before leaving the room.

Sally winked back, her smile wide, pleased too that her daughter had gone back to bed without protest. Though her given name was Angela, with her wide, innocent smile, she soon became Angel to most of the family. Yet by the time she reached eighteen months old it became apparent that this was no celestial being. Spoiled by her grandparents and her father, she became adept at getting her own way. *You spoil her too*, a voice whispered at the back of Sally's mind, and she had to admit it was true. Yes, she spoiled Angel, but after the rotten childhood she'd had, she was determined that her daughter knew nothing but love.

Sally had just set the plates on the table when Arthur

returned, and she walked into his arms, sniffing the familiar smell of Brut aftershave with appreciation. He kissed her again, but then she stepped back, 'Come on, let's eat before it goes cold.'

'I'd rather eat you,' he said, taking a seat opposite her at the table.

Sally shivered at the look in his eyes, but it was a shiver of pleasure. Sexually abused by her uncle when only ten years old, she had grown up terrified of men, but Arthur had changed all that. He had made love to her so gently and tenderly, making her whole again, and now her passion matched his – a passion that hadn't abated in over four years of marriage.

She smiled now as a drop of gravy spilled on to his chin. God, he was so handsome and she was tempted to run around the table to lick it off!

'Now then, stop looking at me like that,' he laughed, reading her well.

She laughed with him, and for a while they ate in silence. Sally then rose to her feet and going to the sideboard she picked up Arthur's present, fingers crossed that he'd like it.

'Happy birthday,' she said again, placing it in front of him on the table and returning to her chair.

He swiftly opened the box, smiling when he saw the watch. 'It's great, Sally.'

'Do you really like it?'

'Yes, I do,' he said, raising his glass in a toast. 'To us, Sally.'

'No regrets, Arthur.'

'None.'

'I didn't realize how much I loved you until you met that girl and decided to emigrate to Australia.'

'If I remember rightly, you hid it well.'

'Can you blame me? She told me she was having your baby.'

'I can't believe I fell for that one. But it wasn't her who turned out to be pregnant, was it? Honestly, Sally, if I'd known that you loved me I would never have left.'

'Do you *ever* regret coming back?'

'Sally, you ask me the same question over and over again,

4

and I give you the same answer. No, of course I don't regret it. As soon as I found out you were pregnant, I couldn't wait to come back to England.'

'If you remember, you left it a bit late. I was giving birth to Angela the day you arrived.'

'How could I forget, but I married you pretty darn quick.'

'Yes, and with a special licence, three weeks after her birth.' She frowned. 'I still worry about her. When Angela grows up she'll find out she was born before our marriage. She'll carry a stigma.'

'Darling, this is the nineteen sixties and attitudes are changing. By the time Angel's an adult, I don't suppose it will matter at all.'

'I doubt that. Getting pregnant before marriage will always be frowned upon.'

Arthur rose to his feet and coming to Sally's side he lifted her from her chair with ease, his huge shoulders hardly straining. 'Stop worrying, woman. Now then,' he husked, 'it's my birthday and I think I've waited long enough.'

Sally leaned against him, her insides melting. She snaked her arms around his neck as he carried her to their bedroom and laying her on the bed he slowly began to peel off her clothes. His own followed, muscles rippling as he came to lie beside her.

Soon they were a tangle of limbs, their bodies slick with perspiration and Sally arched as Arthur entered her, saying a silent prayer, *please, let it happen this time.* They had been trying for another baby for so long, and though the doctor assured her there was nothing wrong, so far it hadn't happened.

She gave herself up to the pleasure, all thought driven from her mind as she groaned in ecstasy. Sally writhed, almost on the point of release when Arthur exploded inside her but, just at that moment, the telephone rang. 'Leave it, Sally, let it ring,' Arthur gasped as he collapsed on top of her.

Yet even as he spoke, Sally knew she couldn't. As the telephone shrilled her body had become covered in goose-bumps and she knew, without a doubt, that something awful had happened.

'I've got to answer it,' she cried, scrambling naked from the bed, and running to the hall.

'Sally,' her mother shrieked as she picked up the receiver. 'Come quick! It's yer gran. I think she's had a stroke!'

Arthur had been marvellous. While she had stood frozen, clutching the telephone receiver, he had come to her side. Gently unravelling her fingers he had taken the telephone, spoken to her mother, and then, urging her to get dressed, he had rung for a taxi. 'Go, I'll stay with Angel.'

And now here she was, sitting beside her mum on a hard bench in the hospital waiting room, both still in shock as they waited for news.

'I wish they'd get a move on, Sal,' Ruth Marchant said, her hands twisting and turning as she looked anxiously at her daughter.

'Me too.' Suddenly thinking of her mother's sister, she added, 'Did you ring Aunt Mary?'

'Yes, she's on her way.'

The door opened, a young man in a white coat entering the room. 'Are you the relatives of Mrs Sadie Greenbrook?'

'Yes, I'm her daughter, Ruth Marchant,' and flapping a hand in Sally's direction she added, 'This is her granddaughter.'

'I'm Doctor Rawlston,' he said, his eyes on Ruth. 'You can see your mother now.'

'How is she?' Ruth asked anxiously.

The young doctor's eyes showed sympathy. 'The stroke wasn't too severe, but she has lost some use in her left hand and her speech is impaired.'

'Oh, Mum,' Ruth murmured as they followed him into a small side-room.

Sally saw the gaunt face on the pillow and felt her stomach twist. She tried, but with tears filling her eyes she was unable to focus on her gran's aura. God, what good was her gift now? A gift she'd had since childhood that had remained undeveloped until Arthur's mother had taken her under her wing. Elsie was a psychic, and instantly saw that Sally had healing powers so had offered to help. With Elsie teaching her, Sally began to understand the meaning of the auras she'd always seen surrounding people, learning to recognize that dark areas signified illness and pain. She'd been able to ease her gran's arthritis, but now, as she ran forward to grasp the old lady's hand, Sally felt helpless, useless, a stroke beyond her healing abilities.

There was an unintelligible gurgle, Sadie looking agitated as she tried to speak.

'My God,' Ruth gasped, hovering anxiously at the other side of the bed.

Once again Sadie tried to formulate words, her eyes frantic with distress.

'Can't you do something?' Sally cried as she turned to the doctor.

'We are doing all we can.'

A nurse poked her head around the door. 'Doctor Rawlston, there's a lady asking to see Mrs Greenbrook.'

'That'll be my sister,' Ruth said.

'Very well, she can come in, but only for a few minutes then you must all leave.'

Mary came in, looking immaculate as usual, but seeing Sadie, her usually upright and dignified stance collapsed. 'Oh, no,' she cried.

The doctor left them, and as the three women stood looking down on Sadie, she flapped her hand. 'It's all right, Mother, don't try to speak, just rest,' Mary urged.

Sadie Greenbrook shook her head, her good arm now waving, and once again feeling helpless, the tears rolled down Sally's cheeks. Her gran was short and tubby, but despite her diminutive height she had always been strong, wise and a tower of strength. Now, lying against the white pillows she looked grey, shrunken, a shadow of her former self.

Sally sank on to the side of the bed, and suddenly felt a hand on her face. With her good arm, Gran was trying to stroke away her tears. A strangled sound then escaped her lips and Sally wondered if she was imagining things. Had her gran said, 'Don't cry'?

'I'm afraid you must leave now,' the nurse said as she came into the room.

Sally stood up, leaning over to kiss her gran's cheek, feeling skin like soft leather beneath her lips.

Ruth and Mary did the same, Ruth saying, 'You'll be all right, Mum. We'll be up again to see you in the morning.'

7

They all looked devastated, Mary putting an arm around Sally as they left the hospital. 'Don't cry, my dear. My mother is a strong woman, and I'm sure she'll get better.'

'Do you think so?' Sally asked, grasping at her aunt's words.

'Of course. Now come on, I'll run you both home.'

It was quiet in the car as they drove back to Battersea, each with their own thoughts. Sally's mind was on the past. As a child her father couldn't stand the sight of her, so much so that she was forced to stay in her bedroom whenever he was in. She had been deeply unhappy, never understanding why he didn't love her, but then her life changed dramatically when he went off with another woman. Sally frowned, remembering her mother's emotional breakdown, but then Gran came to live with them and her world became one of happiness. Her mother had had to work to support them, Gran becoming like a second mother, and she enjoyed a freedom she had never known before. Tears welled in her eyes. Oh, she loved Gran so much. She's got to get better, she's just got to, Sally agonized, unable to imagine her life without Gran in it. She closed her eyes in silent prayer. *Please, God, please don't let her die!*

Two

Two weeks passed, weeks of agonizing worry, but slowly Sadie began to recover. She had regained some use in her arm, and could speak again, though her words were slurred. She was agitated a lot of the time, her eyes showing anger, but the doctor seemed pleased with her progress.

Sally was waiting for Arthur to come home so she could go to the hospital and was relieved when she heard him coming upstairs. Angela was still awake, and hearing her father's voice she scampered out of her room. 'Daddy!'

Arthur swept her up into his arms. 'Hello, princess,' he said, hugging her to him.

'Mary will be here in a minute to run me to the hospital,' Sally said. 'I've left you a salad in the fridge.'

'All right, love. I'll get this little madam to bed first.'

'Read me a story,' Angela demanded.

'Yes, your majesty,' he said, raising his hand in a mock salute.

'I saw Granny Elsie today.'

'Did you now – and I bet she was pleased to see you.'

'Yes, and she gave me sweeties.'

Sally smiled as she watched the scene. She had been ten years old when Elsie and her family had moved to Candle Lane and had vivid memories of seeing Arthur and Ann tumbling out of a removals van. Ann had been ten years old too and they had become fast friends.

'You're miles away, love.'

'I was just thinking about your sister. I miss her since she got married and moved to Milton Keynes.'

The bell rang, and hurriedly giving both Arthur and her daughter a quick kiss, Sally ran downstairs.

'Hello,' she said, climbing into the car.

Mary smiled. 'I would have popped upstairs to see Angela, but we're running a little late. Perhaps next time. Tell me, how is the little minx?'

'She's fine, and twisting Arthur around her little finger as usual.'

'Well, she is adorable,' Mary murmured as they drove down Wandsworth Road before turning into Long Street.

In no time they reached Candle Lane and as they drew into the kerb, one of the neighbours, Nelly Cox, came bustling up. 'How's Sadie?' she asked.

Sally smiled at the tubby old woman, but then frowned worriedly. Nelly looked dreadful, her clothes dirty and creased. She had been devastated when her husband died some years ago and still hadn't got over the loss. He'd had a terminal illness, and Sally always felt guilty that she couldn't do more for the man, her spiritual healing only able to ease his pain. Pushing away her sad thoughts, she answered the old lady's question. 'Gran's improving, Nelly.'

'That's good, and give her my love. I hope she'll be home soon 'cos the lane ain't the same without her.'

'It's about time you got here,' Ruth complained as she rushed out of the house, calling a quick hello to Nelly as she clambered into the car.

'I got held up at work, but we're only ten minutes late.'

'Hello, Mum,' Sally said, thankful that her Aunt Mary had a car. It would have taken a lot longer to get to the hospital by bus, but her mother had failed to appreciate this.

'The doctor said that Mum should be able to come home next week.'

'Did he? Goodness, that's sooner than I expected,' Mary said.

'She's made a good recovery, though her arm is still weak.'

Sally, feeling that her prayers had been answered, felt a surge of joy. Gran would be home soon and things would be back to normal, their lives going on as before. This illusion was shattered when her mother spoke again.

'We'll have to have a powwow soon.'

'Will we?'

'Mum can't be left on her own. I have to work, so we need to get something sorted out.'

10

Mary bristled. 'I work too. You'll just have to stay home and claim National Assistance.'

'No, I ain't doing that!'

'Don't be silly, Ruth. It's the only way.'

'I'm not being silly! When my husband left me, you know I raised Sally on my own. I never went round with a begging bowl, and I ain't about to start now.'

'That's just stubborn pride.'

'No it ain't. Anyway, why should it all fall to me? She's *your* mother too.'

Mary sighed heavily. 'Ruth, I'm not in the position to help and you know that. The only answer is for Mother to go into a nursing home.'

Sally had sat quietly through this whole conversation, but now she stiffened. 'No, don't say that. I can look after Gran. I'll come round every day and as Arthur doesn't usually arrive home until after seven, I can still be home in time to cook his dinner.'

They drew into the hospital car park, and as they climbed out of the car Sally saw the thoughtful look on her mother's face. 'It could be a solution, but it depends on what Arthur has to say about it.'

'Sally, don't be ridiculous,' Mary said. 'You're a young woman and can't be expected to spend all your time nursing our mother.'

'I don't mind. I love Gran, and as a child she looked after me when Mum was at work. Now I can do the same for her.'

'Ruth, tell her she can't possibly take this on.'

'She's offered, and anyway, it won't be that bad. Mum won't need nursing. She just needs someone to be with her during the day.'

Ruth glared at her sister, and fearing a row would develop, Sally said hastily, 'Come on, let's go or visiting time will be over.' Yet as she walked across the car park her fingers were crossed. She had said that Arthur wouldn't mind her going to Candle Lane every day, and prayed she was right.

Sally arrived home intending to tell Arthur that she'd volunteered to look after her gran, but seeing the expression on his face she knew immediately that something was wrong.

'What is it? Is Angel all right?'

'She's fine, but sit down, I've got something to tell you,' and as Sally took a seat beside him on the sofa he took her hand. 'Mr Brooks came up to see me soon after you left. He's sold the shop, along with this upstairs flat. The new owners want to live here and we've been given notice to quit.'

'Leave! Leave here? Oh no!'

'I'm afraid so, darling, but listen, I've got some good news. We've enough saved for a large deposit on a house and I can't see a problem with getting a mortgage. Instead of renting again, we can buy our place, Sally.'

'Our own house,' she said, eyes wide with amazement. Arthur worked with his father in the family removals business and earned a good wage. She had never had to worry about money, Arthur giving her plenty of housekeeping each week, but had never dreamed they could afford a place of their own.

'We can get out of this rotten area, Sally. I'll go to a few estate agents tomorrow to get some details. I rather fancy living in Richmond.'

'We can't move that far away,' she said, and taking a deep breath she told him why, ending with, 'We'll need to buy a house in Battersea, and preferably close to Candle Lane.'

Arthur's face darkened. 'No, I want my daughter out of this stinking area. I want Angela to breathe clean air instead of the polluted muck that taints this part of London.'

'What about my gran? She can't be left on her own, Arthur!'

He stood up and began to pace the room. 'When is she coming out of hospital?'

'In a week's time.'

'If it will make you feel better you can look after your gran for a while. It'll probably take us some time to find just the right house, and then there's the survey and legal stuff to sort out. In fact, it could be months before we're in a position to move in. Surely your gran will be fully recovered by then.'

'Yes, of course she will,' Sally said, feeling a surge of relief, but was then struck by another thought. 'Arthur, when have we got to move out of here?'

'In a fortnight.'

'But until we find a house we'll have nowhere to live.'

'My mother's got plenty of room and we can always put our furniture into storage.'

'But that would mean I'd have to travel from Wimbledon every day, dragging Angela on and off buses. Surely it would make more sense to move in with *my* mother.'

He scowled, obviously not liking her suggestion. 'Christ, Sally, you should have kept up the driving lessons.'

'I can see that now, but I hated driving.'

Arthur now managed a faint smile. 'All right, we'll move in with your mother, but thank the Lord it won't be for long.'

Three

Four months, Sally thought. Four months they had been in Candle Lane, and only her love for Gran kept her going. She had changed so much since her stroke, and was like a different woman. Most of the time she was bad-tempered, belligerent and moody, yet on the odd occasion her former personality shone through, making looking after her at least bearable.

Yet it was Arthur who was worrying her the most. They now slept in the double room with Angel in a small bed alongside them, and she knew Arthur hated living here – hated the lack of privacy. With their daughter sleeping in the same room, sex had become non-existent and she could sense her husband's impatience with the situation.

Yet how could they leave? Sally had studied her gran's aura and though unable to see any darkness other than her arthritis, she had a bad feeling. Gran was still unwell, she was sure of it, despite the old woman's protests to the contrary. She had to be here to keep an eye on her, or living close by, yet Arthur still refused to buy a house in this area. She loved him so much, but why did he have to be so stubborn? What was wrong with staying in Battersea? Candle Lane might not be up to much, but there were nicer streets where they could find a decent house.

Sally went to the street door to check on Angel. The poor child was feeling it too; Gran was often snappy with her, and being cooped up in the kitchen all day wasn't much fun. Though unhappy about it, she'd allowed Angel to play outside, but now her eyes roamed up and down the lane. Where was her daughter? She'd told Angel not to leave the front of the house, but a lot of good that had done. She saw Nelly's neighbour, Maureen Downy, and called, 'Have you seen my daughter?'

14

'She was outside your place a few minutes ago.'

Jessie Stone was standing on her step, her sharp ears pricked. She was a terrible gossip and, like Nelly Cox, Sally had no time for the woman. She stiffened as she spoke.

'If you ask me she's a bit young to be playing in the street.'

Sally bit back an angry retort as she saw Angel flying round the corner, her curly hair bouncing on her shoulders in wild profusion, free of the plaits that Sally had so carefully arranged. Aunt Mary would be arriving soon and she wanted to make sure that Angel looked clean and tidy.

Tommy Walters and his gang were a few steps behind but, as Angel skidded to a halt in front of her mother, they veered off, running to the other side of the lane. Tommy lived next door, and though only seven years old, he was a little hooligan, running wild on the streets.

'Are yer coming out later?' Tommy shouted, his dark auburn hair standing up like a brush.

'Nah, me auntie's coming so I've gotta stay in.'

Sally stared at her daughter in despair. Her freckled face was dirty, her dress smeared with mud, and socks, clean on less than an hour ago, were hanging baggily around her ankles. 'Oh, Angela, your dress is filthy.'

'I don't like dresses. Why can't I wear trousers all the time?'

'You're a little girl, not a boy, and how many times have I told you not to run with that gang?'

'But I like Tommy.'

'He's nothing but trouble. Anyway, I told you not to wander off.'

'But we was playing tag.'

'That's no excuse. Wait till your father comes home and we'll see what he has to say about it.'

'Daddy won't mind,' she said confidently.

Sally sighed. Yes, Arthur would probably side with his daughter, he always did, and she could do no wrong in his eyes. Since moving back to Candle Lane, Angela was becoming impossible. She tried unsuccessfully to discipline the child, but with the rest of her family giving in to Angel's every demand, she was fighting a losing battle.

'Goodness, there's Aunt Mary now. Quick, let's get you washed,' Sally urged as she hustled her daughter into the kitchen.

'Mary's here, Gran,' she gasped, grabbing a damp sponge, and a quick lick was all Angel got before her aunt marched unceremoniously into the house.

'What on earth has that child been doing?' were Mary Taylor's first words. 'She looks like she's been rolling in mud.'

'She's been playing outside.'

'Angela is rather young to be allowed that. You should keep her in.'

'I can't keep her cooped up in this kitchen and she wanted to try out her new skipping rope.'

'The child wouldn't have got in such a state if she was only skipping. It's about time you took her in hand.'

'I do my best,' Sally said, her teeth clenched. She loved her Aunt Mary, but sometimes her hoity-toity ways were difficult to cope with.

Mary pursed her lips but thankfully said no more. She looked immaculate as usual, her perm tight without a curl out of place. Sally shivered. Though she usually avoided thinking about him, the face of Aunt Mary's husband swam into her mind. He was dead now, but as a child he'd been the only man who showed her any affection and she always made a bee line for him when visiting Aunt Mary. With a shudder she fought off the memory of how his cuddles had turned to sexual abuse.

'Come here, darling,' Mary said, smiling as her eyes again alighted on Angel. She then reached into her handbag, pulling out a packet of Spangles. 'Here you are. I know they're your favourite.'

'Fanks, Auntie.'

'The word is *thanks*. Now, say it again.'

'No,' Angel scowled.

'Sally, you shouldn't allow her to be so cheeky,' Mary said, sighing heavily. 'And you really *must* do something about her diction.'

Sally grimaced. Yes, her daughter was cheeky, but how was she supposed to tackle the way she spoke? Gran, along with her mother, and everyone else in Candle Lane spoke in the same way, and since moving back Angel was like a parrot, soaking it all up. Like her aunt, Sally had improved her own speech, but with Angel it had become an impossible task.

'Give over, Mary. The child is fine as she is.'

Sally threw her gran a grateful smile, then sitting Angel down she again tried to brush her unruly locks. God, it was like trying to pull a comb through a mop

'Ouch! Ouch! Stop it. Tell her, Gamma.'

'It's not gamma. It's grandmother,' Mary admonished.

'For Gawd's sake leave the kid alone. I've been gamma since she first started to talk, and anyway, I rather like it.'

Pleased that Gran was sounding more like her old self, and giving up with the brush, Sally said, 'There, that'll do, Angel.'

With the grace of a gazelle the child jumped to her feet, her eyes wide in appeal. 'Mummy, can I go out to play again?'

'No, darling. Daddy may be home soon and it's time for your bath.'

'Let her go out for a while, Sally.'

'No, Gran. I can't give in to her all the time.'

'Well, that'll make a change.'

Sally had to smile. Yes, this was one of the occasions when her gran's old character and humour shone through, and oh, how she wished it would last.

Angel begged to go out again, her voice wheedling, and suddenly Sadie scowled. 'For Gawd's sake shut that kid up. She's giving me a headache.'

Sally closed her eyes. Gran's good humour had been short and sweet. She took her daughter's hand, dragging her kicking and screaming to the bathroom.

'How are you, Mother?' Mary asked as soon as the noise had abated.

'I'm fine. Why shouldn't I be?'

'I only asked, and I'm glad you have Sally here to keep an eye on you. I'd hate for you to be on your own like poor Nelly Cox.'

'Nelly ain't been the same since she lost her husband, but she's a good sort and often pops in to see me. Sally checks on her now and then, and has done since George Cox died. And talking about Sally, I'm worried about her.'

'Why? Is she ill?'

'No, but it ain't right that she has to stay here to look after me. She and Arthur should be in their own place, and I've noticed that he's away from home more and more these days.'

'The firm is busy and they've just expanded again.'

'I know, but I can feel it in me water that something is wrong with their marriage.'

'Rubbish! Arthur adores Sally.'

'Yeah, maybe, but things don't seem the same since they moved back here.'

'I'm sure you're just imagining things.'

'Imagining what?'

Both women looked around as Ruth spoke. She had just arrived home from work, and as Mary studied her younger sister she saw a face drawn with tiredness. Ruth's short brown hair was lacklustre and her complexion pasty. 'You look washed out, my dear. Are you all right?'

'Yeah, I'm fine, but with a new manager coming we're doing a stocktake and it's a lot of extra work. Now, tell me, what is Mum imagining?'

'Oh, nothing really, she's just a bit concerned about Sally and Arthur.'

'Concerned . . . why?'

'I'll let Mum tell you while I make a cup of tea. You look like you could do with one.'

With a sigh of bliss, Ruth sank thankfully on to a chair, pushing off her shoes before fishing a packet of Embassy out of her cardigan pocket. It was only after lighting the cigarette and blowing a cloud of smoke into the air that she spoke, 'Right, Mum, what's this about Sally and Arthur?'

'I'm just worried that they're drifting apart, that's all.'

'Of course they aren't. I know Arthur's away a lot, but with the firm being so busy, Sally understands.'

'They should be out of here and in a place of their own.'

'Maybe, but Sally doesn't mind staying with us until you've recovered.'

'I'm fine now.'

'Well, tell Sally that.'

'I have, but she won't listen, and she's forever looking at me aura. As a kid Sally used to say she was looking at our lights. Do you remember, Ruth?'

'Yes,' she murmured before turning away, her eyes veiled. She'd been against her daughter developing these spiritual gifts, but had to admit that she was marvellous at healing. It had been Elsie who had swayed her decision. When she'd voiced her concerns that the church was against things like clairvoyance, Elsie had spoken of her own philosophy. She said that as far as she was concerned, Jesus had spiritual powers, and said that anything He could do, we could do also. They were God given gifts, she said, so how can the church say it's wrong to use them? By doing so they were saying that God made a mistake in giving them to us.

Ruth sighed, thinking that Elsie made a lot of sense. Sally had the natural ability to ease people's pain, and it would have been a sin to waste such a gift. If Sally sensed that her gran was still unwell, she'd stay to look after her until it was safe to leave.

'Talking about lights,' Sadie said, 'seeing you smoking that fag, I could do with a pinch of snuff.'

Mary turned swiftly, the teapot poised in her hand. 'Mother! Surely you're not thinking of using that disgusting stuff again!'

'It's all right for you, miss goody two shoes, but I miss me snuff.'

'It isn't good for you, especially now you've had a stroke.'

'Don't nag, Mary. I just said I fancied some, that's all.'

There was a shout, footsteps running down the stairs and, as Angel scampered into the room, she dived into Ruth's arms. 'Nanny, Nanny, got sweeties for me?'

'I might 'ave.'

Angel giggled as she settled on Ruth's lap, enjoying the nightly game. 'What did you get me?'

'Let me see. It might be a sherbet fountain, or maybe a gob-stopper and you could do with one of those,' she said, chuckling at her own joke. 'On the other hand it could be some black jacks or penny chews. You'll 'ave to guess.'

'I've already given her a packet of Spangles, Ruth.'

'Oh, is that right,' she said. 'Now then, Angel, if you've already had sweets from Auntie Mary, I'll save mine for tomorrow.'

'No, Nanny. I want them now!'

Ruth moved Angel from her lap, and when the child was standing she gave her a small pat on the bottom. 'You'll get them tomorrow, madam. Now off you go. Mummy's calling you, and I'm not surprised. It's not nice to run around in your birthday suit. Go and get your nightdress on.'

'Sweeties later?'

'We'll see. Now scat!'

With a giggle Angel ran off, and as her little white bottom disappeared, Mary said, 'I hope you're not going to give in to her as usual. One packet of sweets is quite enough and I hate to think what all this sugar is doing to her teeth.'

'Oh, and Spangles are sugarless are they?'

'Touché! Yes, I suppose I'm as bad as the rest of you, but she is irresistible.'

It was quiet for a while as Mary poured the tea. Just as she finished the door opened again and Arthur came into the kitchen.

'Hello, love, you're early,' Ruth said.

'Yes, it was a family moving to Farnham in Surrey today and they didn't have a lot of furniture. Farnham's a lovely little town and I wouldn't mind living there,' he mused, his voice sounding wistful. 'Still, it's nice to get home before seven for a change. Where's Sally?'

'She's upstairs getting Angel ready for bed. Mary's made a pot of tea so you're just in time.'

'Great,' and drawing out a chair he sat down. 'Mum said to tell you she'll be down to see you on Tuesday.'

'Oh, luverly. I still miss your family living next door. Elsie was the best neighbour we ever had, and that lot who moved in six months ago are nothing but trouble.'

'I agree the Walters are a rough lot, but they've only one child so it could be worse.'

'Yeah, but Tommy's a little bugger,' Sadie said. 'Still, at least they're white so I suppose we should count our blessing. We've got West Indians in two houses now and it's getting like the bleedin' jungle round here.'

Mary stomped across the room, her face grim. 'Mother, don't talk about them like that! I can't believe you're so prejudiced.'

'Here we go again, the same old record. Now you listen to me, Mary. Before the 1961 Immigration Act we hardly saw a coloured man in Battersea. I can remember dads telling their kids they'd get a penny for every black man they saw, and they didn't get many I can tell you. Since the immigration act they've flooded in by the thousands, and nowadays kids round here could make a fortune in pennies. And not only that, they're taking our men's jobs and it ain't right.'

'Don't be silly, Mum. The jobs they're doing are ones that employers couldn't fill. They work on the railways, the buses, and in hospitals amongst other things. Our national health and public transport system would grind to a halt without them!'

'Poppycock! Anyway they ain't like us and should go back to where they came from.'

'They came here because our government encouraged companies to recruit them with promises of well paid work. You seem to forget that they're British, and many of the men fought alongside our soldiers during the war.'

'They ain't British!'

'Yes they are, and have British passports. For goodness' sake, they're just people with a different skin colour . . . that's all. They have the same feelings as us, the same dreams, and aspirations. You should listen to yourself. Hitler's prejudice killed millions of Jews, and it sounds like you're adopting his ideals!'

'How dare you say that!'

'Because it's true. Maybe you should think about joining the organized racists.

'Well, someone's got to do something. I reckon Mosley had the right idea.'

'As long as people think like you, Mum, things will never change.'

'I've got a right to my opinions.'

'Yes, but maybe you should keep them to yourself. I don't think it's right that my niece should hear your racial hatred.'

'Come on, you two, calm down,' Arthur cajoled.

21

'I am calm,' Mary said, her expression belying her words. 'But what about you, Arthur? Are you happy for Angela to hear my mother's claptrap?'

He slowly shook his head. 'No, I'm not happy about it, but if she doesn't hear it from Sadie, she'll hear it as soon as she goes to school. In fact it's everywhere.'

'And are you of the same opinion as my mother?'

'No, of course not. I hate the things Mosley stood for, and I think you'll find that the majority of working class people hate his ideals too. Yes, there are those who still follow the man, but these are just ignorant louts who can't think for themselves. Now, if you'll excuse me I'll go upstairs to see my daughter before she falls asleep. I've had just about enough of this conversation.'

On that abrupt note Arthur stomped from the room, leaving the women staring after him open-mouthed. 'Blimey!' Sadie said. 'We certainly ruffled his feathers.'

'*We* ruffled his feathers! No, it was you, Mum,' Ruth said, speaking for the first time since the argument started.

'Yes,' Mary agreed. 'And every time I come to see you, Mum, it's to hear the same old rubbish. Like me, I think Arthur is sick of it. It's almost becoming an obsession with you – and what next? Will you be hanging the Black Shirts flag out of the window?'

'Don't be ridiculous, and show me some respect – after all, I am your mother.'

'Mum,' Mary said, heaving a sigh, 'you have to earn respect. We've always looked up to you, come to you with our problems, and listened to your words of wisdom. But since those two West Indian families moved into Candle Lane you've changed, and nowadays you just sound like a bigot. And I'll say it again – I'm ashamed of you.'

'Watch your mouth, my girl, and show some respect. Anyway what've you got to be so high and mighty about? You're no better than the rest of us, despite talking as though you've got a plum in yer mouth. As for calling me a bigot, well, I ain't standing for that and I've had just about enough of your sanctimon-ious preaching. Now get out of my house, you cheeky bitch!'

'Don't worry I'm going, and you seem to forget that this

is *Ruth's* house – *not yours*,' Mary cried, ignoring her sister's shout as she snatched up her bag before slamming out of the door.

As Mary marched down Candle Lane, her shoulders were stiff, but by the time she reached the corner they were slumped in despair. She shouldn't have lost her temper, yet the things her mother said made her blood boil. *Oh, what am I going to do*, she cried inwardly. *I've got to tell her, and soon*, but she dreaded her mother's reaction.

Four

'Daddy,' Angel cried as she bounced on the bed, and bobbing along the mattress to reach him, her foot became caught in the hem of her nightdress. Unbalanced, she squealed with delight when her father swooped her up into his arms, averting a fall.

His face soft, Arthur planted a kiss on his daughter's cheek. 'You silly sausage, you could have hurt yourself. Now tell me, have you been a good girl today?'

'Yes, I've been good . . . ain't I, Mummy?'

Sally raised her eyes heavenward. 'Other than running with Tommy Walters again, I suppose so.'

'I thought Mummy told you to stay away from that boy.'

Angel hung her head, but then eyes, wide with innocence, rose to meet her father's. 'I didn't mean to play with him, but he asked me to and it would've been rude to say no, wouldn't it?'

Arthur laughed, his arms tightening around his daughter. 'Well, don't do it again. If he asks you to play, just tell him that you're not allowed.'

'Awright, Daddy.'

'Good girl. Now come on – into bed and I'll tuck you in.'

'No, I don't want to go to bed yet. Pleeeease, Daddy.'

'All right, you can stay up for fifteen minutes. Come on, I'll take you downstairs.'

'Arthur!' Sally's voice was sharp.

'I haven't seen Angel all day. Fifteen minutes won't hurt.'

Sally was left looking at her husband's back as he strode from the room, and she sighed. In August they had celebrated Angel's fifth birthday, and the child had been showered with presents. Now though it was the first week in September and on Monday Angel would be going to school for the first time. She would have to get used to early nights, but now, playing with her father, she would become overexcited and it would take hours to calm her down.

'Where's Aunt Mary?' Sally asked as they went into the kitchen.

'She's gone, and good riddance too,' Sadie snapped. 'I dunno who she thinks she is.'

'You cross, Gamma?'

Angel was still perched in Arthur's arms and as Sadie looked up at her granddaughter she smiled wanly. 'Nah, I'm all right, ducks. Come and give me a cuddle.'

Arthur lowered Angel to the floor and she scampered across to Sadie and gave her a quick hug before rushing back to her father. 'Play horses, Daddy,' she appealed.

'Not tonight, princess, I'm afraid my back's playing me up. Go and get a book and I'll read to you.'

Sally smiled at her gran, pleased that she had been nice to Angel. When her daughter returned with a book she climbed up on to Arthur's lap, and Sally heaved a sigh of relief. No rough games – no hysterical giggles, just listening to a story, and with any luck Angel would fall asleep.

As soon as the child was settled – thumb in her mouth as she listened to Arthur's soft voice – Sally went to find her mother. The front room had been turned into a bedroom for Gran many years ago, and it was here that she found her. 'Are you all right, Mum?'

'I just wanted a bit of peace and quiet for a while. Sometimes when your gran gets on her high horse it drives me mad. Since her stroke she's changed, and she seems to think this is *her* house. It isn't, Sally, it's mine, yet she doesn't seem to remember that now.'

'I know, Mum, but she gets confused. I've been reading up about strokes and they're caused by a clot of blood touching the brain. It explains her personality change and we must make allowances for her.'

'Tell me the truth, Sally. How is she?'

'Her aura doesn't look too bad, but her arm is still weak.'

'She was in fine fettle when she was arguing with Mary.'

'Maybe, but it can't be good for her to get in such a temper. We really should try not to upset her.'

'It wasn't me! I hardly said a word, but Mary really got out of her pram.'

'Can you blame her? Working in a doctor's surgery she comes into contact with many immigrants, and from what she's told me they seem to be having a rough time of it. Can you imagine what it must be like for them to face racial hatred every day?'

'There's no need to preach to me. Live and let live, that's what I say. Still, if Mum shouldn't get upset, I'd better have a word with Mary. I'll tell her not to argue with her again, even if she does start spouting racial hatred.'

'Good idea. Now are you coming back to the kitchen?'

'In a minute, love. Did I hear Angel just now?'

'Yes, Arthur brought her downstairs again.'

'It won't hurt for her to stay up for a little while.'

'She'll have to be in bed by seven when she starts school.'

'Yeah, and I feel sorry for her teacher. I wonder how she's going to cope with our little firebrand? Anyway, give me a call before you take her upstairs and I'll come to give her a kiss goodnight.'

'I'll do that, but are you sure you're all right?'

'You should know, Sal. Haven't you looked at me aura thing?'

'Of course I have and it looks fine, but you seem a bit down in the dumps.'

'I'm just tired, that's all. With Mr Wilson leaving we're getting a new boss and I can't say I'm looking forward to it. Old Wilson may be a grumpy old sod at times, but we've rubbed along fine for years. As the saying goes, better the devil you know. Go on back to the kitchen and let me stew in my own juice for a while.'

'I don't like leaving you like this.'

'For goodness sake will you bugger off! Is it too much to ask that I get a bit of peace in me own home?'

Sally's brow was creased as she left the room. She hadn't seen anything wrong in her mother's aura, but she seemed really down. Was it really that her boss was leaving – or was there more to it?

Ruth heard the door as it closed behind her daughter and stepping forward she stared disconsolately out of the window.

26

She was feeling depressed, lonely, but memories of the past always held her back from seeking another relationship. Her marriage had been a disaster, and remembering the way Ken had treated Sally, she was still swamped with guilt. He had been away during the Second World War, and with no news of him for ages she feared he'd been killed in action. It was a moment of madness that led her to meet another man, an affair that left her pregnant with Sally.

Ken survived the war and, when he finally came home, he had begged her to stay with him, promising to bring the baby up as his own. How could she have known that it would all go wrong? When Sally was born with bright red hair, Ken hated her on sight. Instead of bringing Sally up as his own child, he saw her as a constant reminder of the affair, sure that nobody would believe she was his.

Ken changed so much, and fearing his violence she had kept Sally out of his way. God, why had she put up with it? Why hadn't she put her daughter first? Instead she'd been a selfish mother, keeping Sally confined to her room when Ken was around. When the marriage broke up, her mother moved in, and she had watched the growing closeness between Sally and her gran, sometimes resenting it, yet knowing it was no more than she deserved.

Ruth swung away from the window. When Sally had eventually found out that Ken wasn't her father the questions had begun. She wanted to know about her *real* father, but able to tell her little, Ruth knew that Sally wouldn't be able to find him. Andrew had been a married man, with a young son, and had no idea that she had given birth to his daughter.

Her shoulders hunched over. No, she didn't want Sally to find her father. As far as she was concerned it was best left in. the past, but why oh why did the memories continue to haunt her?

Arthur smiled at his daughter, already asleep in his arms and, putting his fingers to his lips as Sadie was about to speak, he carefully stood up.

He carried Angel upstairs, laid her on the bed, and gently tucked her in. For a while he gazed at her innocent face, and then looked around the cramped space. She should be in her own room again, not crammed in here with them, and with a sad smile he remembered the lovely bedroom his daughter used to have, one that he'd so lovingly decorated in pink and white.

His thoughts turned to Sally. Arthur sunk on to the side of their bed as he wondered what was happening to their marriage. When he agreed to come back to Candle Lane it was only supposed to be for a short while. Huh, so much for that plan.

After two months of searching he'd found a house in Richmond, a bit pricey, but the firm was doing well and he could afford the mortgage. But no, Sally stubbornly refused to leave. Her gran was too ill, she insisted, and her mother couldn't cope if she had another stroke. Why not look for a place in Battersea, she'd suggested yet again, close enough for her to stay with Gran during the day. He wasn't having that, and as far as he could see, Sally was overreacting. Sadie looked all right and, though testy at times, she was sounding more like her old self. He still wanted a place in Richmond or the surrounding areas, where Angel could breathe clean fresh air in wide-open spaces.

Four bloody months they'd been here! Well he'd had enough, and that was something Sally would soon find out. They needed to get out of here and he wouldn't beg anymore; instead, one day soon, he'd give his wife an ultimatum.

'Is Angel asleep?' Sally whispered as she came into the room.

He nodded, 'Yes, she's out for the count. Listen, after dinner I've got to pop out for a couple of hours.'

'Oh Arthur, this is the first time you've been home early all week. I hardly see you these days.'

'You know how well the business is doing and we've seen a bigger yard in Clapham. It's just what we need and will hold eight vans, plus there's a small office. Dad wants me to go with him to look it over.'

'Why can't he go on his own?'

'I'm his partner and it's natural that he wants my opinion.'

'But you've been on the road all day. Can't you talk to him about the hours you have to work?'

'Sally, I've told you, we're exceptionally busy at the

moment and it can't be helped.' He wondered if he should mention that he was meeting up with an old friend after he'd been to Clapham. No, he decided, she'd only get upset, but he wanted a break from another night sitting in the kitchen with three women. If Sadie was in a bad mood it was hell, especially if they spoke when she was watching her favourite television programme. God, he didn't know how Sally stood it.

'All right,' she said, 'I suppose you have to go, but what time will you be home?'

'Oh, sometime after ten I should think. Now I'm off to have a wash and a shave.'

Later, Sally kissed Arthur's cheek, trying to look cheerful as she saw him out. Then, her mouth drooping despondently, she went into the kitchen.

'I didn't expect Arthur to go out again,' Sadie said.

'Nor did I, but they've seen a bigger yard in Clapham. He and Bert are going to have a look at it.'

'What! On a Saturday night?'

'They don't get much time during the day. It's amazing when you think about it, from just one removal van, the firm has gone from strength to strength. I suppose I shouldn't complain, but Arthur's rarely home early nowadays.'

'I don't know why he keeps on doing deliveries. Surely they employ enough drivers and there's no reason why Arthur can't work in the office.'

'With the help of a secretary Bert does all the office work, and Arthur doesn't want to put his nose out of joint. With his back problem his father still feels he isn't pulling his weight.'

'Rubbish! It was Bert who started the business, built it up, and it was due to all his hard work that he and Elsie were able to buy their lovely house in Wimbledon. Mind you, I don't blame Elsie for wanting to move away from this dump. It looks so different now and the lane is slowly being surrounded by huge blocks of flats. Nearly all the old streets have been demolished, and I don't suppose Candle Lane will last much longer. And have you seen the way they build them tower blocks, Sally?' Without waiting for a reply Sadie went into full sail again. 'Great slabs of grey concrete

29

lifted into place by huge cranes, and twelve floors are up in a jiffy. I can't believe they're safe and you won't catch me living in one. What's the matter with good old bricks and mortar – that's what I want to know.'

Sally opened her mouth to speak, but Sadie was off again. 'You should get out of this area, my girl; it's gone to the dogs. The factories are still here, belching smoke, and that peculiar smell that drifts in when the wind's in a certain direction still makes my stomach turn. Blimey, you'd think I'd be used to it after all these years.'

'I think with the hops, yeast and other paraphernalia used, it must come from the brewery.'

'Yeah, you could be right, but some people blame the Gartons Glucose factory.'

Sally flopped into a chair, Sadie now asking, 'What's up, love? You look fed up.'

She forced a smile, pleased that Gran was sounding like her old self, this period lasting longer than usual. 'I'm all right, but when Arthur came home early I hoped we could go out, if only to the pictures or something. I think I just need a break.'

'I should think so too! When was the last time you had a night out?'

'It must be a couple of months ago.'

'You're only young and shouldn't be stuck indoors all the time. You need something to do that will ease the monotony.'

'Yes, maybe, but what?'

Both heads turned as Ruth came into the room, her hair wrapped turban-style in a towel. 'I've used all the hot water, Sally. If you want a bath you'll have to wait about an hour for the immersion to heat up again.' Then seeing the expression on her daughter's face, she echoed Sadie. 'What's up, love?'

It was Sadie who answered, 'The girl needs a break, something to do a few evenings a week to get her out of the house. Think about it, Ruth. She's in all day, every day, looking after Angel and me. Arthur is rarely in before eight o'clock and hardly ever takes her out.'

'Why don't you tell him how you feel?'

'Mum, by the time Arthur arrives home he's worn out, and the last thing he wants is to go out again.'

30

'He works too hard. Still, there's nothing to stop you going out on your own. You used to do a healing service in the hall. Why don't you go back to that?' Ruth suggested.

A silence followed whilst Sally digested her mother's words. Yes, why not! Now that Angel was starting school, she'd be in bed early. If her mother wouldn't mind keeping an ear out for her, there was no reason why she couldn't go out a couple of evenings a week. She had to admit that as soon as her daughter had been born, she'd become the centre of her world and her spiritual healing had been put to one side. Yes, she gave Gran occasional sessions to ease her arthritis, but other than that her gift was being wasted. Should she offer her services at the hall again? She chewed on her lip, thinking deeply, suddenly coming to a decision. 'Do you mind babysitting, Mum?'

'No, of course not, and the community hall is only round the corner so you won't be far away.'

'I'd better check with Arthur.'

'He won't mind. Are you forgetting Elsie? His mother has psychic gifts, so he's well used to them.'

'I know, but if I'm going to be out a couple of nights a week, there's his dinner to think about.'

'Gawd, love, I'm quite capable of feeding the man and it's not as if you'll be out all hours. The service is over by ten o'clock.'

'All right then – I'll pop down to the hall tomorrow to see if they'll take me back.'

'Right, that's settled then,' Sadie said bluntly. 'Now, how about a cuppa? I'm spitting feathers!'

Five

'Hello, stranger,' Joe said as Arthur walked into the pub. Arthur grinned, chuffed to see his friend again. He and Joe had hit it off from the start, and had become close as they travelled around Australia. 'It's great to see you, Joe, and you could have knocked me down with a feather when you got in touch. How on earth did you know my mother's address?'

'Well, to be honest, I guessed you were unhappy about something in Oz. I know it was a bit of a cheek to read your letter from home, but I wanted to help and you wouldn't tell me what the problem was. I hoped we'd meet up again one day, so after reading your mother's letter, I took note of her address.'

'I liked Australia, but after finding out that my girl in England was pregnant I was desperate to get back. It was good of you to slip me the fare home, and I'll see that it's returned. Are you here for good?'

'Yeah, but I don't know if I've made the right decision. I came home because my mother's been taken ill and apparently she was pining for me. But blimey, it's freezing! I'd forgotten how awful the weather could be.'

'It's early September, and mild,' Arthur protested, watching as Joe clutched his coat closer to his body.

'Mild! You must be kidding, and as for the money I gave you, forget it.'

'Thanks mate, but I'd rather pay you back.'

'All right, if it'll make you feel better, but there's no hurry. Now tell me, what have you been up to since leaving Australia?'

'I'm a partner in my father's furniture removals firm.'

'Sounds good, and what about the girl you couldn't wait to get home to?'

'I married her and we have a five-year-old daughter.'

'That's great. I'm glad it worked out for you.'

'So, Joe, you're staying in England, and are you working on your father's farm?'

'No. Nothing's changed and we still don't get on. I've got plans for starting something up, but it's only in the early stages.'

'What are you thinking of doing?'

'There's no point in going into it now, but if it's viable financially and I can get it up and running, I'll tell you all about it.'

'Right, I can see you'd rather keep it to yourself for the time being. Are you living with your parents?'

'No, I didn't fancy being in the sticks and have found myself a little flat in Earl's Court. I pop home most weekends to see my mother.'

'How is she?'

'She's had an operation and thankfully is recovering well.'

Time passed quickly as they reminisced, laughing as they remembered their travels around parts of Australia. Then of course the subject of football arose and Arthur went into great detail about England winning the world cup. The choice of players came under review, their positions on the field and the choice of goalkeeper.

Arthur lifted his pint and took a long swig, before saying with a grin, 'We had the best goalkeeper in the world. I can remember watching a football match when a dog invaded the pitch. Gordon Banks showed his all round skills by catching the dog with a flying tackle, and you should have heard the cheers.'

'It was great that England won, but I'm afraid rugby's my game.'

'I don't mind watching a bit of it now and then, but the rules do my head in.'

'What don't you understand?'

'Well, the offside law for one.'

Joe launched into an explanation which Arthur did his best to follow, and finishing his beer he ordered another round. They downed them, still talking sport, until Joe said, 'Sorry mate, I've got to go now, but can we meet up again for a couple of pints?'

33

'Yes, of course. Anyway, as I said, I owe you some money.'

After making arrangements to meet the following week, they parted. Arthur made his way home, pleased to have met up with his old mate again. Christ, Joe sounded like he had big plans, and he couldn't help feeling a pang of envy. The man would make his own way in life and, unlike him, he wouldn't be hanging on to his father's coat tails.

When had his dissatisfaction started? At first he'd enjoyed the removals game – enjoyed travelling around the country, but now he hated it. His father was the boss, and made that plain – almost if he were frightened of being usurped by his son. All Arthur could see was years of the same thing – years of being no different from the other men his father employed. He was just a driver, a humper, with no responsibilities and no say in the running of the company.

'I don't know, Sally, if you start giving healing in the hall again, what about Angel?' Arthur asked as they prepared for bed that night.

'Mum said she'd keep an eye on her.'

'How many evenings are you thinking of?'

'Only two – Tuesdays and Thursdays.'

'What's brought this on?'

'I need to get out of the house, and you're too busy to take me out. I'm in night after night without a break. My days are spent looking after Angel and Gran, and my evenings stuck in front of the television.'

'And *you* don't seem to appreciate that I work like a dog. Oh, poor Sally, stuck in front of the television. Dear me, what a hard life!' Arthur drawled sarcastically.

Sally's eyes widened and she felt a surge of anger. 'I'm twenty-three, Arthur, not eighty-three, and when was the last time I had a bit of fun? It feels as though life is passing me by. The swinging sixties! What do I ever see of the bloody swinging sixties?'

'Don't swear, Sally. It doesn't become you.'

'Is that a fact! Well, I'll swear if I want to, and if you want the truth I'll give it to you. I'm fed up, bored, and when was the last time you made love to me?' As soon as the words left her mouth, Sally flushed. Shame filled her and she lowered her eyes. What was wrong with her? Why had she spoken like that? Yes, she felt frustrated, but suddenly realized that it wasn't the only reason she was feeling low. For weeks now she had been on tenterhooks, almost as if instinctively waiting for something awful to happen.

'It was you who insisted on moving back to this dump,' Arthur snapped, 'and it was only supposed to be for a short while. We could have a place of our own, but instead we have no privacy, and I refuse to make love to you whilst my daughter is in the same room. What if she woke up? After all, you aren't exactly quiet, are you?'

Sally flushed again. Yes she was noisy, but when making love Arthur brought her to such a pitch that she was unable to stifle a scream of ecstasy. But how could he throw *that* in her face? Oh God, what was happening to them – to their marriage? They hardly saw each other these days. They were drifting apart and becoming like strangers.

'I'm sorry, Sally. I shouldn't have said that. I'm afraid I was in a bad mood when I came home, but I've no right to take it out on you.'

She looked up now, and seeing the shamefaced look on her husband's face she flew into his arms. 'I'm sorry too. It's all right, I won't go out, but can you at least promise to be home earlier a few nights a week?'

'I wish I could, but we're so busy that it's unlikely. You go to the spiritualist hall, and if I can get away at any time I promise I'll take you dancing or something.'

Arthur's arms tightened around her and Sally pushed herself closer, feeling a surge of passion. She felt his own desire mounting, hard against her, and, turning, she led him towards the bed.

Angel was asleep, thumb in mouth as usual and as Arthur's eyes flicked towards her, he said, 'No, Sally, we can't.'

'Please, Arthur, I'll be quiet, I promise,' she begged, her frustration mounting as she pressed close to him again.

His eyes became dark with passion and with a soft groan he unbuttoned her blouse, his eyes feasting on her breasts. In moments they fell on to the bed, both now frantically pulling off their clothes, and as Arthur's lips fastened on her nipple, Sally groaned softly. Oh, it had been so long, so long, and unable to wait, she whispered, 'Please, darling. Please take me.'

As Arthur entered her, Sally arched her back in ecstasy, matching his passion and mindlessly forgetting her surroundings as he pounded into her. The frantic coupling was quick, her nails unconsciously digging into Arthur's back. She was nearly there, almost on the point of release, her mouth wide as she screamed, 'Yes, yes! Now, Arthur – now!'

Yet at that moment a small voice intruded, 'What are you doing?'

Sally frantically pushed Arthur off and they collapsed, both unspent and panting. She saw her husband's eyes were wide with horror as he desperately tried to cover himself, but it was too late, Angela asking, 'What's that, Daddy?'

'See . . . see what you've done,' Arthur growled, at last managing to pull a sheet over his rapidly diminishing erection.

Sally scrambled off the bed, hastily wrapping the spread around her naked body. 'It's all right, darling. Come on now, go back to sleep,' she urged as she hurried to Angel's side.

'You was screaming, Mummy. Was Daddy hurting you?'

'No, of course not. We were just playing. Now be a good girl and go back to sleep.'

'Want milk.'

'All right, Daddy will get you some,' Sally answered, her eyes holding an appeal as she looked at Arthur.

He glowered at her, but as Sally placed herself in front of Angel's view, he was able to pull on his dressing-gown, tightening the belt angrily as he left the room.

Sally sat stroking Angel's hair, her body still screaming and unfulfilled. That was it! The thing Arthur dreaded had happened, and he would never attempt lovemaking again whilst his daughter slept in their room. How much longer could this situation go on? How much longer could their marriage survive? It was hell for both of them, but she couldn't leave her gran while she was still in danger. Tears filled her eyes, and as Angel drifted off to sleep again, Sally wondered what the future held.

Six

Sally stood in the Spiritualist Hall, waiting for a client, her thoughts drifting back. Angel's first day at school had initially proved to be traumatic; though she was fine on the walk there, as soon as they'd arrived in the playground her daughter had gone into a panic. She refused to enter the building, clinging desperately on to her hand, until Tommy Walters came to the rescue.

'Come on, don't be a baby,' he'd said, and though two years older than Angel he'd taken her under his wing.

Sally was amazed when she went off with Tommy, the boy turning back to give her a triumphant grin. Tommy Walters looked like a ragamuffin, whilst Angela had been scrubbed and groomed to within an inch of her life, the two making an incongruous pair. It surprised her that Tommy had taken charge of Angel, and she doubted it would do much to his credibility with the gang he ran wild with. Thankfully, since that day, Angel had gone to school without a murmur, and Sally was doing her best to keep her daughter away from the boy.

Now, as September drew to a close, she was in despair over her marriage. On their fifth wedding anniversary Arthur hadn't taken her out. There had been a bunch of flowers, but no card, and just lately he'd begun to act strangely. At one time all he had talked about was buying a house, but now he longer mentioned it, and she could sense he was hiding something.

Her stomach churned, and feeling nauseous at the thought, she wondered if he had another woman. On occasions he'd gone out in the evening, always with a feeble excuse, but somehow she couldn't face confronting him, dreading what she might hear. At other times she berated herself for even thinking such a thing, deciding it was all in her imagination. Yes, Arthur seemed preoccupied, and yes he'd been out without telling her where, but was that enough reason to think he was being unfaithful?

She was sure that living in Candle Lane was the main cause of their problems and at times she was tempted to suggest that they find a place of their own again, even one out of the area. Yet every time she came near to making the decision, something held her back. Perhaps it was intuition, she didn't know, but at the thought of leaving she was filled with dread. Was it her gran? Was she going to have another stroke?

It was a welcome relief to be out of the house a couple of evenings a week, and she now came to the hall to join three other healers, two of whom she already knew and liked. Yet even when out of the house for these few hours her mind constantly turned to her gran. Her mother had promised to ring the hall immediately if she became ill, yet even with this reassurance, Sally was unable to completely relax. It affected her healing powers. She was able to help people with simple problems, but had to pass those she couldn't touch to the other healers.

A woman now approached and, after inviting her to sit down, Sally gently questioned her, finding out that she suffered from attacks of migraine. She smiled reassuringly, telling the lady to relax, and then stood behind her chair, lifting her head in a silent prayer for guidance. Her hands hovered over the woman's head as she tried to concentrate, opening the channel and allowing the healing energy to flow through her palms.

Elsie, her mother-in-law, had been so patient when teaching her, and Sally remembered her first attempt at healing. After the session, though amazed at how it eased her gran's pain, she'd been left feeling dreadfully tired. Elsie explained that she must allow the energy to flow through her, not from her, and once she'd mastered this technique, her healing energies flowed more naturally. Sally knew that without her mother-in-law's help she would never have been able to develop her gifts, and though able to use clairsentience to prophesy on occasions, she preferred to concentrate on healing.

Since moving back to Candle Lane she didn't see so much of Elsie and missed her once-regular visits to Wimbledon. Now, with looking after Gran all day and Arthur arriving home late every evening, they were a thing of the past. Elsie called to see them as often as she could, but Gran or her mother monopolized her time and she missed their cosy tête-à-têtes.

As her hands continued to hover, Sally could feel the familiar tingle as it radiated from her palms and closed her eyes. It was quiet, the atmosphere peaceful, calm, but then the double doors swung open and Angel catapulted into the hall.

'Mum,' she shouted, running full pelt across the wooden floor and skidding to an ungainly halt in front of her. 'Mum, you've got to come! Gamma's shouting and Nanny's crying.'

Sally turned swiftly to her client. 'I'm so sorry, I must deal with this. Would you like to wait for another healer?'

The woman was smiling at Angel, an effect her daughter usually had on people the first time they saw her. 'I can see you have a problem and don't mind waiting for someone else. She's adorable,' she added, nodding towards Angel.

'Looks can be deceiving,' Sally said ruefully. As the woman walked to the other side of the hall, she crouched down in front of her daughter. Angel's coat had been thrown over her nightclothes and she had slippers on her feet. 'Why aren't you in bed? And who is Gamma shouting at?'

'Gamma's shouting at the black man.'

'What black man?'

Placing her arms akimbo on her hips, her stance like a miniature adult, Angel sighed with exasperation. 'The one wiv Auntie Mary of course.'

Bewildered, Sally stared at her daughter. What was Aunt Mary doing with a black man, and how had Angel left the house on her own? 'Does Nanny know you've come to the hall?'

'No, I ran out before she saw me. Mummy, please come home. I'm frightened.'

Sally's face creased with anxiety. If Angel was frightened the situation at home must be bad. She grabbed her daughter's hand and called out a hasty goodbye to the other healers before hurrying from the hall.

39

'Slow down, Mummy, pleeease,' Angel cried, but Sally hardly heard her daughter's protest as they skidded around the corner into Candle Lane, at the same time seeing the door to number five flying open. A man shot out as though propelled by a cannon, landing in a heap on the pavement.

Mary came running out to solicitously help him to his feet, and close behind Sadie Greenbrook, her voice raucous as she cried, 'Get him away from here or there'll be murder done!'

'He's got a name, Mother. It's Leroy, and I can't believe you're acting like this.'

'And *I* can't believe that you're going to marry *him*! He . . . he's . . .'

'Black! Yes, he's black, but unlike my first husband, Leroy is a decent man.'

'Why couldn't you find a decent *white* man? It ain't right, Mary, and if you go ahead with this I'll wash me hands of you!'

'All right, Mum, if that's how you feel then there's nothing else to say. Except that I'm pregnant! Yes, that's knocked the wind out of your sails hasn't it?'

The neighbours were now on their doorsteps, obviously enjoying the spectacle, with only Nelly Cox looking at them with sympathy. Sally pushed her way between her gran and aunt. 'For goodness' sake, you two! Do you want the whole street to know our business?'

'They can't bleedin' miss it when she turns up with the likes of *that*!'

'What do you mean – *that*?' Mary cried. 'He's a human being and as I said, a decent one.'

'He's a bleedin' nigger!'

'Mother! Don't you dare use that word!'

'What's a nigger, Gamma?'

On hearing her great-granddaughter's question, Sadie had the grace to look shamefaced. 'It's not a nice word and I shouldn't have said it. Take no notice of Gamma.'

'Mum!' Sally cried. 'Didn't you even notice that Angel had left the house?'

'No, I'm sorry,' Ruth said. 'With all this going on it ain't surprising.'

Sally then looked on in amazement as her impossible, yet

40

sometimes sensitive daughter walked over to Leroy and, taking his hand, she stroked it gently. 'You've got a cut. Does it hurt?'

'No, darlin', it's just grazed and I'm fine.'

'Why is your skin black?'

''Cos I comes from Jamaica.'

'Where's that?'

'Angel, that's enough. There's no need to interrogate the man,' Sally gently admonished.

Leroy smiled. 'It's all right, I don't mind, and this is one cute child.'

'Get away from him, Angel!' Sadie called.

'Why, Gamma?'

'Just do as I say!'

'Mother, he isn't contagious,' Mary snapped.

'Come on, it's best we go,' Leroy urged, taking her arm.

'Yes, you're right. It's obvious we aren't welcome here.'

'There ain't many places we is,' Leroy murmured sadly.

With a sniff Sadie turned on her heels and marched back indoors, but it seemed she wanted the last word as she cried, 'And don't bring him to my house again!'

The door slammed shut and with a groan Ruth turned to her sister. 'I warned you about upsetting Mum. She ain't well, and you shouldn't have brought him here. And why on earth upset her even more by saying you're pregnant?'

'Because I am.'

'What, at your age! Don't be bloody stupid.'

'Don't call me stupid!'

'I'll call you what I like, but I ain't standing here arguing. Gawd knows what effect this will have on Mum's health and I'm going in to make sure she's all right.'

'Huh, she can't be that ill. Not after the way she shoved Leroy out of the door.'

'In that temper, I think she could've shoved a bus outside. You'd better stay away for a while, Mary, and as I said, don't bring *him* here again. You know how she feels.'

'She had to know sometime.'

Ruth's lips tightened as she turned away from her sister. Flinging a look at Sally she said, 'I'm going in. Are you coming?'

'Yes, in a minute, but I'd like a word with Aunt Mary first.'

41

'Your gran probably needs you, so make it quick,' and on that sour note Ruth went inside.

'Leroy, this is Sally, my niece,' Mary now said. 'And you've already met her daughter, Angela.'

'Pleased to meet you.'

Sally smiled pleasantly at her aunt's boyfriend as she shook his hand. 'Hello, it's nice to meet you too.' Leroy was tall, with very dark brown eyes, and black, tightly curled hair. His suit was grey and double-breasted, with very wide-legged trousers narrowing to turn-ups at the ankles. There were several Jamaican families now settling in Battersea, and many of the men seemed to adopt this style of dress. She was amazed by her aunt's bravery. If a white woman was seen with a black man, she became scorned, and Mary must think a lot of Leroy if she was prepared to face becoming an outcast.

'It seems that at least one member of my family is prepared to take your hand, Leroy.'

'I'm not prejudiced, Aunt Mary, but you know what people are like around here and it's going to be hard for you.'

'Yes, we know, and others before Leroy have run the gauntlet of landladies with signs saying "No Blacks" on their doors.'

'When are you getting married?'

'As soon as we can arrange it. Will you come, Sally?'

'Of course, and I'm sure my mother will too.'

'Huh, can you see my sister going against your gran? No doubt you'll be under pressure to stay away too.'

Before Sally could answer, Angel tugged at Mary's sleeve. 'Can I be a bridesmaid, Auntie?'

'No, I'm sorry darling. We aren't getting married in church so there'll be no bridesmaids.'

Seeing the rebellious look forming on her daughter's face, Sally quickly intervened. 'Go indoors now, Angel.'

'No, don't want to.'

'Do as I say, and right now!'

Angel's lower lip began to tremble but, knowing her daughter's wily ways, Sally kept her expression stern, suppressing another smile when with a huff of outrage Angel did as she was asked. No sooner had her daughter gone inside, than she came running out again.

'Mum! Gamma said you've got to come in now.'

'Goodness, Aunt Mary,' Sally said, 'you'd think I'm still a child to be ordered around. Still, it's best that your gran stays calm.'

'Goodbye, my dear,' Aunt Mary said and, taking Leroy's hand, they began to walk away.

With a small wave Sally watched them running the gauntlet of Candle Lane. Mrs Stone from number nine spat at Mary's feet as she passed. Her temper rose and she wanted to fly at the woman, but knowing it would take a miracle to overcome the prejudice, she just sadly watched until Mary and Leroy turned the corner. Then she went indoors.

No sooner had Sally entered the kitchen than her gran started, her voice full of venom as she said, 'I can't believe it! My daughter marrying a bloody black! God, and she said she's pregnant. That will mean she'll have a bleedin' half-caste. Well I disown her and she's no daughter of mine. In fact, if she comes to my house again she'll get the door shut in her face.'

'I don't think she's pregnant,' Ruth said. 'Are you forgetting how old she is?'

'She seems to think she is, and pregnant or not I'm finished with her.'

Sally, still upset about the treatment her aunt had received from the neighbours, found her temper rising again. 'This isn't your house, Gran, it's my mother's, and if you don't mind I'd rather you stopped spouting racial hatred in front of my daughter!'

'If you don't like it you know what you can do!'

'Don't speak to Sally like that,' Ruth shouted, joining in the argument.

'I'll speak as I bloody well like!'

'No shout . . . no shout!' Angel cried.

Sally, seeing the distress on her daughter's face, fought to bring herself under control. 'I'll take Angel upstairs,' she said, marching from the room, determined now that it was time she and Arthur found a place of their own. Yet as her temper cooled, nagging intuition rose again. She couldn't leave Candle Lane, she just couldn't. She still had a dreadful feeling that something awful was going to happen. And if so – what, and when?

Seven

It was the second week in October when Nelly Cox opened her street door, peering at the young woman standing on her step.

'Mrs Cox?' she asked.

'Yeah, that's me. What can I do for you, love?'

'My name is Janet Kemp and I'm a social worker. May I come in?'

'Well, I suppose so, but what do you want?'

'Just a little chat,' she said, stepping inside and, as they entered the kitchen, Nelly noticed the young woman's eyes flicking rapidly around the room.

Feeling uneasy, Nelly gripped the back of a chair. 'What do you want to talk to me about?'

'May I sit down?'

'Yeah, all right.' Once the woman was seated at the kitchen table, Nelly sat opposite her.

Without preamble the social worker said, 'I understand that you have no family, Mrs Cox, and that you live alone.'

'Yeah, that's right.'

'How do you manage?'

'Manage! What do you mean?'

Janet Kemp smiled gently, her voice soft, 'It seems you have difficulty coping on your own.'

'What! Who told you that?'

'I'm afraid I'm not at liberty to say, but a letter was sent to our department.'

'Who sent this letter?' Nelly cried.

'I can only say that it was from someone who was concerned about you. Now then, Mrs Cox, I'm only here to help so please don't upset yourself.

'Help! I don't need any help.'

'I can see you aren't managing to do your housework.'

Nelly's face reddened. 'Well, I must admit that I've been a bit lax since I lost me old man.'

'It's very cold today, and you don't seem to be dressed appropriately for the weather. Are you having financial difficulties?'

'I ain't wealthy, but I manage.'

'Do you have any problems with your memory?'

Nelly reared to her feet. 'Now you listen to me, young lady. I ain't answering any more of your questions. I don't know what you've been told, but it's all rubbish, and I certainly ain't lost me marbles!'

'Please, as I said, there's no need to get upset. It isn't unusual to become a little forgetful when one gets older.'

'I ain't bleedin' forgetful.'

'All right, Mrs Cox, but it isn't healthy to live in a house that's infested with vermin.'

'Vermin! Vermin!' Nelly screeched, suddenly realizing that she sounded like a parrot. 'Who told you that I've got vermin?'

'I'm afraid I can't tell you, but what I can do is offer rehousing. We have a place in Osborn House if you would like it.'

'But that's an old folk's home!'

'You're seventy-six, Mrs Cox, and qualify for a place. I'm sure you'd be very happy there.'

'I ain't going into a home! I've lived here for over fifty years, and won't leave unless it's in a coffin.' Nelly found herself panting, and placed a hand over her chest.

'Please, please calm down,' the young social worker urged. 'We aren't forcing you to leave your home. Perhaps there are other ways we can help.'

'I've told you before – I don't need any help. In fact, I want you to leave.'

'Very well, but I could call to see you again next week?'

Nelly drew in a breath, saying in a very dignified voice, 'Thank you, but that won't be necessary.'

Janet Kemp's smile was tinged with sadness. For a moment Nelly decided she could like this young woman, but then her anger reasserted itself. Someone in Candle Lane, some nosy parker, had put the social worker on to her, and she intended to find out who it was. And when she did – oh, would they get a piece of her mind.

After closing the door on the young woman, Nelly returned to the kitchen, collapsing on to a chair. Who? Who had said she was incapable of looking after herself?

She thought back to what the social worker had said and as the penny dropped she sat bolt upright in her chair. It must have been that young piece who had moved in next door. Nelly had only invited Maureen Downy in once, and that had been soon after the young family had moved in. The invitation hadn't been returned, but it didn't worry her. She hadn't taken to the sniffy young woman and nowadays they rarely spoke.

Maureen Downy, yes, she was the one. Only last week she'd seen her chatting to Jessie Stone, but as she had walked towards them the conversation had stopped, both looking furtive. Yet she had caught the tail end of what they were saying, and it was something to do with mice. Anger flared again as she rose to her feet and in no time Nelly was banging on the young woman's door.

'Oh, hello,' Maureen Downy said, wiping her hands on a tea towel.

'How dare you!' Nelly cried. 'How dare you try to have me put in a home!'

'A home! I don't know what you're talking about.'

'Yes you do, you lying cow! I've had a social worker at me door and you told her I had vermin.'

Maureen bristled, and then spat, 'You have! Your place is bloody disgusting and I found mouse droppings in my kitchen last week that must have spread from your house. I've got me kids to think about, and I don't know why I should put up with your muck infesting my home. And come to that, just look at the state of you! When was the last time you had a decent wash and put clean clothes on?'

In shock, Nelly found that her tongue felt as though it was stuck to the roof of her mouth as she fought for words, only managing to splutter, 'Why . . . you . . . you . . .' and before she could think coherently, Maureen spoke again.

'If you ask me, an old people's home would be the best place for you.'

And on that note she slammed the door in Nelly's face.

For a moment she stood panting, staring at the door and about to raise her hand to the knocker again, but then Nelly sagged as the young woman's words rang in her head. Dirty – she was dirty – and she had mice! Stumbling now she returned to her own house – and as she went inside it was as if she were seeing it for the first time.

Yes, it *was* dirty, in fact filthy. Nelly was filled with shame, her eyes brimmed with tears, but then she dashed at them impatiently. Crying wouldn't solve anything. There was only one thing to do. She would clean the house, and herself. Until that was done she would keep her head down, and then, if that social worker called again, she would show her that she was quite capable of looking after herself.

Eight

A week had passed; Sally paused in the act of pouring porridge into a bowl as her mother spoke.

'It's nice that Angel is staying with Elsie on Saturday night.'

'Yes, but with Ann's twins too, it'll probably be a mad house.'

Ruth chuckled. 'Yeah, and I don't envy Elsie.'

Sally glanced at the clock and then looked worriedly at her mother. 'Have you seen the time? If you don't get a move on you'll be late for work.'

'I'm taking a couple of days off. I can't stand the new manager, and if I ain't there for couple of days he might appreciate how much I do. Will you ring the shop and say I'm ill?'

'Oh Mum, you know I hate doing that. What am I supposed to say is wrong with you?'

'I dunno, but I really do feel knackered. He only took over a fortnight ago and it's been non-stop. First it was another stocktake, and now he's decided he wants all the shelves rearranged. Honestly, Sal, it's just too much and I don't know why he can't leave things as they are.'

Sally found herself thinking about the time she had worked in a haberdashery shop and said with a wry smile, 'When I first went to work for Sidney Jacobs I too rearranged all the stock. Like me, I expect your new boss just wants to make an impression.' With a start she realized that it had been months since she'd been to see her old boss, and with her mother off work she was struck by an idea. 'Mum, as you're home, do you mind if I go out for a couple of hours?'

'Of course not, but I was going down to see Nelly. She's hardly shown her face for over a week and I'm a bit worried about her.'

'I'll pop in to see her if you like.'

'Yeah, all right, but ring the shop first.'

The call made, Sally hurried from the house, glad to be away from her gran for a couple of hours. She'd been hard going for the last few days, and it would be a treat to have a bit of time to herself.

Mrs Stone was standing on her doorstep, surveying the lane, and seeing Sally approaching she folded her arms under her ample bosom, chin lifting as though in readiness for a confrontation. Sally kept her head low, not wanting to speak to the woman, but it seemed Mrs Stone had other ideas.

'Is your aunt still seeing that man?' she asked.

'I don't think that's any of your business.'

'Your grandmother certainly gave her what for, and I should think so too. She should stick to her own kind.'

Sally tensed, but then decided to ignore the remark. Like Gran, and many other people, the woman was a racist and it would be a waste of time arguing with her. Did her aunt put up with this every time she went out with Leroy? Yes, probably, and Sally's heart ached for her.

Saying nothing in reply she hurried past Mrs Stone and was soon at Nelly's house.

'Watcha, Sally,' the old lady said as she opened the door. 'Are you coming in for a cuppa?'

'How are you?' she asked as they stepped inside, her face stretching into a grin when she saw how clean and tidy the kitchen was.

As if reading her mind Nelly gestured her to a chair. 'I can see how surprised you are, but after a visit from a do-gooder social worker, I decided I'd better pull me socks up. She was talking about me going into an old people's home. Bloody cheek!'

'It looks lovely in here,' Sally said, and meant it.

'When my George was alive, I used to keep the place spotless, but after he died I sort of lost interest.' Shaking her head sadly Nelly continued. 'Not only that, the Lane just ain't the same anymore and I miss me old mates.'

Sally reached out to grasp the old lady's hand, her heart aching for her.

'It was that young piece next door who reported me, and

at first I was hopping mad. But then I took a good look at myself and realized she was right. I *have* let myself go. I was ashamed, Sally, ashamed to see how dirty this place was.'

'It looks lovely now, Nelly.'

'Yeah, it ain't too bad, but between you and me it's been bleedin' hard work to get it up to scratch again.' Her voice lowered. 'I even had to buy some mouse traps. Yeah, I've got mice, Sally.'

'Oh dear, have you got rid of them?'

'The traps were empty this morning, but I'll keep putting them out just in case. Don't let the buggers beat you, that's what I say, and that goes for flippin' Maureen Downy too. If that social worker calls again she'll see that I ain't ready for the knacker's yard yet, and let's hope there's no more talk of an old people's home.'

'Listen, Nelly, if you can't manage the housework you only have to say. I'd be pleased to come and give you a hand.'

'Bless you, love, but now I've got on top of it, I can manage fine. You've got enough on your plate with looking after your gran. How is she?'

'About the same.'

'Is she still being difficult?'

'Yes, at times.'

'I should pop down to see her more often, but to be honest I find her hard going nowadays. She seems to do nothing but moan, and now that your aunt is seeing that coloured chap she's even worse. Mind you, I'm surprised at Mary.'

'Not you too! Is it really so awful?'

'For Mary it is, and your gran's right. Your aunt should stick to her own kind.'

A shadow passed the window and before Sally could respond, Nelly pursed her lips. 'Look at that girl from number seventeen. If you ask me she wants her arse tanned. Have you seen the length of the skirts she wears? Huh, skirts, they're more like belts and if she bends over you can see her knickers.'

Sally smiled wryly. She shouldn't be surprised at Nelly's attitude. After all, like her gran, the old lady was stuck in a

50

time warp. Deciding to leave the subject of her aunt, she now focussed on Nelly's latest comment. 'It's the fashion. All the youngsters wear miniskirts now.'

'You don't.'

No, Sally thought, she didn't wear the latest fashion, and once again found herself thinking that life was passing her by. Models like Jean Shrimpton looked great in the latest fashions, sometimes wearing straight cut minidresses and knee high white boots. God, what must it be like to shop in Chelsea, buying clothes from Mary Quant? There was the Biba Boutique in Kensington too, a shop she would love to explore. Oh, there was so much she was missing out on. Dancing at the Streatham Locarno, or going to see the latest pop group performing live. Instead she felt like a staid old married woman, only seeing groups like The Beatles or The Rolling Stones on television when they appeared on *Ready, Steady, Go.*

'You're miles away, love,' Nelly said.

'Yes, sorry, I was just thinking that I could do with smartening myself up a bit.'

'With your red hair and green eyes you always look lovely, and there's nothing wrong with your clothes.'

'They're out of date, and I rather fancy dressing like that model, Twiggy.'

'Twiggy! Blimey, I can remember seeing a picture of her in the paper earlier this year. She was standing on top of a car modelling a plastic, transparent, halter neck dress. No, love, I don't think Arthur would like you to wear clothes like that.'

'I wasn't thinking of transparent dresses, Nelly.'

'I've told you, Sally, you look nice as you are. Anyway, that Twiggy is as thin as a rake. Men like women with a bit of meat on their bones.'

Sally smiled wryly, thinking she was mad to expect someone of Nelly's age to understand. Perhaps she should treat herself to a miniskirt and boots. Arthur always admired her legs, saying they were long and shapely. Wearing a short skirt might make him sit up a bit. It would be nice to see an appreciative look in his eyes again, and their marriage could certainly do with a bit of spark. Angela would be at

Elsie's on Saturday night, so you never know, she thought, crossing her fingers.

She rose to her feet now and gave the old lady a quick kiss on her cheek. 'I'm sorry, Nelly, but I must be off. I'll pop along to see you again soon.'

'Yeah, do that, love. I enjoy our little chats.'

Sally hurried down Candle Lane and was just in time to jump on a bus as it drew in at the stop. In fifteen minutes she was in Wandsworth and as she entered Sidney Jacobs's haberdashery shop her mouth tightened. A young girl was slumped over the counter, reading a magazine, her jaws working rapidly as she chewed on gum. Her hair was long, straight and dark, with a fringe that reached low over her eyebrows, almost touching her heavily made-up eyes. Black eyeliner lined the top and bottom lids, and thick false eyelashes blinked when she spoke, 'Can I 'elp yer?'

'Where is Mr Jacobs?'

'Who's asking?'

'I'm a friend of his. Is he upstairs?'

'Yeah, but he ain't well so you'd better not disturb him.'

'Not well!' Sally exclaimed, rapidly making for the door that led up to Sid's flat. She heard the girl's protest, but ignored it as she ran upstairs, bursting into the sitting room and paling at the sight of her old boss. He was sitting in a chair by the fire, a blanket around his shoulders, his once chubby face white and drawn.

'My life, Sally, you gave me a fright,' he croaked.

'You look awful.'

'It's nice to see you too,' he managed to gasp before doubling over with a fit of coughing.

'Have you seen a doctor?'

'Don't fuss. It's just a cold.'

'It looks more than a cold to me and you should be in bed.'

'I can't take to my bed when there's the shop to see to.'

'How long has that young girl been working here?'

'What's this, twenty questions? She's been here for six weeks. Now enough already and put the kettle on.'

Sally felt Sid's forehead, finding it hot. 'All right, I'll

make you a cup of tea, but you're burning up and as I said, you should be in bed.'

'What if Trudy needs me in the shop?'

Sally tilted her head, her thoughts racing. Yes, why not? She was free until Angel came out of school. 'I can stay until about two thirty, and if I think the girl is competent she can manage until closing time.'

'I doubt she'll cope. She's called me twice this morning.'

'If I don't think she can manage I'll close the shop at two thirty and send her home.' Sid was about to protest but she held up her hand. 'For goodness' sake, your health is more important than the shop. If you don't take care of yourself this could develop into pneumonia.'

'All right, you win, but I can still put myself to bed so you get the kettle on.'

With a sigh of relief Sally watched Sid as he shuffled from the room. He really did look awful and if there were no sign of improvement she'd insist that he see a doctor. The tea made, she took him in a cup, solicitously tucking the blankets around him before making her way downstairs.

'All right was he?' Trudy asked.

'No, he isn't all right and I'm staying to help out for a while. If you can't manage after that, we'll have to close early.'

'You don't 'ave to stay. I can manage.'

'We'll see. Now I think the counter and those wooden drawers could do with a polish – so let's get on with it.'

'Hold on. Who are you to give me orders? I ain't a bleedin' cleaner and I told Mr Jacobs that when I took the job. He does the polishing.'

'I used to work here and practically ran the place. Mr Jacobs is ill and it's up to us to see that the shop is neat and tidy.'

'No fanks. If you want to do it, that's fine, but I ain't busting me nails doing flippin' cleaning.'

Sally bit back the reply that sprung to her lips, and shaking her head she began the task herself. Behind the counter was a tower of mahogany drawers which she had once taken pleasure in buffing to a beautiful shine. The brass handles that she'd lovingly restored to their former glory were once again tarnished, but it would take more than one day to bring them up to scratch. The door opened as a customer came in, and intent on rubbing beeswax into the wood, she let Trudy attend to her.

'Yeah, can I 'elp yer?'

'I'd like to look at some knitting patterns. Have you any for cardigans or twin sets?' the elderly lady asked.

'You might find some in them books,' Trudy said, pointing to the untidy pile at the end of the counter. She then leaned forward again, her elbows on the counter and head buried in her magazine.

'Which one has patterns for double knit wool?'

'I dunno, but there's one there somewhere.'

Sally gritted her teeth, determined not to interfere. She needed to see if Trudy could be left on her own, and this was the only way to do it. Surreptitiously she studied the girl, and when the customer finally found a knitting pattern she asked to see some wool.

'What colour do yer want?'

'I'm not sure. Can I see what you have?'

With a discernible tut, Trudy pulled a drawer from the glass-fronted counter, slapping it on to the surface. 'That's all we've got at the moment.'

The customer fingered the wool. 'I think I'll have beige as it'll go with anything. Do you always have it in stock?'

'I fink so.'

'You don't seem so sure. I can't afford to buy it all now, so can you put the rest by for me?'

'No, we don't do that. We've had too many customers who ask us to put stuff by, but then they don't bother to collect it.'

'I wouldn't do that.'

'That's what they all say, and anyway, as I said, we usually carry this colour in stock.'

Sally's brow creased. When had Sidney stopped putting by wool for the customers? He'd always done it when she worked there, and as few people could afford to buy all the wool at once, it was expected. If he'd discontinued the service a lot of his customers were probably going elsewhere.

'All right,' the woman said, 'I'll take four balls for now, and have you got a cable needle?'

Trudy sighed again, but pulled out a selection. One was chosen, and then the customer said, 'How much does it come to?'

Sally, whilst still appearing busy, was keeping an eye on the transaction, watching as Trudy now scribbled the prices on a scrap of paper before adding them up.

At least she can do arithmetic, Sally thought as the customer proffered the money. Trudy rang up the sale and, without so much as a smile, she gave the customer her change.

The woman had barely closed the door when Trudy said, 'I need to go to the toilet. I won't be a minute.'

There was something in her attitude that worried Sally, a sort of shiftiness, and her suspicions were aroused. With a swift look at the scrap of paper Trudy had used to add up the sale, she went to the till, her eyes widening at the last amount on the till roll. Six shillings had been rung up, but the sale was for one pound, six shillings. Had Trudy just made a mistake, or was something more sinister happening?

For the next couple of hours Sally kept busy, but continued to watch the girl, and when several customers had been served, she again checked the till. Two sales for goods under a pound had been rung up correctly, but the others for larger amounts were again short. 'Get your coat on and get out,' she finally snapped.

'What?'

'You heard me. You've been on the fiddle and if you're not out of here in two minutes I'll call the police.'

Trudy's face paled, and without argument she took her coat. 'I'm going, but you'll be sorry, you stuck-up bitch. My brothers will sort you out, just you wait and see.' And with a flounce of her head she left the shop, slamming the door behind her.

Sally felt the girl's threats were just bravado and stood tapping her nails on the counter. God, what had she done? Because of her swift action, Sid was now without an assistant. Yet what choice had there been? She frowned; perhaps a warning would have been better? No, Trudy was a thief, depriving an old man of his livelihood and she didn't deserve a second chance. With a sinking heart Sally suddenly realized that she should have consulted Sid first. After all, what

55

if he wanted Trudy prosecuted? A glance at her watch showed her that it was one o'clock so, turning the shop sign to closed, she went upstairs.

Sally knocked softly on Sid's bedroom door before opening it, and seeing he wasn't asleep she approached the bed. 'I . . . I've got something to tell you.'

'Spit it out then.'

'I . . . I sacked Trudy.'

'My life, girl! What did you do that for?'

'I caught her fiddling the till.'

'Humph, well I can't say I'm surprised. Takings have been down since she started, but I didn't manage to catch her at it.'

Sally frowned worriedly as she looked at Sid. It had only taken her a few hours to find Trudy out, and she couldn't understand how this normally shrewd old man had failed. 'I'm sorry, Sid, I should have asked if you wanted her prosecuted.'

His rheumy eyes clouded, 'She's made a real shmuck outta me, and I doubt she's the first, but I can't be bothered any more. I think I'll have to pack it in, Sally. I can't manage the shop on my own, and since you left I can't seem to find a decent assistant. It's time for me to retire.'

'I wish I could come back, but I'm looking after my grandmother and I only leave her to pick Angel up from school.'

'I know,' he said with a small sad smile. 'And talking about Angel, how is that little fireball?'

'She's fine, but what will you do with the shop?'

Sid was taken by another bout of coughing before he could speak. 'I don't know what I'll do with the business, but for the time being it can remain closed. To be honest I'll miss it. I moved here with my Rachel when I was just a young man, and have known most of my customers for years. I suppose I could lease the shop and just keep this flat.'

'What about your son? Wouldn't he be interested in taking it on?'

'There's no chance of that. He's got his own jewellery business and he's not short of a bob or two. As for his wife, huh, all she thinks about is entertaining her friends. In fact, I can't remember the last time they came to visit me.'

Sally remained chatting to her old boss for a while longer,

but seeing his eyes beginning to droop she decided it was time to leave. There was an old flask under the sink which she filled with tea, and after making a sandwich she left both on his bedside table. 'I'll come to see you again tomorrow, Sid, but if you're still in bed I'll need the keys.'

'Yes, take a set, and don't worry about me. I'll be fine.'

Sally left the shop, still worrying about Sid. She hoped he would recover quickly, but what if he didn't? Her mother only had a couple of days off, and with Gran to look after she wouldn't have time to check on her old boss too.

With no time now to stop off at Clapham Junction for a look around the shops, Sally arrived home to find her mother and Gran discussing a dreadful disaster in South Wales. The news when it broke was awful. In the mining village of Aberfan a slag heap had collapsed and over two million tons of mine waste had engulfed Pantglas School.

'Ain't it dreadful,' Ruth was saying as Sally slipped off her coat. 'They're saying that over a hundred have died and most of them children.'

'Yeah, it's terrible,' Sadie agreed. Seeing Sally she added, 'Hello, love, did you have a nice day out?'

'Yes, thanks. I went to see my old boss, Sidney Jacobs.'

'Huh, at least you had a decent boss.' Ruth grimaced. 'Gawd, I'm sick to death of working in the grocer's. My old boss was a grumpy old sod, but this youngster that's taken over is driving me mad.'

Sally gazed at her mother, suddenly struck by a thought. 'Mum, you're not going to believe this, but I might have another job for you.'

'Oh yeah, doing what?'

'Sidney Jacobs's latest assistant was fiddling the till, and now he's talking about retiring. I know he'd be lost without his little shop, but if you work for him it would solve both your problems.'

For a moment Ruth was silent. But then she shook her head. 'No, I don't think so. At least the grocer is just at the end of the lane, but if I work for Sid it'll mean getting a bus to work every day. I'd have to leave earlier, and I'd be home later.'

'It only takes about fifteen minutes on the bus, and as you'll be virtually running the shop, the pay will be better too.'

'Running the shop!'

'Sid used to leave all the ordering of stock to me. Once you get the hang of things I'm sure he'll do the same with you. He's a lovely old man, Mum, and I know you would love working for him.'

Sally held her breath as she watched the range of expressions that ran across her mother's face. First doubt, then calculation, and finally a smile as she said, 'All right, Sally, I'll give it a go.'

Nine

'Hello, Elsie, come in,' Ruth said.
  'How's Sadie?'
  'About the same, and how are your lot?'
  'They're fine, and it was nice to see Ann on Saturday. Since she moved to Milton Keynes I don't see her so often, but with her brood it isn't surprising.'
  'Yeah, with three kids, and two of those twins, your daughter has certainly got her hands full.'
  'You can say that again, but I miss them and wish she hadn't moved so far away.'
  'Did Angel behave herself?'
  Elsie grinned. 'To be honest, my place was like a madhouse. They all got over tired and it was a job to get them off to sleep.'
  As they stepped into the kitchen Sadie smiled, and Ruth heaved a sigh of relief. At the moment her mother was in a good mood, but for how long?
  'Watcha, Elsie. How are you?'
  'I'm fine, Sadie, and how are you?'
  'Not so bad, but have you heard about my Mary?'
  'Yes, Arthur told me.'
  'I ain't standing for it. She'll marry that man over my dead body.'
  'Arthur said you were against it, but would it be so bad? From what I've heard he's a nice chap and Mary deserves a bit of happiness after what she's been through.'
  Ruth saw her mother's eyes darken and, recognizing the signs of a change in her personality, she spoke rapidly to change the subject. 'How about a cup of tea, Elsie?'
  It was no good. Her face now livid, Sadie shouted, 'Elsie

Jones, if you're going to take Mary's side you can get out of my house!'

'Now then, there's no need for that. I'm not taking sides.'

'It sounds like you are to me!'

Elsie moved to Sadie's chair, and leaning forward she grasped the old lady's hand. 'Come on, love, I don't want to fall out with you. Let's just forget I said anything and start again.'

'Yeah . . . well . . . just don't mention Mary's name again.'

'All right,' Elsie said, her eyes full of sympathy as they met Ruth's. 'I've popped down because I want to talk to you out of Bert's hearing. It's his birthday in January and I thought we could arrange a surprise party.'

'Blimey, love, it's only the third week in October, aren't you being a bit previous?'

'No, not really, there's a lot to sort out. I'll need to rope Arthur and Sally in with the planning too. Aren't they in?'

'No. Sally's doing a healing service at the hall, and I've no idea where Arthur is.'

'Really! But as he only had a local job today I expected him to be here.'

Ruth glanced at the clock, a frown on her forehead. It was eight o'clock, and if Arthur only had a local delivery, what was keeping him? 'Perhaps he ran into a few problems,' she suggested.

'I don't think so or Bert would have mentioned it when he came home. I should have telephoned first to check that you were all in, but with Bert hovering it was impossible.'

'I expect Arthur will be home soon.'

'I hope so. The trouble is I can't stay long. Bert thinks I've gone to bingo, and has no idea I was coming here. Do you know, I can't believe he's going to be fifty in January. Where has all the time gone?'

'He's still just a whippersnapper,' Sadie commented, her good humour returning. 'So, you're going to throw him a party. Where are you having it?'

'I thought I'd book the hall. I know we don't live around here now, but most of our friends are still in this area.'

'Yeah, good idea. Right, what can we do to help?'

A list was drawn up: food, drink, music, the guests and

then Ruth said, 'I seem to remember helping you with another party some years ago. The one you threw for Arthur before he went off to Australia.'

'Yes, and our first grandchild was conceived that night. It's about time those two had another child, so you never know,' she said with a suggestive wink.

They all carried on reminiscing for a while, Elsie disappointed that Angela was asleep, but nevertheless creeping upstairs to have a peep at her. Then at nine thirty she said, 'Bert will be wondering where I am if I leave it any later. Honestly, Ruth, I can't imagine where Arthur is. Does this often happen?'

'Yeah, he's always late home when he's doing a long-distance delivery.'

'But I've told you. It was only a short journey today.'

Ruth shrugged. 'He knew Sally would be at the hall tonight so I expect he popped into a pub for a drink.'

'Yes, that's possible, but I can't wait any longer and had better ring for a taxi.'

When Elsie came back into the kitchen she said, 'A cab is coming straight away. Will you let Arthur know about the party and tell him I'll need to speak to him out of Bert's hearing?'

'Yes, all right, love.'

Soon after there was the toot of a horn as the taxi arrived, and as Ruth escorted Elsie outside her mind was churning. She was sure Arthur was up to something, and though hiding her concern from Elsie, she was filled with suspicion.

'Bye, Ruth,' Elsie called.

'Bye,' she called back, and when the taxi drove off she went back inside, frequently glancing at the clock until half an hour later, Arthur appeared. 'Hello, lad,' she said. 'Have you had a busy day?'

'Yes, I had a delivery to Devon. A big load too.'

As she lit a cigarette, Ruth looked at him from under her lashes. He was lying, but why? The same awful suspicion filled her mind again. No, surely not? Surely Arthur wouldn't be unfaithful to Sally! Should she say something? Should she confront him?

She opened her mouth to speak, but then the door opened

as Sally arrived home, entering the room with a flurry. 'Hello, darling,' she said, her eyes going immediately to her husband.

Ruth studied Arthur's reaction, saw the fondness in his eyes and berated herself. No, it couldn't be another woman, it just couldn't. So what *was* he up to?

When everyone had gone to bed, Ruth sat alone in the kitchen, her mouth drooping despondently. When Mary had turned up with a bloke, albeit a black man, she had begun to feel her own loneliness again and there were times when she craved a man's arms around her. She lit another cigarette, wondering if she dare take the chance again, but even if she did, what hope did she have of meeting anyone? Taking a final drag on her cigarette she threw it into the hearth, her shoulders still slumped as she made her way to bed.

Ten

The following morning Sally was humming as she absent-mindedly flicked a duster over the furniture. The night Angela had stayed with Elsie was still fresh in her mind. She and Arthur had spent the whole night making love and it had been wonderful. She had been silly to suspect Arthur of having an affair and knew that now.

'What's that bleedin' racket outside?' Sadie snapped.

Sally moved across to the window, her mouth setting in a grim line when she saw Tommy Walters' mother, red-faced with temper, giving her son a thrashing. Angel was watching the scene, obviously distressed as the boy screamed in agony. Sally had no time for the lad, but no matter what he'd done, surely there was no need for Laura Walters to lay into him with a belt.

'I won't be a minute, Gran,' she called as she rushed outside.

A few neighbours were on their steps, all looking decidedly uncomfortable at the treatment Tommy was receiving, but none intervening. Sally rushed up to Laura, grabbing her arm, and as the woman turned to spit abuse, Sally was sickened by the stench of alcohol on her breath. She'd heard rumours that Laura Walters was a drinker, but this was the first time she'd seen any sign of it. 'Let the boy go,' she urged.

'Mind your own business! He deserves a beating, and that's what I'm giving him.'

'Why, what has he done?' Sally asked, relieved that at least the woman was distracted enough to stop laying a belt across Tommy's legs.

'That's my business too,' she spat, but in the process she let go of Tommy's ear. In a flash the boy was gone, his little legs pumping until he reached the end of Candle Lane and skidded around the corner.

'I'll get you later, you little bugger!' Laura screamed and, throwing a scowl at Sally, she staggered back indoors.

'It's disgraceful, that's what it is,' Mrs Stone said, shaking her head with disgust. 'One o'clock on a Saturday afternoon, and if you ask me the woman's as drunk as a skunk.'

Other women nodded, joining in the gossip, but Sally grabbed Angel's hand, dragging her back inside. 'But I want to wait for Tommy to come back,' she protested.

'Inside,' Sally insisted as she pushed Angel ahead of her into the kitchen, her mind still on Tommy Walters. He was a holy terror and the bane of her life, so why was she feeling sorry for him?

'What was all that about?' Sadie asked.

'Laura Walters was giving young Tommy a hiding.'

'Huh, I expect he deserved it.'

'No child deserves to be thrashed with a belt, Gran, and I think the woman was drunk.'

'Yes, as a skunk,' Angel said. 'What's a skunk, Gamma?'

'Gawd, where did she hear that?'

'From Jessie Stone.' Not wanting Angel to hear any more of this conversation, she urged, 'Listen, darling, why don't you go upstairs to get a jigsaw puzzle. Gamma and I will help you to put it together.'

'Don't want to.'

'Well then, choose another toy.'

With a little more persuasion Angel finally left the room to find a toy, Sadie then saying, 'I've heard that Laura Walters likes the booze, her old man too. In fact Nelly Cox said she thinks they're both alcoholics.'

'Goodness, Gran, no wonder Tommy runs wild and it explains why his clothes are like rags. Laura Walters can't be much older than me, but she looks awful, thin and scraggy.'

'I think Nelly said she's around thirty, but she won't see old bones if she keeps boozing.'

'Dreadful though that is, it's Tommy I'm concerned about. Maybe I should report her to the authorities.'

'Keep your nose out of it. It's none of our business and do you really think the child would be better off in care?'

'If getting beaten is a common occurrence, then yes.'

'What makes you think it's common? Have you ever seen or heard him beaten before?'

'Well . . . no.'

'There you are then, as I said, keep your nose out of it. Now how about making us both a drink?'

Sally moved to pick up the kettle, her thoughts still on Tommy as she filled it. No, she hadn't seen any other signs that the child had been thrashed, but that didn't mean it wasn't happening. She just hoped that Laura Walters calmed down before Tommy showed his face again, and now partially understood why the boy was allowed to roam the streets. He might be streetwise, but he was only seven years old, and it wasn't right, despite what Gran said to the contrary.

She paused momentarily, feeling a flush of guilt. When Tommy tried to walk with them to school, she chased him off. Yet what choice did she have? Tommy's language was terrible, and only recently he'd been caught trying to pinch apples from a market stall. No, she didn't want her daughter mixing with him, and as she lit the gas under the kettle, Sally was sure she was doing the right thing. After all, she had to protect her daughter from his bad influence.

When Ruth arrived home that evening she was waxing lyrical about her new boss. Sidney Jacobs had recovered from his awful cold, and her mother had taken to the job like a duck to water.

Sally couldn't help feeling a twinge of envy. Now that Angel was at school she could have worked for Sid again, if only part time, but she had to stay home to look after Gran. Oh, she loved her, she really did, but just lately the house had begun to feel like a prison.

'Mind you, Sal, there was a bit of bother today.'

'Why – what happened?'

'That young girl you got rid of came in. She had her brothers in tow and they were looking for you.'

'Really! My goodness, what did you do?'

'I put the fear of God into them, that's what. I told them I'd call the police.'

'Did they leave?'

'Well no, not straight away, and they caused a rumpus until I dialled 999. They scarpered before the police arrived, but I told Trudy I'd give them her name and address if she showed her face again.'

Sally hoped it was the last her mother would see of Trudy, then the thought was driven from her mind when there was a knock on the door. She opened it to see her Aunt Mary. Instead of her usual upright and proud demeanour, she looked awful. Her hair was lank, and her face wan as she almost slunk inside.

'Well, look what the cat's dragged in,' Sadie snapped. 'And if that coloured geezer's with you, then drag yourself out again.'

There was no curt response, no argument; instead Mary looked at them, her eyes bruised with pain.

'You look awful, Auntie,' Sally cried. 'Are you ill?'

Mary shook her head, whilst Sally focussed on her aura. There were no dark patches, no signs of illness, so why did her aunt look so distressed?

'Mary, sit down before you fall down,' Ruth ordered. 'Come on, tell us what's up?'

'I'm not pregnant.'

'Of course you aren't. I told you that.'

'But I thought I was! Oh I'm a stupid, stupid woman.'

'Does this mean you ain't gonna marry that West Indian?' Sadie asked.

'I won't be getting married and Leroy has gone.'

'Gone . . . gone where?' Sally asked.

'I . . . I don't know.'

Sadie smiled with satisfaction. 'Good riddance to bad rubbish.'

At last Mary showed a bit of her old fire; eyes suddenly blazing she glared at her mother. 'Leroy is a wonderful man and I won't have you talking about him like that.'

'If he's so wonderful, how come he buggered off?'

'Because I told him to go.'

'But why,' Sally blurted out as she went to kneel by her aunt's side.

Mary crumbled, her eyes flooding with tears, and jumping up she fled the room. Ruth made to follow her, but Sally scrambled to her feet. 'No, Mum, let me talk to her.'

'Yeah, all right. You two were always as thick as thieves and I don't think I'm in Mary's good books at the moment.'

Sally found her aunt in the bathroom, perched on the edge of the bath and leaning forward with her arms wrapped around her waist. She rocked as though in pain as she sobbed, 'Oh, Sally, I've been such a fool.'

'Why? Is it because you broke up with Leroy?' Sally held her breath, wondering if her aunt would confide in her.

Mary spoke again, her voice cracking with emotion. 'Oh Sally, I never expected to meet someone like Leroy. Since your uncle's death, I've occasionally been out with men, but I've never been able to . . . to have sex. Leroy changed all that and somehow broke through my barriers. Then, when I thought I was having a baby, I almost burst with happiness. God, what a stupid, stupid woman I am.'

As her aunt sobbed, Sally sat beside her on the edge of the bath, wrapping an arm around her shoulders. 'I'm so sorry you lost your baby, but why did you send Leroy away?'

'I . . . I didn't lose the baby, Sally.'

'I don't understand.'

Mary dashed tears from her eyes. 'I'm eight years older than Leroy, but it didn't seem to matter, and he was thrilled when we thought I was pregnant. But I'll never be pregnant . . . I'll never have a baby. It's too late!'

'But why?'

'I went to see the doctor and felt such a fool when he told me I wasn't pregnant – in fact I've never been pregnant! It was the change, Sally, the change of life, and I was too stupid to realize that.'

The change! Sally closed her eyes, working out her aunt's age, suddenly realizing that though she always took great care of her appearance, looking years younger, she was well into her forties. 'I still don't understand why you broke up with Leroy. All right, he was younger than you, but surely that doesn't matter.'

'He was over the moon when he thought I was having a baby and told me he couldn't wait to have a family. How could I marry him after that? He needs to meet a younger woman, one who can give him the children he wants.'

'Did you tell him that?'

'No, I just told him the pregnancy was a false alarm, and then went on to say I didn't want to marry him after all.'

'But if you had told him the truth it might not have mattered.'

'He may have stayed with me, but eventually he would resent the fact that I can't have children.'

'Oh, Auntie,' Sally sighed.

Visibly straightening, Mary managed a small lopsided smile. 'I feel better for talking about it, thank you, my dear.'

'Aunt Mary, there's no need to thank me. I'll never forget how you took me in when I fell pregnant with Angel.'

'Yes, well, I wasn't going to let your mother force you into having an abortion. Now come on, let's go back to face the others, and at least my mother will be happy.' She took a deep breath, adding firmly, 'It's time to put on a front again.'

'You don't have to pretend with me.'

'I know, and I'm glad that you and I have always been able to talk so openly.'

And the talk must have helped, Sally decided as she watched her aunt calmly telling the others what had happened, her stance once again dignified.

'I hope you've learned your lesson, and in future stick to your own kind,' Sadie remarked.

'Yes, I thought you'd say that,' Mary said, before telling them that she was leaving.

'But you haven't even had a cup of tea,' Ruth protested.

'I know, but I think it's better I leave before saying something to Mum that I might regret.'

'If you've got anything to say to me, let's hear it!'

'No, Mum. Some things are better left unsaid, and anyway, knowing how you feel it would be a waste of time.'

Sally followed her to the street door, laying a hand on her aunt's arm. 'You will come to see us again soon, won't you?'

'Yes, but let me lick my wounds a bit first. To be honest, knowing what my mother's reaction would be I don't know why I came here today. It was silly to expect sympathy. Yet somehow I suppose I hoped to see my old mum, the one who was wise and tolerant, and one I could always go to with my problems.'

'She's still in there somewhere, and at times her old personality shines through.'

'Well it wasn't showing today.' A loud bang made Mary jump, her mouth grim as she said, 'Kids with penny bangers, they drive me mad, and every five minutes there's a child asking for a penny for the guy. I don't know why their parents allow it; after all, it's tantamount to begging.' She grimaced. 'Oh, listen to me, moaning like an old woman, yet since finding out that I'm going through the change, I feel like I've aged overnight.'

'You're not old, Auntie.'

'But I'm past having children.' Leaning forward she planted a kiss on Sally's cheek. 'Bye,' and with a small wave she marched stiffly along Candle Lane.

Sally went back to the kitchen, her mouth tightening as she listened to her mother and gran talking about the event, both happy that Mary had broken up with Leroy, both forgetting the pain her aunt was in.

Was this what had been worrying her? Was this the awful thing she intuitively knew was going to happen? She felt a shiver. No, somehow she doubted it.

Eleven

On November the fifth, Sally was outside with Angel, smiling as her daughter squealed with delight, a sparkler in her gloved hand. The pinpoints of light reflected on Angel's happy face and Sally's heart swelled with love. Oh, she was so beautiful.

'Why can't we have a bonfire, Mummy?'

'We haven't got anywhere to light one, but maybe next year.'

'Tommy's having a bonfire. He's got loads of old stuff piled up in his back yard.'

'That's nice, dear,' Sally said, keeping her eyes peeled for Arthur.

'I wish Daddy was here.'

Sally's eyes flicked along the lane. Arthur had promised to bring home some fireworks, but so far there was no sign of him. The lane was thick with smoke, and from back yards the occasional rocket whooshed into the sky, exploding in a bright shower of tumbling lights.

'Will Daddy be home soon?'

'I hope so.'

A group of small boys ran into the lane, one throwing a penny banger in their direction, and as it exploded Sally grabbed Angel's hand, pulling her indoors before she had time to protest.

'No, Mummy,' Angel cried as Sally hurriedly closed the door.

'Your sparklers are all gone now, darling.'

Angel ran into the kitchen, her voice wheedling as she said to Ruth, 'Nanny, I want to go outside again.'

'You can when your daddy comes home.'

Sally glanced worriedly at the clock. 'Mum, I'm supposed to be at the hall by eight.'

'Don't worry. You can leave this little madam to me.'

'All right, but don't give in to her. There are kids outside throwing bangers and I don't want her hurt.'

'It's always the same on firework night, and last year the little buggers tied a jumping jack to a cat's tail. The poor thing was terrified, bolting down the lane with it trailing behind and going off with a bang every few seconds.'

There was still no sign of Arthur, but Sally had to leave. 'I'd best be off,' she said, leaning down to kiss her daughter. 'Be a good girl for Nanny.'

'Where's Daddy?'

'I don't know, darling, but I'm sure he'll be home soon.'

'He said he'd buy some fireworks.'

Sally hated seeing the disappointment on Angel's face, but surely Arthur would be home shortly? With a small wave she left the house, frowning again as she walked down the lane.

Since that wonderful night of lovemaking when Angela had stayed with Elsie, she had thought things were fine again, but soon after Arthur had become distant and distracted. He'd gone out a few times without telling her where, annoyed if she tried to question him. She was fighting her suspicions, telling herself she was being silly. He couldn't be having an affair, he just couldn't.

The hall was almost empty, with only one healer working on a client when Sally walked in. Perhaps the smoke and fireworks had put people off, she thought as she wandered across the hall to talk to one of the other healers.

By nine o'clock she'd only had one client, and still worried about Arthur, Sally asked the other healers if they minded her leaving early. She wanted to get home, to see if he was there. Surely he had kept his promise to Angela?

The smoke was dense as she turned into Candle Lane and Sally coughed, holding her scarf over her mouth. A fire engine drove past, and suddenly worried she quickened her pace.

When Sally walked into the kitchen it was to find her mother sitting on the sofa, cuddling a small sobbing form. 'What's the matter with Angel?' she cried, but when the small form came fully into view the breath left her body in a rush. It wasn't Angel. It was Tommy Walters, his face streaked with dirt and eyes red from crying.

'Tommy burned his hand and I brought him in to have a look at it. Mind you, it ain't too bad, but it's giving him a bit of gyp.'

'How did he manage to burn it?'

'The silly bugger lit a bonfire in his backyard, but it got a bit bigger than he expected. Blimey, love, you've missed all the excitement. Luckily for Tommy, Mr Stone was in his back yard and saw it over the wall. It was a big blaze by then and he called the fire brigade.'

'But where were Tommy's parents? Didn't they see the fire?'

'His dad wasn't in, and Laura Walters was in her front room with no idea what was going on until the fire engine arrived.' Throwing a look at Tommy she mouthed, 'Drunk.'

The boy was too astute. 'Yeah, me mum was pissed.'

'That isn't a nice word,' Ruth told him, unable to hide a smile of amusement.

'Isn't Arthur home yet?'

'No, and he hasn't rung. I had the devil of a job getting Angel to bed.'

'Where's Gran?'

'In her room.'

'I'd better go and check on Angel. Is she asleep?'

'I dunno. I got a bit sidetracked when Tommy turned up with this burn on his hand, but I haven't heard a peep out of her for a while so I expect she's drifted off.'

Sally hurried upstairs, but as she stepped into the bedroom there was no sign of Angel. Her bed was empty. 'Angela, where are you?'

There was a muffled cry and then the wardrobe door flew open, her daughter tumbling out. 'Mummy, Mummy, there was a fire and Tommy got burned,' Angel sobbed, flying into her arms.

'He only hurt his hand, darling.'

'No! I looked out of the window and saw him on top of the bonfire.' Her voice rose in hysteria, 'When the flames got really big he fell inside. He got deaded!'

'Come on, come with me,' Sally insisted, disengaging her daughter's arms.

Sally led Angel downstairs, watching her daughter's eyes widen when she saw Tommy sitting on the sofa. 'I thought you got burned,' she said.

'I did, look at me hand.'

'But you was on top of the fire, and . . . and then you fell inside.'

'Nah, you silly sod. That was a guy I dressed in me old clothes. You can't have a bonfire without a guy on the top.'

'I found Angel in the wardrobe and she was very upset.'

'I thought she was asleep,' Ruth cried, colouring with guilt. She then turned to Tommy. 'I think it's time you went home.'

'But I've got a burn.'

'It ain't that bad and doesn't even need a bandage. I've put some margarine on it and it'll be better in no time.'

Tommy reluctantly rose to his feet, grinning at Angel as he walked across the room. 'You daft bugger! Fancy thinking I got burned in the fire.'

Sally hated his language but held her tongue as the boy scampered out. Angel, calmer now, ran across the room to kiss her nanny, and then Sally took her daughter back upstairs.

'Why didn't Daddy come home, Mummy?'

'I expect he got held up at work, darling.'

'But he promised.'

Arthur had let the child down and Sally fought to stay calm. She began to hum a lullaby, relieved when at last her daughter settled. Angel had had a bad fright, and now Sally's lips tightened again, annoyed with Tommy's parents. How could they let the boy light a bonfire without supervision? What sort of parents were they!

Half an hour later Sally returned to the kitchen, and as she walked in her mother asked, 'Is Angel all right?'

'She was a bit overexcited, but she's asleep now. I'm worried about Arthur though. He said he'd be home by seven.'

'I expect he got held up.'

Sally flopped on to a chair. Yes, that was probably it. Sometimes when the van arrived at a house, the other people hadn't finished moving out and there would be a delay before they could unload the furniture. Yet on this occasion he should have rung, if only to let Angel down gently.

It was after ten o'clock before Arthur turned up, and after a short greeting he sat by the fire, staring into the flames.

'Arthur, you said you'd be home early and that you'd buy some fireworks for Angel.'

'Did I? Sorry, I forgot.'

'Why didn't you ring?'

'Look, I've got a lot on my mind. Now just leave it will you.'

Sally stared at him, unable to believe his attitude. He was leaning forward, still staring into the fire, his mind obviously elsewhere. What was he thinking about – or who? Once again she felt sick, wondering if there was someone else. 'I . . . I'm going to bed,' she said.

Her mother said goodnight, but Arthur was still in a world of his own and didn't even raise his head.

With one foot on the stairs, Sally paused as tears filled her eyes. This couldn't go on, it just couldn't, and oh, how she wished she'd agreed to them finding a place of their own, even if it was out of the area. Once again she wondered why Arthur never mentioned moving now. She knew he hated living here – he had made that plain, so why had he changed his mind? Did he have another woman? Was he going to leave her?

Twelve

On Saturday Sally felt as though her feelings were on an emotional rollercoaster. Arthur arrived home early, immediately asking her if she wanted to go out, if only to see a film or something. She stared at him, confused. Earlier in the week he had been distant, distracted, but now he was full of smiles, offering to take her out.

'I know, shall we go dancing, Sally? That's if your mother doesn't mind babysitting.'

'Of course I don't mind,' Ruth said. 'You two go out and enjoy yourselves.'

'Right, get your glad rags on, Sal, and we'll go to the Hammersmith Palais.'

She didn't need asking twice and ran upstairs to have a bath, emerging in the kitchen less than an hour later. Arthur was still in the bedroom putting his suit on, but they would soon be off.

'You look nice, Sally,' Sadie remarked.

Angel touched her arm. 'Yes, you look pretty, Mummy.'

'Well thank you both, but I could do with something a bit more modern to wear.'

'That dress is fine. It's a classic style that will never go out of fashion.'

Sally looked down at her black dress, hoping that she wouldn't look too out of date at the Palais. She had brushed her hair until it shone, and applied mascara to her lashes. A touch of lipstick completed her make-up, and she hoped the black, strappy high-heeled shoes made her ankles look slim.

When Arthur came downstairs he made no comment, but Sally noticed that he eyed her legs with appreciation. 'Right, we're off. Be a good girl, Angel,' he said, picking the child up to give her a kiss.

75

'I want to come with you, Daddy.'

'Not tonight, princess,' and after giving her a quick cuddle he placed her on to the floor again.

'It's not fair. I want to come too!'

'Why don't you get the playing cards, Angel,' Ruth urged. 'We'll play snap and I bet I beat you this time.'

Sally smiled gratefully at her mother as Arthur grabbed her hand, both hurrying out before Angel could react.

They climbed into the car and were soon on their way to Hammersmith, but as Sally gazed out of the window, she was still confused. What had brought about this change? She wanted to talk to Arthur, to confront him, but then decided to say nothing. Maybe this evening out would bring them closer and she didn't want to spoil it.

When they reached the Palais, it didn't take Arthur long to park, and then they were queuing outside the dance hall for a ticket. The sound of Motown music reached Sally's ears, her foot beginning to tap. She liked British female singers like Dusty Springfield, and Sandie Shaw, but Motown music was fast becoming a favourite. Amongst others there were Diana Ross and the Supremes, Martha and the Vandellas, black female singers who brought a new sound. There were male groups and singers too who were becoming increasingly popular: Smokey Robinson and the Miracles, Marvin Gaye and The Four Tops coming to mind.

As they walked into the dance hall Arthur made straight for the bar, whilst Sally loitered to watch the dancers. Miniskirts and dresses were in abundance, and for a moment Sally felt frumpy amongst the young girls, but then Arthur shoved a glass of Babycham in her hand and the moment passed.

They found a table, and soon after Sally urged Arthur to dance. He agreed, if a little reluctantly, but then Sally became hardly aware of her husband as she gave herself up to the loud exciting music.

The tempo suddenly changed to a ballad, and hearing the voice of Matt Munro singing *A Portrait of my Love*, she walked into Arthur's arms. The lights dimmed, and the huge mirrored ball suspended above the dance floor spun, sending a myriad of tiny twinkling lights over the couples as they swayed together. 'I love you, Arthur,' Sally whispered.

'I love you too, darling,' he husked, his lips softly kissing her neck.

Sally closed her eyes. He meant it, she was sure of it, and wished this moment could go on forever.

All too soon the song ended, Arthur urging, 'Come on, I want another drink.'

As he went to the bar again, Sally sat at their table looking around the room. She had rediscovered the joy of dancing and was having a wonderful time. Then, as Arthur placed another Babycham in front of her she grinned up at him. 'Thanks, love. I can't wait to get back on the floor.'

'In a minute, Sal, let me have a beer first.'

Sally took a sip of her drink, tapping her feet to the beat of the music, and after half an hour, Arthur stood up, saying with a little bow, 'May I have this dance, madam.'

'Thank you, kind sir,' she said, jumping to her feet.

Once again Sally gave herself up to the music and when the rhythm of an old rock and roll song started up, they began to jive.

Sally laughed as Arthur spun her back and forth and when the music came to an end they were both gasping for breath. Arthur led her back to the table where Sally flopped on to her chair whilst he went off to the bar again.

In the next hour they danced again once or twice, but then it was time to leave, Arthur saying as they drove home, 'Did you have a good time, love?'

'Yes, it was great. We should do it more often.'

'If I can get away early next week, we'll try the Streatham Locarno.'

Sally placed her hand on Arthur's thigh, loving the feel of his muscular leg. She felt a little tipsy, and also felt like making love. Perhaps if Angel was fast asleep they could risk it, she thought, her hand once again squeezing her husband's leg.

Her hopes were dashed when they arrived home to find their daughter restless with a tummy upset, and suspecting she had been given too many sweets, Sally heaved a sigh of disappointment.

It took Angel some time to finally settle, and when Sally climbed in beside Arthur, she found him asleep. She snuggled up behind him, an arm around his waist. It had been a wonderful night out. Arthur had held her, told her he loved her, and as Sally closed her eyes she sighed with happiness. He couldn't be having an affair, he just couldn't.

Thirteen

Arthur was busy for the rest of the week, only home before eight on one occasion, but when Saturday came round again, he arrived home early.

Sally smiled as she placed his dinner of fried liver and bacon on the table. 'Are we going dancing?'

'No, sorry, I've got to go out again.'

'Oh, Arthur. Why?'

'I've got a bit of business to sort out.'

'What sort of business?'

He kept his head low as he ate, saying dismissively, 'It's just something I have to take care of.'

Sally tensed. It didn't seem possible after their wonderful night out last week, but now, once again, Arthur was being evasive. Unable to help herself she blurted out, 'Arthur, what are you up to?'

'Up to! What do you mean?'

'You're hiding something from me.'

'No I'm not.'

'It sounds like you are to me,' Ruth commented.

His face darkened. 'What's this? Have I got to answer to *both* of you now?'

'Are you cross, Daddy?'

Sally saw the worried frown on her daughter's face and said hurriedly, 'Daddy's just tired. Come on now, it's time for your bath.'

Only ten minutes later, Arthur appeared and, sitting on the edge of the bath, he playfully splashed water over Angel. Sally watched for a moment then, trying to keep her voice calm she said, 'Arthur, why won't you tell me about this business that you have to take care of?'

'There's nothing to tell. It's just work – something in the

79

pipeline,' he said, his voice dismissive.

Sally felt her stomach churn. It felt as though Arthur had put a wall up again, one that she couldn't penetrate. Surely there wasn't any business to sort out on a Saturday night, so where was he really going? 'If there are estimates to price – how come you're involved? I thought your father handled all that. You only have to do the removals.'

'Yeah, that's me, the donkey, and I don't need you to rub it in. If you must know I'm sick of it. If I could find a way out, I would.'

'But you've never said anything before! I thought you were happy working with your father.'

'I was to start with, but nothing changes. Dad gets the work and along with the other drivers, I do the humping.'

'Have you told him how you feel?'

'What's the point? Now just shut up about it!'

'No shout, Daddy,' Angel cried, her face crumbling with distress.

'Christ,' Arthur said, leaning over the bath to stroke Angel's cheek. 'Sorry, sweetheart, I didn't mean to shout.'

'Lift me out now,' she appealed, holding up her arms.

'Mummy will see to you, darling. I've got to go now.'

'No, Daddy.'

'If you're a good girl I'll take you to the park tomorrow. Now give Daddy a kiss.'

Arthur then turned to Sally. 'I'm sorry, love, I shouldn't take my frustration out on you, but will you get Angel out of the bath now? I need to have a wash and shave.'

Sally stared at him, wanting to question him further, but with her daughter's eyes on them, she just nodded. She lifted Angel, wrapping her in a towel, leaving the bathroom to Arthur. Her thoughts were raging as she got her daughter ready for bed, and telling her to go downstairs to say good-night to Nanny and Gamma, she waited for Arthur to come out of the bathroom.

He emerged a few minutes later, and without preamble, Sally said, 'Arthur, where are you really going tonight?'

Arthur walked over to the wardrobe, his back towards her as he took out a clean shirt. 'I've already told you. I've got some business to take care of.'

80

'Will your father be with you?'

As Arthur added a tie, he swung round, his voice hard with impatience. 'What's this, the bloody Spanish Inquisition? No, my father won't be with me and I don't need all this hassle from you.'

Sally was about to respond, but Angel ran into the room. 'Nanny said I can stay up for a while.'

'Did she now,' Arthur said and, picking up his jacket, he bent to kiss Angel. 'I'm off now. Be a good girl and as I said I'll take you to the park tomorrow.' His eyes hardened as he turned to Sally. 'See you later, and don't bother to wait up.'

Sally tried to hide her feelings as she took Angel downstairs, thankful that her mother said nothing until the child was engrossed in a game of snap with Sadie.

'So, Sally, Arthur's gone out again. What's he up to?'

'I don't know, but he said it's to do with business – something in the pipeline.'

'He certainly works hard, doesn't he,' Ruth commented, a hint of sarcasm in her voice.

'Snap,' Angel shouted.

Wanting to escape her mother's questions, Sally rose to her feet. 'Come on, it's time for bed.'

'No, Mummy.'

'I said bed!' Sally said briskly, brooking no argument as she glared at her daughter. 'Say goodnight.'

Angel's eyes filled with tears, but she did as she was told and, ignoring the stunned looks on the faces of both her gran and mother, Sally took her daughter upstairs. The child was subdued as Sally tucked her into bed and, feeling a surge of guilt, Sally dragged her into her arms.

'I'm sorry, darling.'

'Was I a naughty girl, Mummy?' she asked, looking confused.

'No, of course not and I'm sorry for shouting at you. Come on, I'll read you a story.' Sally grabbed a book, Angel's favourite at the moment, her voice soft as she read 'The Princess and the Pea'. Soon Angel's eyes began to droop and, as she fell asleep, Sally rose to her feet. She made her way downstairs cursing herself for confronting Arthur in front of Angel, their row upsetting the child. She could remember her own childhood, the constant arguments she'd heard, and didn't want Angel to suffer that too. It was frustration as well as disappointment that had made her confront him, his evasiveness driving her mad, but somehow in future she would have to avoid speaking to Arthur in front of Angela.

Another evening stretched ahead of her, another evening sitting in front of the television, her mother speaking as soon as she walked into the kitchen.

'What rattled your chain? There was no need to snap at Angel like that.'

'I don't want to talk about it.'

'Do you two mind! I'm trying to watch the television,' Sadie complained.

Ruth raised her eyebrows, shaking her head in annoyance as Sally slumped on to a chair, and for the next few hours conversation was sparse.

'How about a cup of cocoa?' Sadie said at half past ten.

'All right, I'll make it,' Sally said as she rose to her feet. 'And then I'm going to bed.' There was no sign of Arthur and once again she was unable to stop the suspicion that he was having an affair from churning in her mind.

She made the drinks and then gave her mother and gran a perfunctory kiss before going upstairs, finding that instead of getting ready for bed, she was standing at the window looking out on to Candle Lane.

The sky was clear, the lane bathed in the moon's silvery glow and looking almost pretty, an illusion that would be shattered in daylight. There wasn't a soul to be seen, emphasizing her bleak feelings. Why was she feeling like this? Why was she so suspicious? It was the way he avoided meeting her eyes that made her sure he was hiding something. Yet if there *was* another woman, could he really dance with her, hold her close and say he loved her?

Oh where are you, Arthur? Sally cried inwardly. *And who are you with?*

Recalling the expression on Sally's face, Arthur had been kicking himself as he drove to the pub. He was anxious about the huge step he was thinking of taking, his nerves keyed up, but he shouldn't have taken his feelings out on his wife. Maybe he should tell her what he was up to, but until he made a decision, one way or the other, he didn't want to take that step. Now, as he sat beside his friend, he was still unsure.

Joe took a swig of beer before speaking. 'Well, Arthur, are you in or out?'

'I want to say yes, but it's such a big risk. It means putting every penny of my savings into the venture, and scrapping any chance of buying a house.'

'I thought you said your wife would be happy to stay in Candle Lane.'

'Yes, she'd jump at the chance, but I want something better for my daughter. Candle Lane isn't the environment I had in mind.'

'Leave it out, Arthur. Both you and your wife grew up there, and I can't see that it's done you any harm.'

'When do you need my final decision?'

'I'm still scouting around for land, but could do with your answer within a month.'

'Would you mind showing me the paperwork again?'

'Of course not, and as I've said so many times before, you'd be a fool to miss out on this.'

Arthur scanned the architect's drawings, but remained undecided as he discussed the salient points with Joe. Yes, he had been brought up in a working class area of London, and had the means to buy a house, but that was on the tail of his father's success. Without that security, would he and Sally have considered buying a place of their own? Would working class couples take the risk? 'I still don't know, Joe. What makes you so sure these houses will sell?'

'Times are changing. Young couples are earning more nowadays and moving away from rented accommodation. They have their eyes set on the future, and the property ladder. These houses will be the first rung on the ladder.'

'But if they don't sell we'll be up the creek without a paddle.'

'They will sell, I'm sure of it. We've looked at every angle, and once the show house is up the rest will be snapped up before they're even built.'

Arthur stared at the plans again, his thoughts racing. If Joe was right they could make a fortune on the fifteen houses. The builder was already on board, and now there was just the land to find and purchase. He couldn't put in as much money as Joe, but enough of a share to show a good profit. Dare he risk it? He thought about the years working for his father and the years that stretched ahead. This was his chance – a chance to show what he was made of, and one that may never present itself again. If this venture worked it would be followed by others, and in a few years' time they could be in clover. 'All right, Joe, after I've talked it over with Sally, I'll give you my answer.'

'Fair enough. Now, how about another pint?'

When the drinks arrived Arthur downed his, another following. The pub was closing before both men left, and as Arthur drove home his mind was still turning. If he agreed to go in with Joe it would mean telling his father he was leaving the firm and he dreaded the confrontation – dreaded seeing the disappointment on his father's face.

The doubts returned, but there was no getting away from the fact that he hated the removal business. Years of doing the same old thing, years of back-breaking lifting, maybe ending up almost crippled with pain like his father. No, he didn't fancy that. He wanted to build something on his own endeavours, a business he could be proud of.

For a moment a memory surfaced and he saw himself all those years ago at the docks, waiting to board the ship that would take him to Australia. God, his father had looked devastated, his mother and sister too. Yet he couldn't hold that up as a comparison. After all, he wasn't leaving the country this time! He was just thinking of leaving his father's firm. He drew close to Candle Lane, his mind almost made up, and if Sally was still awake he'd tell her of his plans.

It was almost midnight when Ruth heard Arthur coming in and her lips compressed. She wasn't usually awake at this time, but found herself tossing and turning. Arthur was up to something, she was sure of it, and wondered if she should talk to her daughter. She could sense that something was worrying Sally so perhaps she was equally suspicious. But surely – unlike *her* husband – Arthur wouldn't be unfaithful.

It was about fifteen minutes later when Ruth heard voices in the lane, someone shouting, and then a door slammed. It was probably that lot next door, she decided. Another five minutes passed, and still she was unable to calm her mind.

The room felt clammy, airless, and she wondered if there was a storm brewing. With an impatient sigh she threw back her blankets and padded to the window, opening it a little wider.

She was just about to return to her bed when she heard a noise and her brows creased. It was faint, but sounded like muffled sobs. Puzzled, she stuck her head out of the window, straining her neck to gaze along Candle Lane.

At first Ruth could see nothing, but then, in the faint light from a street lamp, she could see a small figure sitting on the kerb, feet in the gutter. A child! What was a child doing out after midnight?

She threw on her dressing-gown, and careful not to make any noise she slipped downstairs, her face stretching as she stepped out into the lane. The small figure sitting hunched in a thin jumper was Tommy Walters. His head was bent and as she approached it was obvious that he was crying. 'What are you doing out here at this time of night?'

The boy sniffed, cuffing his face with his sleeve. 'Me muvver chucked me out.'

Ruth found anger rising. What sort of woman threw a child on to the streets at this time of night? 'Why, Tommy?'

''Cos I was sent to buy her a bottle of booze earlier, but I dropped it on the way home.'

'Tommy, I don't understand. If this happened earlier, why has she chucked you out at this hour?'

'I managed to keep out of her way until now, but she caught me hiding in me bedroom.'

'Hiding! Weren't you in bed?'

'Nah, I was asleep underneath, but she found me.' His sobs rose and once again he cuffed his face with his sleeve. 'She gave me another belting too.'

'Come on,' Ruth said, holding out her hand. 'I think I should have a few words with your mother.'

'No missus!' he cried, scrambling to his feet. 'She'll go mad.'

'I can't leave you out here all night.'

Tommy straightened his shoulders, now saying bravely, 'I'll be all right. I'll wait until me mum and dad are asleep and then I'll sneak back in again.'

'Have you got a key?'

'Nah, of course not, but me bedroom's at the back. I can climb over the wall and then shin up the drainpipe.'

'But you might fall!'

'Course I won't. I've done it before and it's a piece of cake.'

Ruth shivered, clutching her dressing-gown closer to her body as she eyed Tommy's thin clothes. His mother must be mad, and despite the boy's protests, she wanted to give the woman a piece of her mind. 'I can't leave you out here, Tommy. I think it would be better if we knock on your door.'

'No! No, don't! I . . . I'll run away.'

Ruth could see the fear in the boy's eyes and her heart went out to him. 'All right, but it's freezing out here so you'd better come into my place for the time being.'

All might have been well, but as they stepped inside Sadie came out of her bedroom. In other circumstances her appearance might have been comical as she stood with arms folded across her chest, blue hairnet askew, and dressing-gown gaping to reveal a long flannelette nightdress. Toothless and lisping, she demanded, 'Why are you bringing that bleedin' hooligan in here at this time of night?'

'Because his mother chucked him out.'

'Humph, no doubt he deserved it. Now get him out of my house.'

'No, Mum. It isn't safe for him to go home yet and I'm not leaving him on the streets.'

'But look at the state of him. He's probably alive with fleas. Now as I said, get him out of my house.'

'This ain't *your* house, Mum, it's mine, and *I'll* say who comes in and out of it.'

'Don't talk to me like that, my girl!'

Ignoring her mother and turning away from the indignant look on her face, Ruth touched Tommy's shoulder. 'Go into the kitchen and I'll get you a bite to eat.'

'What! You're gonna feed the little bugger too?'

'It's all right, I don't want nuffin,' Tommy said, his eyes shining with unshed tears.

'Go into the kitchen,' Ruth urged again, giving him a small shove on the back.

When the boy was out of sight she turned back to her

mother. 'He's only two years older than Angel, and I'd like to think that if she was in trouble, someone would help her. Now go back to bed, Mum, and keep your nose out of it.'

Perhaps it was something her mother saw in her face, Ruth didn't know, but instead of arguing Sadie huffed loudly. 'Sod yer then. I'm going, and you can do what you like.'

Ruth entered the kitchen and in no time she had cut a doorstep of bread, spreading it liberally with margarine and strawberry jam. With a small smile she gave it to Tommy, and wide-eyed, without protest, he took it, cramming it hurriedly into his mouth as though scared it would be snatched from his hand. The slice rapidly disappeared, leaving jam smeared across his face. 'Cor, thanks, missus. That was bleedin' lovely.'

Tommy was perched on the edge of the sofa, his face pinched and blue with cold. Ruth's heart ached for him. He may be a little hooligan, his language appalling, but when all was said and done he was just a seven-year-old child. She poured him a cup of milk and then sat beside him, her questions gentle. 'Do you get many beltings, Tommy?'

'Nah. Most of the time I keep out of me muvver's way.'

'What about your dad?'

'He's all right. When he's had a skinful he just goes to sleep.'

Seven, he's only seven, Ruth thought again, yet already he sounded so streetwise. She was about to question him again, but saw him sinking back on the sofa, his eyelids drooping. Instead she sat quietly beside him, and as he drifted off to sleep she studied his face, finding that in sleep he looked so sweet and innocent.

Ruth lit a cigarette, taking a deep drag. There was something about the child – something that drew her, and seeing an old blanket on her mother's chair, she gently tucked it around him. He stirred, but didn't awake, and she decided to leave him there until the morning. There would probably be hell to pay, not only from her family, but the Walters too. Yet how could she turn the child out into the night to climb drainpipes?

With one last glance at the sleeping child, Ruth made her way to bed, finding that this time she drifted straight off to sleep.

87

Fourteen

When Sally awoke the following morning, she found Arthur's arm around her waist, and as she shifted slightly, his hand came up to cup her breast.

She found herself instantly aroused. Her hand reached down to grasp him, finding that he was equally ready and, half awake, he groaned softly.

'Arthur, please,' she whispered, and with another soft groan he gathered her into his arms.

Their lips met, but then Arthur became fully awake. 'No!' he cried, flinging himself around to look at Angel.

'It's all right, she's asleep,' Sally told him, her hand once again snaking down below his waist.

'We can't. She might wake up.' Firmly removing her hand, he flung back the blankets and headed for the bathroom.

Sally squeezed her eyes shut against his rejection, fighting tears of frustration. Yes, Angel had woken up the last time they had attempted to make love, but that was nearly three months ago. Since then, other than the night Angel had stayed at Elsie's, Arthur had barely touched her and she wondered at his self-control. He must be equally frustrated, yet was it willpower, or did he have another woman? He came back into the room now, barely glancing at her as he began to dress.

'Arthur, is there someone else?'

'Someone else,' he echoed, looking puzzled.

'Have you got another woman?'

'What! Don't be ridiculous, of course I haven't.'

Angel awoke, rubbing her knuckles sleepily into her eyes, and as Arthur went to her side he hissed, 'Sally, we've got to talk, but not in front of *you know who*.'

She stared up at her husband, feeling her heart pounding

against her ribs. Arthur had initially denied an affair, but had he changed his mind? Was he going to confess? Oh, God, I can't bear it, she thought, barely listening as Arthur spoke to Angel.

'Why don't you go downstairs to see Nanny.'

'Come too, Daddy.'

'I'll be down in a minute, so will Mummy.'

Angel scrambled out of bed, and making sure she had her warm dressing-gown on, Arthur tightened the belt. As she ran from the room he turned with a smile on his face. 'I don't suppose we'll be on our own for long.'

How can he look so cheerful, she thought, unaware that her eyes were dark with pain. 'Are you going to leave me?' she blurted out.

'Sally, I don't know what you're talking about. Why would I leave you?'

'To go off with her.'

Running a hand through his hair, Arthur sat on the side of the bed, his expression bewildered. 'I don't know where you've got this idea from, but I can only say again that I'm not being unfaithful.'

'You've been out lots of times without telling me where.'

'I know, but it hasn't been to see another woman,' and as tears spurted in Sally's eyes he gathered her into his arms. 'Maybe I should have put you in the picture earlier, but I didn't see any point in discussing it until I'd made up my mind.'

'I . . . I don't understand.'

'No, of course you don't. Right, I'll start at the beginning. You see an old friend of mine, someone I met in Australia, has asked me to go into business with him. I've been meeting him to discuss the details. There's been a lot to sort out, a lot to look into, but I've come to a decision now.'

'God, Arthur. You should have told me instead of letting me worry myself sick.'

'I thought you trusted me.'

'I did . . . I do, but you've been so distant lately and I didn't know what to think.'

'Yes, I suppose I have been distracted, but there's been so much to take into consideration.'

'Surely you're not thinking of leaving your father's firm.'

'Huh, that says it all. It's *his* company – not mine.'

'He's your father and takes it for granted that the firm will one day go to you.'

'Yes, *one day*, but he isn't fifty yet and will carry on working for at least another fifteen years. He doesn't really need me, Sally. I just do deliveries, day in day out, and he can easily replace me. I hate the job.'

'I thought you liked the removals business.'

'It was all right at first. I enjoyed travelling around the country, but now it's just a daily grind.'

'What sort of business are you thinking of going into?'

As Arthur began to talk about his plans, Sally's face stretched in amazement. She thought about her father-in-law, a man she had grown to love. Bert, like Arthur, was a giant of a man, and she knew that if Arthur made up his mind to leave the firm, he would be devastated. 'Are you sure you're doing the right thing?'

'Yes, I'm sure, but before giving Joe Somerton my answer, I thought it best to talk it over with you.'

'What's to talk about? It sounds to me like you've already made up your mind.'

'I'll be using all our savings to set up this business, and that means we can't buy a house for the foreseeable future.'

'Well that's all right. We can stay here.'

'No, we need a place of our own again,' and as Sally was about to protest he held up his hand. 'Look, I know you still feel that your gran needs looking after, but there's no reason why we can't rent a flat close by. You can look after Sadie during the day, and in the evenings we can be in our own home.'

Sally nodded, seeing the sense of his words. She had been wrong in thinking that Arthur had another woman, but perhaps this served as a warning. If their marriage was to survive they had to have the privacy of their own place again. Yet would they be able to manage financially? 'Arthur, if you're putting all our savings into this business, what will we do for money?'

'Joe and I are going to pay ourselves a small wage until the houses are sold, but it'll be nothing like the money we're used to. We'll just have to pull our horns in.'

'We'll have rent to pay.'

'I know, but I'm sure we'll manage.'

For the first time, Sally began to realize how lucky they had been. Arthur was well-paid and they'd never had to worry about money. Now, for the first time, she would have to learn to economize. Well, she'd had a good teacher in her mother and knew how to make nourishing meals from cheap cuts of meat and vegetables. If her mother could do it, so could she. Not only that, Elsie had supported Bert when he started up his own business, and she would do the same. With a smile she said, 'All right. I'll start looking for a flat straight away.'

Arthur's face lit up with delight, but at that moment Angel burst into the room again. 'Mummy, Daddy, come and see who's downstairs.'

As Sally stepped into the kitchen she was surprised to see Tommy Walters. The boy's ragged clothes were rumpled and he was perched at the table, tucking into a bowl of cereal. 'What's going on, Mum?'

'His mother threw him on to the street last night so I let him sleep on the sofa.'

'Threw him out! But he's only a child.'

'I know, and Laura Walters is a bloody disgrace. Unlike you, Sally, she ain't fit to be a mother.'

Angel scrambled on to a chair opposite Tommy, grinning as she said, 'Can he live with us now, Nanny?'

'Well, I don't know about that, ducks.'

'Of course he can't live with us. Don't put silly ideas into her head, Mum. As for his mother throwing him out, you should report it to the police.'

'I ain't a snitch.'

'So you think she should be allowed to get away with it?'

'No, but if the police become involved the boy will end up in care.'

'Yes, *care*, and it seems to me he'd be better off.'

Ruth stepped closer to her daughter, and out of Tommy's earshot she hissed, 'Don't be daft, of course he wouldn't. I ain't reporting it to the police, but I will have a word with his mother.' She moved away smiling at Tommy, 'Now, lad, would you like some more cereal?'

'Yes please, missus,' he said with a wonky-toothed grin.

'I've bleedin' told her she shouldn't bring him in here,' Sadie said as she stepped into the room, her face set in disapproval as she looked at the boy.

Arthur followed, looking equally surprised to see the lad, but unlike Sally he sat beside him at the table. 'Hello, young man, and what are you doing here?'

'Me muvver chucked me out and she,' he said, pointing at Ruth, 'fetched me in here.'

'She,' Arthur gently admonished, 'is Mrs Marchant. Why did your mother throw you out?'

''Cos I dropped her bleedin' bottle of gin.'

Arthur roared with laughter, obviously finding the boy amusing, but Sally's lips compressed. 'Don't swear, Tommy.'

'Swear! But I didn't swear.'

'Yes you did. You said *bleeding.*'

'But that ain't swearing, and she just said it,' Tommy protested, his eyes flicking to Sadie. 'Now if I'd said, fu—'

'Don't you dare!' Sally cried before the boy had time to finish the word. 'Where on earth did you learn such bad language?'

'Me dad says it all the time. He calls me a little bugger too.'

Arthur roared with laughter again, but Sally's smile was thin. She said quietly in her mother's ear, 'Mum, I don't like Angel hearing all this bad language. She's drinking in every word he's saying.'

'I know, but you've got to feel sorry for the kid,' and turning back to Tommy she added, 'Come on, love, it's time you went home.'

Tommy scrambled from his chair, blurting out before he ran from the room, 'Thanks for 'aving me.'

There was silence for a few moments, before Ruth said, 'That was nice of him. He's not such a bad boy really.'

'Mum, how can you say that? You heard his appalling language.'

'You can't blame the boy for that. He's only repeating what he hears at home.'

'Maybe, but I still don't want Angel mixing with him.'

'But I like Tommy,' Angel protested.

'I want you to stay away from him.'

'Sally, you should listen to yourself,' Ruth commented. 'You sound as snobbish as your Aunt Mary. Tommy is no different from the other kids in the street.'

'I know, and I don't want her running with them either.'

'Both you and Arthur grew up in Candle Lane and it didn't do you any harm. Now you act as if the place isn't good enough for you.'

'There weren't kids like Tommy Walters around then.'

'Yes there were, but you have a selective memory. As for language, Angel has heard swearing before, mainly from my mother, but she hasn't picked it up.'

'Here, Ruth, you swear too,' Sadie protested.

'Not as much as you, Mum!'

'Come on, let's all calm down,' Arthur said. 'Anyway, we both have something to tell you.'

Yes, Sally thought, they had something to tell them, and after this morning's events she found herself looking forward to moving out of Candle Lane. She would have to find a flat that wasn't too far away, but hopefully in a better part of Battersea.

Sadie and Ruth listened to Arthur, both silent until he came to the part about them finding a place of their own. It was Ruth who then turned to Sally, saying, 'But what about your gran?'

'I'll still look after her all day, and only go out to pick Angel up from school. When you come home from work I can leave, and you can take over.'

Ruth's head went down, her shoulders slumped, and for a moment it was quiet until Sadie broke the silence, 'Yes, it's about time you had your own place again, and I don't see why you have to stay with me. I keep telling you that I'm fine, but you don't seem to listen.'

Sally bit on her lower lip, knowing that despite her gran's protests, she really couldn't be left on her own all day. 'I'll stay with you until the doctor gives you the all clear.'

'He's an old fusspot and hell might freeze over before that happens.'

'Are you trying to get rid of me, Gran?' Sally asked, trying to lighten the atmosphere.

'Of course I ain't, you silly mare.'

'What's a silly mare, Gamma?' Angel asked.

'It's a funny horse, me darling.'

'Can I have one?'

Arthur picked Angel up and swung her high before putting her on to the floor again, laughing as he said, 'If you ever have a horse of your own, you won't want a silly one. What do you say, Ruth.'

At last Ruth raised her head. 'Your dad's right,' she said before turning to Sally, her voice contrite, 'I've been selfish, and I'm sorry. Yes, I agree, it is about time you had your own home again, and if you can still come here during the day, I don't see any problem.'

'Good, that's settled then,' Arthur said. 'Now, Sally, how about feeding me and then I'm off to Wimbledon to break the news to my father.'

'He ain't gonna like it, lad,' Sadie observed. 'Are you sure you're doing the right thing? You've got security working for your father, and that ain't something to be sniffed at.'

'I know, but believe me I've given this a great deal of thought before making my decision.'

'I don't doubt it, but your father is still going to be upset.'

Sally watched as Arthur lowered his eyes, and like Gran, she knew her father-in-law was going to be devastated. With a small sad shake of her head she began to prepare Arthur's breakfast, but as goosebumps suddenly ran up her spine, her hands shook. Her intuition was aroused again, and once again she had a terrible feeling that something awful was going to happen. Was Gran in danger? Was she going to have another stroke?

Fifteen

Arthur drove to Wimbledon, his nerves keyed up. Should he delay telling his father until he saw him at work in the morning? His hands gripped the steering-wheel and he was almost on the point of turning back, but then he bit his lower lip. No, it would be better to get it over with, and anyway there were too many prying ears around in the office, especially those of his father's secretary.

As he parked in the drive his eyes roamed over his parents' house, once again appreciating why they had chosen it. The mellow red bricks added warmth to the façade, and though bleak now, in summer the gardens would be ablaze with his mother's favourite flowers.

Arthur rang the bell; his mother looked harassed when she opened the door. Hearing the sound of children screaming with laughter, it didn't take long before Arthur's nephews tumbled into the hall. No wonder his mother looked worn out.

Ann, his sister, chased behind, and seeing him her face lit up. 'Arthur! How lovely, but why isn't Sally with you?'

'I've only called in for a quick word with Dad.' Arthur gazed at his sister, thinking that after the trendy clothes she used to wear, her appearance was now almost matronly, and her face was lined with tiredness. 'If we had known you were visiting, Sally would have insisted on coming.'

'It's a surprise visit and Mum wasn't expecting me either.'

'Darren, Jason, stop that!' Bert bellowed as he came into the hall to see the boys pulling the cat's tail. The animal raised its hackles, hissing as it ran off to safety whilst Bert put a restraining arm around the twins, his smile warm as he said, 'Hello, son. What brings you here today?'

'I want to talk to you, but with this lot around, I don't think I'm going to get the chance.'

'If it's important we can talk in my study, and woe betide you lot,' he said with a mock growl, 'if you disturb us.'

'Surely it can wait until you've had a cup of coffee,' Elsie protested.

'Of course it can,' Arthur told her, and now that the moment he dreaded had arrived, he found himself relieved that it had been put off for a while.

His mother's usually immaculate sitting room was now strewn with toys, but it didn't seem to bother her as she smiled happily at her grandchildren. 'What a shame that Sally didn't come with you. Angel would have loved to see her cousins.'

'Yes, I'm gutted,' Ann said. 'Sally's my best friend, and I miss her.'

'Well you chose to move out to the sticks, Sis.'

'I know, but it wouldn't hurt you to drive down to see us more often.'

'Give me a break, Ann. I only have Sundays off and by then I'm whacked.'

'It isn't that far, and you know my hubby can't drive.'

'It's about time he learned. After spending six days a week on the roads, a day without driving is a luxury for me.'

'Now then, you two, if you don't stop this will develop into an argument. Arthur, can I get you something to eat with your coffee?'

'No thanks, Mum, I had a big breakfast before I left.'

'How's Sadie? She didn't look too bad the last time I popped down to Candle Lane.'

'She's all right, except for her changeable moods. I don't know how Sally puts up with it.'

'Nor do I, but I saw in the tarot cards that things are going to change. I'm not sure how, and must admit I was a bit worried when I saw the spread.'

His mother was looking at him, a strange expression on her face, almost as if she knew what his plans were. Arthur blanched. 'Change . . . what sort of change did you see?'

'It wasn't clear, but I think we're about to find out. Isn't that why you've come to talk to your father?'

Unable to meet his mother's eyes, Arthur lowered his head, relieved when she left the room to make the coffee. When he looked up again it was to see his father gazing at him, his eyes puzzled. Arthur found his hands trembling, but then the children began to squabble over a toy, breaking the tableau, and he breathed a sigh of relief.

For a while chaos reigned until Ann was able to break the boys up, but in the meantime the noise had woken the baby, the little girl squalling in her carry-cot.

'Arthur, bring your coffee to my study,' Bert said, his tone brooking no argument. 'We might as well have our talk now and perhaps when we come back this lot will have settled down again.'

He followed his father to the small room at the back of the house and as Bert sat behind his desk, Arthur took a chair in front of it, his hands twisting and turning in his lap.

'Well, son, this is obviously important, so let's hear it.'

'I . . . I'm leaving the firm.'

'Leaving the firm! But why?'

'I want to strike out on my own and I've been given a wonderful opportunity to take on a partnership with an old friend of mine.'

'But you're already in partnership with me!'

'It isn't official, and in reality I'm no different from all your other drivers.'

'What do you mean, no different? You're my son!'

'Dad, I'm fed up with it. Fed up with lugging furniture – fed up with being on the roads day in and day out.'

'We're a removals firm so what else did you expect?'

'It's *your* firm, one *you* built up and I had little hand in it. I want to achieve something for myself, something I can be proud of.'

'Are you going to start up your own removals company?'

'No, I'm going into the construction game. Joe Somerton and I are buying a plot of land and will be building low cost houses.' Unable to keep the enthusiasm out of his voice Arthur went into the details, waxing lyrical about the project, the builders and the architect.

'But you know nothing about building. Have you thought about the risks involved?'

'I won't be involved in the actual construction. Joe and I will be project managers, and it will be up to us to sell the houses.'

'And if they don't sell?'

'They will, Dad. We've looked at this from all angles. Young couples are looking to get on the property ladder and the time is ripe.'

'It all sounds a bit pie in the sky to me. Have you forgotten you've got a wife and child to support?'

'Of course I haven't. Until the houses are sold, Joe and I will be paying ourselves a small wage. Sally and I will just have to pull our horns in for a while.'

There was a moment of silence and then the questions began again. 'What do you know about this friend of yours? You're talking about going into business with him, so have you checked him out? How much money is he putting into the venture? And is it as much as you?'

'Joe's a great bloke and he's risking far more money than me. He's putting in the lion's share.'

'So how is it a partnership?'

'It'll still be a partnership because I'll be taking less of the profit when the houses are sold.'

'Where is *his* money coming from? And has he got any experience of the building game?'

Arthur sighed, fed up with this inquisition. He knew what he was doing, but it sounded as if his father took him for a complete fool. He wasn't a child and it was about time his father realized that. His patience stretched, Arthur found his voice high as he snapped, 'Joe inherited money from his grandparents, and no, he was brought up on a farm so hasn't any experience.'

'A farm! Christ, son, this sounds worse and worse. *Your* only experience is with removals and Joe's a carrot cruncher, a farmer's boy. What do the pair of you know about running a business? Nothing!'

'You started yours with no idea if it would succeed. You uprooted us from Wimbledon to Battersea and sank every penny you had into the venture. If it worked for you, why shouldn't it for me?'

'I'd been employed in removals for years and at least had some experience. You on the other hand know nothing about the construction industry.'

'Then I'll learn, and at least I won't spend the rest of my

life humping furniture!' Arthur saw the pain in his father's eyes and hung his head. 'I . . . I'm sorry, Dad,' he mumbled.

'Arthur, go back to the sitting room. I want to be on my own for a while.'

His father's voice sounded husky with emotion, and unable to think of anything to say, Arthur left him.

Ann was nursing her daughter as he stepped into the sitting room, the boys now playing quietly, and as he met his mother's eyes, she said, 'What have you done, son?'

'I've told Dad that I'm leaving the firm.'

'How has he taken it?'

'Not very well.'

'Why are you leaving?'

Arthur perched on the edge of a chair, explaining his reasons, once again finding his voice full of enthusiasm.

'You have a family to support and at least with your father you have security.'

'Yes, Dad pointed that out, but I can't let this opportunity pass me by.'

His mother sighed, whilst Ann sat watching the scene, her eyes wide but saying nothing. Arthur bit hard on his bottom lip, hating upsetting his parents, but this was something he just had to do. 'Please, try to understand, Mum.'

'I am trying, but it's a lot to take in. How does Sally feel about it?'

'She's supporting my decision.'

'Well, son, I hope you make a success of this new venture, but I'm still not happy about you leaving the firm.'

'Thanks, Mum, now if you don't mind I think I'll go now.'

'Yes, that might be for the best.'

Arthur quietly said goodbye to them all, and leaving the house he found his heart heavy. He flung himself into the driving seat, still seeing the hurt on his father's face, his mind distracted as he drove down West Hill. Had he done the right thing? Was this new venture too risky?

Arthur hadn't seen the traffic lights turn to red, and didn't realize he'd jumped them until he heard the screeching of tyres. He swiftly turned his head, just in time to see the lorry almost on top of him.

Unable to react, eyes wide with horror, he felt the lorry

hit with the deafening sound of metal crunching against metal. Arthur was thrown violently sideways, his body rebounding against the door as the car slewed across the road.

More deafening noise and then pain! Agonizing pain! He screamed, but then – mercifully – there was nothing but blackness.

Sixteen

Sally was humming as she finished peeling the potatoes, smiling at the antics of her daughter sitting perched on a cushion at the kitchen table, playing cards with Sadie.

'Snap!' she yelled, giggling as her small hands avidly grabbed the cards.

'Gawd, you're too good for me,' Sadie said, holding up her hands in defeat.

'Play again, Gamma?'

'All right, but just one more game.'

Ruth looked up from basting the roast lamb, her face pink from the heat of the oven. 'It's nearly two o'clock and there's only the potatoes left to roast. I hope Arthur's home in time for dinner.'

'He left before eleven so should be back in plenty of time. Would you like me to peel some parsnips?'

'Yuk, no, Mummy!'

Sally grinned. Angel hated parsnips, but Sadie smacked her lips, her reply an affirmative. She bent back to her task, her mind now on Arthur again. He sounded so excited about this new venture, but should she have tried to talk him out of it? He was sinking so much money into it, in fact every penny saved over the last five years. What if it all went pear shaped – what then? This was a new chapter in their lives, the future uncertain, and she couldn't help feeling apprehensive.

Her mind slewed again, wondering how her in-laws were reacting to the news. Bert was a wonderful man, someone she looked up to, and having no real father of her own he had filled a void in her life.

Angel yelled with glee as she won the game of snap, and Sally turned from her task as Sadie spoke.

'No more games, Angel. I'm fair worn out.'

'Gamma doesn't want to play, Mummy. Can I go out?'

'No you can't.'

'Pleeease, Mummy.'

'I said, *no*.'

'Half an hour won't hurt, Sally.'

'Gran, the last time I let her play outside she went off with Tommy and his gang.'

'She won't do that again – will you sweetheart?' Sadie said, her eyes on Angel.

'No, I'll stay by the door.'

'See, she's learned her lesson. Let her go out for a while, Sally. She'll be fine and it can't be a lot of fun for her stuck in here.'

Sally sighed heavily as her mother joined in the conversation, also taking Angel's side. 'Go on, let her go out for a while.'

Angel could play in the yard if it wasn't so full of her mother's old junk – junk she refused to get rid of, saying it might come in useful one day. Her mother was a hoarder, with every spare cupboard and drawer stuffed with things that would never be used. Old clothes, old curtains, china, books, and a myriad of other bits and pieces that drove her mad when she wanted to find anything. Honestly, Sally thought, the sooner they got a place of their own the better, a home with a garden for Angel to play in.

'Please, Mummy,' Angel appealed again.

'All right, but for half an hour and no more. And woe betide you, my girl, if you leave the front of the house.'

'Yippee!' Angel yelled as she made to run outside, coming to an abrupt halt when Sally grabbed her.

'Put your coat on,' she demanded. A scarf was then tucked around her daughter's neck, followed by a bobble hat, and when she was wrapped up to Sally's satisfaction she let her go, watching as Angel grabbed her skipping rope before flying out of the door.

'You mollycoddle that child,' Sadie said.

'It's freezing outside so how is making sure she's wrapped up mollycoddling her?'

'Blimey, when I was a kid we was lucky if we had shoes on our feet, let alone hats and scarves.'

'Yes, well, that was a long time ago. I don't want Angel to catch a cold.'

'See, mollycoddling her,' Sadie murmured.

Sally closed her eyes in exasperation, but kept her mouth shut. She had learned that it was pointless to contradict her grandmother, and now checking that the potatoes were part boiled she drained them before piling them around the lamb joint.

It was over an hour before Sally called Angel inside, her mind elsewhere as she ignored her daughter's protests. Dinner would be ready soon and there was still no sign of Arthur. She glanced along the lane, hoping to see his car, and then decided to ring Elsie to see if he was still in Wimbledon.

When they had first moved back to Candle Lane Arthur had insisted on paying to have a telephone installed, and now she thankfully reached for the receiver. It was a luxury few other families in the lane had, but one that acted as a lifeline should Sadie have another stroke.

'Go into the kitchen, Angel. I won't be a minute.'

'No, Mummy. I want to play outside again.'

'I said go into the kitchen!'

Angel puckered her face in disgust, but at last did as she was asked, and in another couple of minutes Sally was frowning as she replaced the receiver. Elsie said that Arthur had left them at twelve thirty, so where was he? Her frown then turned to an expression of annoyance. Had he gone off to see his friend again? And if so he could have at least rung to let her know. God, he drove her mad sometimes.

There was a knock on the door, and composing her face she opened it, her complexion paling when she saw a police constable on the doorstep.

He didn't need to speak, didn't need to tell her, she just knew. Something awful had happened to Arthur! The hall spun, strange pinpricks of light floated before her eyes, and then her knees caved under her.

Sally became aware of the policeman's arms as he helped her to straighten, but she still felt light headed. The kitchen door then opened, Angel appearing on the threshold, her eyes wide as she took in the scene.

103

'Nanny, Nanny, there's a policeman!'

'What's going on?' Ruth snapped as she too stepped into the now crowded hallway.

'Mrs Jones?' the policeman asked.

'No, I'm Mrs Marchant. This is Mrs Jones. Sally, are you all right?'

'Arthur,' she gasped.

'Fetch her into the kitchen,' Ruth ordered.

With the constable's support, Sally was able to stagger to a chair, her face still white and eyes rounded with fear as she waited for the dreaded words. For a moment the policeman just looked at her, but then, as he cleared his throat to speak, she gasped, 'He's dead isn't he.'

'No, Mrs Jones, but your husband was involved in a traffic accident and has been taken to hospital.'

Not dead! Arthur wasn't dead! Sally slumped as all the air seemed to leave her body, but almost immediately she reared up again. 'What hospital has he been taken to?' she cried. 'I must go to him.'

Still reeling with shock, Sally sat by Arthur's side, thankful that her mother had taken over. Her one thought had been to get to the hospital, but as she had scurried around, seemingly in circles looking for her shoes, her mind had felt frozen.

Though the hospital was in Wimbledon, to Sally it felt like déjà vu. Earlier in the year she had sat with her mother, anxious for news when Gran had her stroke. Now, once again she was in a hospital, this time with Elsie, and frantic with worry.

'Oh, why won't he wake up, Sally?'

'I don't know, but I wish the doctor would get a move on. What's taking him so long?' The emergency department was buzzing with noise, children crying, yet in the small curtained cubicle it sounded muffled, almost as if they were apart from it all.

'He's looking at Arthur's X-ray results,' Elsie said, both looking up expectantly as the curtains drew back.

It wasn't the doctor; it was Bert, his face grey. 'Hasn't Arthur come round yet?'

'No,' Elsie said. 'And if that bloody doctor doesn't come back soon, I'll find him myself.'

'God, I wish I could get out of here. I hate hospitals,' Bert growled.

Elsie said crossly, 'Look, I know you've got a phobia about them, but that's our son lying there.'

'Yes, sorry, love. I'll try to pull myself together. God, how did this happen? Arthur is a good driver and I intend to find out how he got hit by a bloody lorry.'

A nurse appeared, her stiffly starched, white apron rustling as she moved them to one side whilst she took Arthur's blood pressure. 'There really shouldn't be three of you in here,' she murmured. 'When the doctor returns you'll have to wait outside.'

Bert ran a hand through his hair, his voice echoing his frustration. 'Look, we've been here for an hour now and still don't know the extent of my son's injuries.'

'The doctor will be here soon,' was the nurse's only comment as she took Arthur's notes from a clipboard at the end of the bed, entering his blood pressure results.

Bert was about to speak again, but then the doctor arrived, and motioning them outside he spoke quietly, his eyes on Sally. 'I've made arrangements for your husband to be admitted to an orthopaedic ward. The porters will be here shortly to move him.'

'Is . . . is he going to be all right?' Sally croaked.

'We're concerned that he hasn't regained consciousness, but the X-ray results only show a hairline fracture to his skull. There are no symptoms of compression and his pupils are equal. His leg is badly damaged with a fracture to the tibia, and fibula, one of them compound and requiring surgery. There is also a nasty flesh wound near his ankle.'

Sally hardly took in one word, only able to gasp again in a voice that was cracking, 'Is . . . is he going to be all right?'

'We haven't found any other injuries, but your husband will be closely monitored to make sure there are no signs of pressure to the brain. However, as I said, the X-ray results show no indication of compression.'

105

'And if there is pressure on the brain?' Bert now asked.

As though Bert hadn't spoken the doctor said, 'Ah, here are the porters. You can follow them up to the ward.'

'Wait – what are the symptoms of compression?' Bert insisted.

Seemingly annoyed the doctor rattled off a list. 'Noisy breathing, flushed face, pulse strong and slow, pupils unequal and a high temperature. Now I understand your concern, but as I said, none of these symptoms are present.'

Elsie laid a hand on Bert's arm, saying softly, 'Calm down, love.'

'Calm! How can I be calm when my son's lying unconscious on a hospital bed?'

Sally pressed the heels of her hands to her eyes, but then the porters flung back the curtains and began to wheel Arthur towards the lift. She fought the rising tears, following with a soft prayer on her lips. 'Please, God, please let him be all right.'

For another agonizing hour they sat outside the ward, only allowed in one at a time for a brief glimpse of Arthur. He'd been seen by another doctor who repeated what they had been told in the emergency department, and they could see that Arthur's condition was being constantly monitored. The ward sister advised them to go home, but they refused, until finally, when Sally was by his side, Arthur opened his eyes, groaning softly.

'Nurse!' Sally cried.

Both a doctor and nurse responded. They ushered Sally away but she hovered outside the now drawn curtains around Arthur's bed. When the doctor emerged with a smile on his face, Sally felt a surge of relief, her knees giving way.

She was dimly aware then of sitting in the ward sister's office, of the relief on her in-laws' faces, and then the doctor's words finally penetrating her fuddled mind. Arthur hadn't sustained any brain damage, but now they were going to operate on his leg.

'How bad is it?' Bert asked.

'The compound fracture needs surgery as soon as possible. We wouldn't normally operate so quickly following a concussion, but I'm afraid it can't wait.'

The doctor then left and they were allowed to see Arthur. He managed to smile tiredly at them, his attention drifting, but shortly after the ward sister came to their side. 'I suggest you all go home,' she said. 'There's nothing you can do and he'll be going down to theatre soon. You can ring the ward for information on his condition, and then return tomorrow.'

'Can't I see him after his operation?' Sally asked as she released her grip on Arthur's hand.

'Mrs Jones, it will be very late by the time your husband returns to the ward.'

'I don't care . . . I want to stay.'

Very well, but you will only be able to see him for a minute or two.'

Sally bent to give Arthur a kiss, but he hardly seemed aware of her presence.

Elsie too kissed her son on the cheek. 'Don't worry, son. You'll be all right,' she choked.

As Arthur was given his pre-med, all three were again asked to leave, and not knowing what else to do they made for the canteen, hardly speaking as they sat sipping strong, acrid tea.

'Do you want a sandwich or something?' Elsie asked.

'No, I'm not hungry.'

'We could be here for hours and you need to keep up your strength. Try to eat something, love.'

'Later, maybe later.'

'I can't believe this has happened – and why didn't I see something in the cards?' Elsie then blurted out, her face lined with distress.

Sally gripped her hand. 'I've had a feeling for some time that something awful was going to happen. I thought it would be my grandmother – not Arthur. Oh, Elsie . . .'

'Come on now,' Bert cajoled. 'You heard the doctor and he said Arthur's going to be fine.' He then yawned widely. 'Sorry, but with Ann and the children down for the day, we're a bit worn out.'

'Why don't you go home? I can ring you as soon as there's any news.'

'What, and leave you on your own! No, we'll stay. Bert rang Ann earlier and she's decided to stop over.'

'Oh God, I should ring my mother,' Sally cried.

'It's all right, love. Bert rang your mother too and she said to tell you that Angel's fine.'

Angel, yes Angel – when had she last thought about her daughter? Her whole focus had been on Arthur and Sally now recalled the tears on the child's cheeks as she had rushed from the house. 'I'll still ring, and maybe say goodnight to Angel. I doubt we'll be home before her bedtime.'

Bert glanced at his watch, and seeing it was after six he nodded in agreement. 'Have you got some change for the telephone?'

'I didn't bring my handbag. I . . . I didn't think . . .'

'Oh course you didn't. Here, take this and there's a phone over there,' Bert pointed.

Sally spoke to Angel, reassuring her daughter that her daddy was going to be fine, her mother then coming back on the line. 'When will you be home?' she asked.

'I don't know . . . I suppose soon after Arthur returns from theatre.'

'All right, but I'd better ring Sidney Jacobs to tell him I won't be in tomorrow.'

'Why?'

'Sally, wake up. I expect you'll want to return to the hospital in the morning so you won't be able to look after your gran. I'll have to stay at home, but it's a bloody nuisance and I'll lose a day's pay.'

Her pay, Sally thought, with all that had happened her mother was worried about a paltry few quid. She fought to quell the tide of hysterical laughter that rose, but found it impossible, bending double with mirth, the receiver now dangling by its cord as she dropped it.

'Come on, come and sit down,' Elsie said, leading her back to her chair. 'Now, what brought that on?'

'My mother,' Sally spluttered, hiccuping as she gained her composure. 'Arthur is in theatre, his leg smashed, but all my mum seems worried about is money. She said she'll stay home tomorrow, but is moaning that she won't get paid.'

'I expect it was nervous tension that caused your hysteria, but don't take any notice of what your mother said. We all react differently to stress. I'm sure she's upset about Arthur too.'

'Oh, Elsie, you always see the best in people, but my mother can be very selfish at times.'

'Nobody's perfect, and your mother's had a hard life. She spent years when your father left worrying about money, and it's a hard habit to break.'

'Ken Marchant wasn't my father.'

'No, of course he wasn't.'

Bert came back to the table, and sitting down he reached across, his huge hand enveloping Sally's. 'I've had a word with your mum and reassured her that you're all right. You are aren't you?'

'Yes . . . sorry, I lost it for a minute. Thanks, Bert. God, how much longer will we have to wait to find out how Arthur is?'

'It's only been an hour since he went down to theatre, but if you like I'll pop up to the ward to see if there's any news.'

'We'll all go,' Elsie said firmly.

No, they were told, Arthur wasn't out of theatre yet, but the ward sister allowed them to wait in a small side-room where they sat quietly, each with their own thoughts and prayers.

An hour passed, an hour in which Sally flicked through magazines, barely seeing the words, and then finally a nurse poked her head around the door. 'Mr Jones is back from theatre and sister says you can see him for a minute or two.'

All stood up quickly. 'I'm sorry, but one at a time please.'

Sally tiptoed into the ward, her face registering distress when she saw Arthur. He looked so pale! She took his hand and he briefly opened his eyes, yet it was obvious that he was hardly aware she was there. His leg was encased in plaster, but he seemed unaware of that too as his eyes closed again. She bent forward, kissing his cheek, her voice a murmur as she said, 'I love you, darling.'

When her in-laws had been to see Arthur the ward sister came out of her office, saying kindly, 'The operation went well, and he'll look a lot better in the morning.'

'Thank you,' Sally said, feeling faint with relief and, she now realized, hunger.

They were on their way home again, all feeling exhausted, yet happy to know that Arthur was going to be all right. 'I'm so tired,' Sally murmured.

'It's stress, love, but you can relax now. The worst is over.'

Sally registered Elsie's words and they played a drumbeat in her mind as her eyelids drooped. Yes, the worst was over, and she thanked God for listening to her prayers.

When they arrived in Candle Lane, Sally wasn't surprised to see her Aunt Mary sitting in the kitchen, all three women looking at her expectantly as she walked into the room. Like most families, past rows were forgotten when an emergency arose, and Sally asked, 'How did you know about the accident, Aunt Mary?'

'Your mother rang me of course. Now tell me, how is Arthur?'

Sally managed to answer, but then to her surprise she found the room spinning. She swayed on her feet, Bert rushing forward to help her on to the sofa.

'She's as white as a sheet and it's probably delayed shock. I think she needs to be in bed,' Elsie said.

'Yes, and a drop of brandy wouldn't hurt,' Bert added.

The room came back into focus again, the dizziness passing, and as a cup of strong tea was placed in her hand, Sally gulped it down greedily.

'Are you feeling better now?'

'Yes I'm fine, but must admit I could do with something to eat.'

'I should think so too,' Elsie said. 'You've eaten nothing and no wonder you felt faint.'

'I'll make you something,' Ruth said, bustling over to the cupboard.

'Right, Sally, I'll have to pop into the office in the morning to sort out drivers and deliveries. After that I'll be down to run you to the hospital.'

'I'll be with him,' Elsie said, and after Sally assured her again that she was all right, they said they had to leave.

Sally watched wearily as her in-laws said their goodbyes. Then, after managing to sit up to eat a sandwich, she listened to her aunt, mother and Gran chatting, relieved that they had forgotten their differences.

During a lull in the conversation Sally told them she was off to bed, but despite her exhaustion, sleep was impossible as she went over the events of the day. She should have known that Arthur had been in an accident – should have sensed something. Huh, so much for intuition.

She recalled her anger when Arthur hadn't returned from Elsie's, her mind accusing him of going off somewhere without telling her. God, how awful! She'd been berating him when at the time he'd been lying injured.

Round and around her thoughts went, her head beginning to ache. She turned on to her back, and then it happened! A familiar glow was forming, something she hadn't seen since Angel's birth. The room began to glimmer with a strange but beautiful translucent light. Her friend was here, the lovely presence had come, and as the soft light began to enlarge, she smiled with joy.

Softly it seemed to drift towards her, and then Sally found herself enfolded, cocooned, peace and wonderment replacing her tormented thoughts. She closed her eyes, a smile still on her lips, and as soft fingers seemed to caress her hair, she finally drifted off to sleep.

Seventeen

When Sally awoke the next morning she was smiling gently, remembering a familiar dream, one she'd often had as a child. She'd been flying, free as a bird, skimming low over the rooftops. The dream was so real, so vivid, and she could still feel the exhilaration coursing through her veins.

She turned over, luxuriating in the warmth of the blankets, but then little niggles of worry began to pick at her mind. Last night the spiritual presence had come, one that as a child she had called her friend. When she was upset, hurt, or worried, this friend had always come to comfort her as it had last night.

Since her marriage to Arthur, she no longer saw it, sensing that perhaps it had disappeared because she no longer needed it. After all, she was now an adult and happily married, the pain of her childhood gone.

So why now? Why had it come back now? Suddenly frightened, she shivered and flung back the blankets. Had Arthur taken a turn for the worse? Was that why the presence had come? Without stopping to put on a dressing-gown or slippers, she ran downstairs, frantically dialling the number of the hospital. Come on, come on, she thought impatiently as she waited to be put through to the ward.

'What are you doing up so early?' Sadie asked as she came out of her room.

'I could say the same to you,' Sally said, but then pressed the phone closer to her ear as she was finally put through. She was aware of her grandmother listening as she spoke to a nurse, and then her shoulders slumped with relief as she replaced the receiver. 'He's all right, Gran. Arthur's still all right.'

'Sally, you're shaking with the cold. Put your dressing-

112

gown on – and crikey, your feet are bare. Do you want to get chilblains?'

She smiled happily at her grandmother, her footsteps light as she ran back upstairs, calling, 'I'll be back in a minute.'

In no time Sally returned to the kitchen, wrapped in her thick dressing-gown, and after making a cup of tea she sat sipping it, wondering again why the spiritual presence had returned. 'Are you feeling all right, Gran?'

'Yeah, I'm fine. Ain't you looked at me aura?'

Sally adjusted her eyes, studying the halo of light surrounding her grandmother. There were dark patches, but these were familiar ones caused by her arthritis. 'Remind me to give you some healing later. I can see your arthritis is playing up.'

'You always know when I'm in pain and it still gives me the willies.'

Seeing nothing else to worry about in the aura Sally was perplexed. Her gran was fine, the ward sister said that Arthur was comfortable, so why the visitation?

She glanced at the clock, deciding to get ready herself before getting Angel up for school. However, at that moment there was a flurry of movement as her daughter scampered into the room, hair tousled and a worried look on her face.

'Where's my daddy?'

'He's still in hospital, darling, but don't worry, he's fine.'

'I want to see him.'

'Not today, but soon, I promise.'

'But I want to see him now!' And as Ruth walked into the room, Angel cried, 'Nanny, tell Mummy.'

'Tell Mummy what?'

'That I want to see my daddy.'

'Come here, pet.'

Angel ran to her nanny, and leaning forward Ruth gently stroked her granddaughter's cheek. 'Your daddy is a bit poorly and needs to rest. When he feels better you can go to see him, and when he comes home you can be his nurse. We'll get you a nurse's uniform. Would you like that?'

'Yes, Nanny, and can I give him medicine?'

'Of course you can.'

Peace reigned then, and later, just after her mother left to take Angel to school, Bert and Elsie arrived. 'You're earlier than I expected,' Sally said as she opened the door.

'Elsie came to the yard with me, pestering me to get a move on. The drivers have been sorted out and my secretary can manage for a while. What about you, are you ready to go?'

'Do you mind waiting until Mum comes back? She's just taken Angel to school and won't be long.'

'We don't mind and it'll give us a chance to say hello to Sadie.'

Sally took them through to the kitchen, hardly listening as they chatted to Sadie, her thoughts again on Arthur. The ward sister had said he was comfortable, but was she just being kind?

As Ruth walked down Candle Lane, Angel's hand gripping hers, she saw Tommy Walters, and with a cheeky grin he fell into step beside them.

'Watcha, Angel. Where's yer muvver?'

'My daddy's in hospital and she's gone to see him.'

''Ospital! Why's 'e in 'ospital?'

'He got run over.'

'No he wasn't, Angel,' Ruth said. 'Your dad was involved in a car crash, but thankfully not a bad one.'

'Has he got broken bones?' Tommy asked, his eyes wide.

Puffing with importance, Angel said, 'Yeah, loads of them.'

'Angel, that isn't true!' Ruth protested. 'He's broken his leg, that's all.'

Tommy fixed Angel with an accusing glare. 'Gawd, you ain't 'arf a fuckin' liar.'

'Now that's enough of that language!' Ruth snapped, cringing as she hoped Angel didn't repeat the word in front of Sally. She hastily changed the subject. 'Do you have school dinners, Tommy?'

'Nah.'

'Have you got a packed lunch then?'

Tommy shook his head, but before she could question him further he shouted, 'Come on, Angel, race yer to the end of the lane!'

Like a flash they were off, both skidding to a halt when Ruth screeched, 'Come back here!' She hurried towards them, crouching down to take one of Tommy's grubby hands in her own. Christ, she thought, that Laura Walters is a bloody disgrace. Fancy sending the kid to school without so much as a wash, and had the child had any breakfast? 'If you don't have school dinners, or a packed lunch, what do you get to eat?'

'Stuff,' he said, his eyes lowering. 'I manage.'

'I always save him some of mine, Nanny.'

'Oh, is that a fact. And how do you get it out of the dinner hall?'

'I shove it in my pocket.'

'What! If you've ruined your coat your mother will kill you,' Ruth exclaimed, pulling Angel to one side and hastily checking her pockets.

'It's all right, Nanny. I don't put any runny stuff in there.'

'She gave me her jam sponge on Friday, and even though there wasn't any jam left on it . . . it was smashing.'

Ruth sighed heavily, her heart going out to this little ragamuffin. 'Here,' she said, taking some money out of her purse. 'This week you'll have school dinners.'

His large eyes rounded, 'Cor, fanks, missus. Blimey, I wish you was my nanny too.'

Still holding his hand, they began to walk again, and as Tommy looked up at her with a cheeky grin, Ruth's heart flipped over. Dirt and all she was drawn to the child.

When they reached the school gates, Ruth bent to kiss Angel. 'Now, be a good girl.'

Tommy's little chest puffed, and with a look of importance he said, 'Don't worry, missus. I'll look after her.'

Unable to resist, Ruth pulled him into her arms. 'Yeah, I know you will.'

Shooting her a look of surprise, but pink under the grime with pleasure, Tommy grabbed Angel's hand. 'Come on, that's the bell.'

Ruth watched the two of them as they ran into the playground, then turning she made her way home again, hoping that tomorrow she'd be able to return to work. Sidney Jacobs might be a nice old boy, but she'd only been working for him for a short while and doubted he'd be happy if she took another day off.

* * *

115

As soon as they reached the hospital it was obvious to Sally that Sister Moody wasn't pleased to see them. She frowned as they approached, saying, 'It isn't visiting hours yet and the consultant will be arriving soon to do his rounds. We have a strict routine that must be adhered to.'

Bert seemed to stretch, towering over the woman. 'We would like to see our son, if only for a few moments.'

At first it looked like the woman would refuse, but then with an impatient nod of her head she said, 'Very well, but only for five minutes. Visiting time is between two and three during the afternoon, and between seven and eight in the evenings. If Mr Jones were in any danger there would be leniency. However his operation was successful, and in future there is no reason why you can't keep to visiting hours.'

'Thank you, Sister,' Elsie whispered as they all moved towards Arthur's bed, Bert hovering anxiously at the foot whilst Sally and Elsie took a side each.

'Hello,' Arthur said, his voice weak.

Sally forced a smile, thinking that he still looked awful and not a lot better than last night. 'Hello, darling.'

'How are you feeling, son?' Elsie asked.

'Not so bad, Mum.'

Sally focussed her eyes, her vision just slightly off centre as she studied Arthur's aura. His head area still showed darkness, but there was an improvement. Her eyes now ranged over his body, seeing that other than his leg injury, all seemed well.

There was a slight groan as Arthur tried to adjust his position in the bed and, determined to show a cheerful face, Sally said, 'That'll teach you to argue with a ten-ton truck.'

'Yes, and you were lucky,' Bert said, now moving to stand next to Elsie. 'How did it happen? The lorry driver says you jumped a red light. Is that true?'

'To be honest, Dad, I can't remember. I was driving down West Hill, but other than that my mind's a blank. Is the driver all right and what's happened to my car?'

'He's fine, but I'm afraid your car is a write-off.'

The ward sister approached the bed, her white starched cap as stiff as her body as she said firmly, 'You'll have to leave now. Mr Hardcastle has arrived to do his rounds, along with Dr Willis.'

'Mr Hardcastle?' Bert queried.

'The surgeon who operated on your son's leg.'

'I'd like a word with him please.'

'I'm afraid that won't be possible at the moment, but I'm sure Dr Willis will be able to spare you a few minutes this afternoon.'

'Huh,' Bert said, amazing Sally when he ignored the women and marched down the ward to the surgeon, immediately engaging the man in conversation.

Unable to hear what they were saying, Sally turned back to Arthur, grasping his hand. He smiled wanly, but his eyelids were beginning to droop, their visit obviously exhausting him.

'You really must go now,' the ward sister insisted. 'Your husband needs to rest.'

Sally kissed Arthur gently, finding his lips felt unnaturally dry. Elsie kissed his cheek and after whispering goodbye they moved down the ward to join Bert.

His conversation with the surgeon was obviously over as Mr Hardcastle, along with Dr Willis, moved off towards the first bed, neither man looking at Sally. Bert was frowning, but refused to answer any questions until he'd hurried up the ward to say goodbye to Arthur.

'He was asleep,' Bert said as he returned to their side. 'Come on, let's go home.'

'He still looks terrible. What did the surgeon say?' Elsie asked as they now walked through the stark hospital corridors.

'He said it would be some time before Arthur will be able to use his leg.'

'Some time! What does that mean? Weeks? Months?'

'He couldn't say for sure. It depends on how well the injuries heal.'

'Oh, dear,' Sally gasped.

'Now then,' Bert cajoled. 'Last night we were worried that Arthur might have brain damage, so let's count our blessings. His leg is damaged, but it will get better, even if it takes a while. Let's look on the bright side.'

'Yes, you're right, love,' Elsie said. 'What do you say, Sally?'

'I was so worried last night, but feel reassured today. As Bert said, Arthur was lucky. He was hit by a lorry, shoved yards along the road, his car a write-off, yet all he really sustained is a damaged leg.'

'Someone up there must have been looking after him,' Elsie commented.

For a moment Sally's steps faltered as she found herself thinking about the spiritual presence again. Why had it come to comfort her? Stop it, stop worrying, she told herself, and as Bert said, count your blessings. Arthur was going to be fine, and that's all that mattered.

Eighteen

If only the hospital was nearby, Sally thought as she once again prepared to visit Arthur. Nearly a week had passed since his accident, and unable to leave her gran, she could only visit in the evenings. Elsie went every afternoon, and on Sunday they would all meet up, though God knows what the ward sister would say. Bert, despite his phobia about hospitals, would be there on Sunday, but now that Arthur was recovering, Elsie would probably have to drag her husband, kicking and screaming to the ward.

She'd been to the hall to tell the other healers that she wouldn't be able to join them for a while, gratified when they offered to put out absent healing for Arthur. She had assured them that he wasn't in any danger and was recovering well, adding that she would be back to join them as soon as possible.

It was nearly time to leave and she dreaded the journey, the buses few and far between, but maybe Arthur would be able to come home soon, leg in plaster or not. She heard a knock at the door, but left her mother to answer it as she grabbed her shoes before making her way downstairs, surprised to see a man on the doorstep.

'Sally, this man says he's a friend of Arthur's.'

'Hello,' she said hesitantly, struggling to see the man in the dim light.

'My name is Joe Somerton and I was wondering if I could have a word with your husband.'

'Joe! The Joe that Arthur met in Australia?'

'Yes, that's me.'

'You'd better come in,' Sally said, and as he stepped into the light she gasped. God, the man was gorgeous. Tall and rugged, he had blond hair above chiselled features. There were signs of a fading tan, his blue eyes were vivid, and as he reached out to shake her hand she felt a tremor running through her body.

Confused her voice was unnaturally high. 'I'm afraid Arthur had an accident and he's in hospital.'

'Strewth! Is he all right?'

'He's got a badly damaged leg, but he's on the mend.'

'Would it be all right if I visit him?'

'I don't see why not. As a matter of fact I'm just on my way to the hospital now.'

'May I join you?'

'Er . . . yes, I suppose so. I get a bus at the end of the lane and then change at Clapham Junction.'

'I have my car and can drive you.'

'Oh, wonderful, and it will save me so much time.' Sally was aware that she was babbling, but this man had a strange effect on her, making her stomach flutter.

Angel came running into the hall. 'Mummy, can I come to see Daddy too?'

Sally dragged her eyes away from Joe, her voice still sounding high when she spoke to her daughter. 'Not tonight, darling, but I'll give him your love.'

'But I want to see my daddy!'

'Come on, Angel. Come with Nanny,' Ruth said. 'And I think we might find some sweeties in my handbag.'

As usual the thought of sweets placated her daughter, and now turning to grab her coat, Sally threw it on. 'Thanks, Mum,' she mouthed. 'See you later,' and as Angel ran back into the kitchen with her grandmother, Sally followed Joe outside to his car.

'She's a little beauty,' he commented, unlocking the passenger door.

Sally climbed into the Jaguar, admiring the leather upholstery and walnut dashboard. As Joe climbed in beside her she said, 'Yes, it is a lovely car.'

He laughed, a deep pleasant rumbling sound. 'I was talking about your little girl.'

'Oh,' Sally said, feeling herself going pink.

They drove to Putney, the conversation mainly about Arthur, and as they walked into the ward he smiled brightly.

120

'Joe, great to see you. I guessed you might wonder where I'd got to and was going to ask Sally to ring you tonight.'

'I pipped you at the post then. How's the leg?'

'Not too bad.'

'How did it happen?'

'I'd made up my mind to go into business with you and went to tell my father. Unfortunately, on the way back it seems I tangled with a lorry, but to be honest I can't remember much about it. It seems I jumped the traffic lights and I've had an intention to prosecute notice from the police. I've been lucky though. My father has been told there were no witnesses and was tipped the wink by a copper he knows that they aren't going to take it any further.'

'Strewth mate, that is a bit of luck. So, you're coming in with me – that's great.'

Arthur frowned. 'I could be laid up for some time, Joe. It might be better if you find another partner.'

'If you haven't changed your mind, there's no need for that. I can carry on without you for a while and once you're up and about you can get involved. I've also got a bit of good news.'

'You've found some land?' Arthur asked, his eyes lighting up with enthusiasm.

'Yup, and it's going for a fair price. It's just outside Reading, in Berkshire, ideal for commuting to London, and once the deal's been finalized we can get to work.'

'What about planning permission?'

'There's outline permission in place, but a lot will depend on our architect's drawings. I've an appointment to see the planning officer tomorrow.'

'Good luck, mate.'

Feeling like an appendage, Sally settled down beside Arthur, listening as they enthused about the project. She found her eyes drawn to Joe again and grew hot with shame. What was the matter with her?

As if aware of her scrutiny he smiled apologetically as their eyes met. 'Sorry, Sally, I seem to be taking all of Arthur's time.'

'That's all right,' and as Arthur took her hand she returned the pressure.

'I'll come to see you again as soon as there's any news, Arthur, but now I think I'll leave you two lovebirds alone. I'll wait outside to run you home, Sally.'

'Thank you.'

'Bye for now, Arthur.'

'See ya, mate.'

They both watched Joe leaving the ward, Arthur saying, 'Well, what do you think of him?'

'He seems nice.'

'He's a good bloke, and I'm relieved that he still wants me to go into partnership with him. I just hope I'm out of here soon.'

'You will be,' she said, and after talking for a while longer, the bell sounded to signal the end of visiting time. Reluctantly Sally stood up. 'I'll see you tomorrow, love. Is there anything you need?'

'No, nothing, but how about a kiss?'

Sally leaned across the bed, and as she kissed Arthur there was the sound of wolf whistles from several beds. Arthur grinned, enjoying the camaraderie. 'None of us in this ward are ill, it's mostly broken bones so we have a few laughs.' He then turned away from her, shouting, 'Shut up you lot. You're just jealous.'

Pink with embarrassment Sally whispered goodbye again, and as she hurried out of the ward, more wolf whistles accompanied her.

During the drive home, Sally found that instead of thinking about Arthur, she was studying Joe's profile. Once again a tremor ran through her. *Stop it, stop it*, she berated herself, quickly averting her eyes. How could she feel attracted to someone else when Arthur was lying injured in a hospital bed? In the five years of their marriage she had never looked at another man, her love for Arthur deep, so why now? Unbidden she heaved a sigh.

'Are you all right?' Joe asked.

Angry with herself and determined to fight these feelings, Sally found her voice clipped and sharp. 'Yes. I'm fine.'

'Don't worry about Arthur. He'll soon be on the mend.'

Sally didn't answer, deciding to keep conversation to a

minimum. This man had an effect on her, one that she was ashamed of, and she was determined to see as little of him as possible.

As the car drew into the kerb outside number five, Sally, with one hand on the passenger door, held the other up towards Joe. 'Please, there's no need for you to get out.'

'Right. Goodbye, Sally, I expect I'll see you again soon.'

He grinned and Sally's heart lurched. Shame filled her and scrambling red faced out of the car she mumbled a quick goodbye. The car drove away, but Sally didn't turn her head to look as she hurried inside.

After assuring both her mother and her gran that Arthur was making progress, Sally spent the rest of the evening in front of the television. She tried to fight it – tried to concentrate on the programme, but it was no good and her thoughts kept returning to Joe. At ten thirty, unaware of what she was watching on the screen, she decided to go to bed.

Sally snuggled down under the blankets, missing the feel of Arthur's body beside her, yet behind closed lids it was Joe's face she saw. She found herself wondering what it would be like to be held in his arms, and to feel his lips on hers. *No! Stop it!* her mind screamed. What was the matter with her? She loved Arthur and shouldn't be thinking about another man. Frustration, that was it – just frustration, and once she and Arthur had a place of their own again they could have a proper married life.

She turned over and thumped her pillows, wishing that her friend would come to soothe her tortured thoughts. She scanned the room but there was no sign of the presence – no translucent light, no magical glow, and in despair she closed her eyes.

Nineteen

On Monday, when Joe reached the outskirts of London, he put his foot down on the accelerator. Since meeting Arthur's wife he'd been unable to put her out of his mind. She was a real beaut, and no wonder Arthur had been in such a hurry to leave Australia. If he'd had someone like Sally waiting for him, he'd have rushed back too.

Pack it in mate, he told himself, knowing that she was out of bounds, yet despite that she remained on his mind. There was something about her, something that drew him from the first moment he'd laid eyes on her, and had he imagined that she was similarly affected?

Yes, of course he'd imagined it, and seeing her with Arthur it was obvious that the pair were in love. He shook his head, thinking that Arthur was a lucky man, and the less he saw of his wife the better for his peace of mind. Determined now to concentrate on the road, he finally forced thoughts of Sally away.

The meeting with the planning officer appeared to go well. Joe had already submitted the drawings to the local council, and after the man suggested a few alterations, he said he'd accompany Joe to the site.

Joe stuffed the papers back into his briefcase, and once he arrived at the plot of land the planning officer parked alongside him. The man climbed out of the car, looking around with pursed lips, and for a moment Joe's heart froze.

Slowly they began to walk the plot, questions being asked about the infrastructure that Joe, with the help of the builder, was able to answer.

'Right,' the man said, 'I've seen all I need to see.'

'Does this mean we'll get the go-ahead?'

'I don't foresee any problems. The District Council has

agreed the plans, but they have to be passed by the Parish Council too. You should get their decision in writing within the next few days.'

'Does that mean I've got it?' Joe asked again.

The man smiled faintly before saying, 'As I said, you'll hear in a few days.'

Joe heaved a sigh of exasperation. Time was money and he was anxious to get the building underway. But now his tummy rumbled, and after the planning officer drove off he turned to the builder. 'Eddy, do you fancy joining me for lunch?'

'Yeah, thanks. Lead the way in your car and I'll follow you.'

Joe pulled up outside a country pub that he'd tried before and knew served good home-cooked food. Though still worried about planning permission, he was hungry.

Eddy climbed out of his van, his ruddy face breaking into a smile. 'Don't worry – I reckon we'll get the green light.'

'What makes you say that?'

'The planning officer more or less said so.'

As they walked into the bar, Joe once again appreciated the décor. A huge log fire burned in the enormous hearth, and well-polished horse brasses were tacked along the thick, wooden mantel. The ceiling was low, with more brasses nailed along the beams and, as he approached the mahogany bar, mirrors behind it reflected his image.

'Hello, what can I get you?' the portly publican asked.

'What's on the menu today?'

The man indicated a blackboard and, after both he and Eddy settled on the home-made steak and kidney pie, they moved to a seat by the window. Until the meal arrived they talked about the building project, but when the publican put their pie and vegetables in front of them, both tackled the golden pastry with gusto. As Joe cut into his pie, rich gravy spilled out, making his mouth salivate in anticipation, and it wasn't until he had almost cleaned his plate that he spoke again. 'Have you got your team on board, Eddy?'

'Yes, all but the labourers, and I'll see about recruiting some as soon as we get the go-ahead.'

'Good,' and swallowing the last of his pint, Joe stood up. 'I'm sorry it's a rushed lunch, but I've got to go.'

'All right, and let me know when you hear from the council so I can start ordering materials.'

'I'm glad you said when, and not if,' Joe said. After paying for both meals he began his journey back to London. Traffic was light for a while, and Joe's thoughts turned to Arthur. They were definitely forming a partnership and it was time to put something in writing. He prayed the news from the council would be good or they'd be back to square one, but there was no point in worrying Arthur at the moment. He'd wait until he heard one way or the other before paying him a visit.

When Joe arrived at the hospital four days later, Sally was there, sitting by Arthur's side. She looked up as he approached, and for a moment looked pleased to see him, but then it was as though a veil came down over her eyes. With what looked like a false smile, she said, 'Hello, Joe.'

'Hello, mate,' Arthur said. 'How did it go with the planning officer?'

'I heard this morning that we've got the go-ahead.'

'That's great, but I should be helping you. Christ, I wish I was out of here.'

'The builder will start the foundations, but other than that there isn't much we can do yet.'

'We could see about the cost of advertising and getting some brochures printed. How about getting an artist's impression of what the development will look like? It would look great on the front page.'

'Yes, good idea and I'll get on to it straight away.'

'We'll need to see that estate agencies get the brochures.'

'I'll get on to that too. Blimey, mate, talk about a slave driver,' Joe said, his smile belying his words.

'We'll need a name for the development too. Have you thought of one?'

'No, but it's a lovely spot with beautiful views over the Berkshire countryside. Any ideas?'

Arthur closed his eyes momentarily, and then suggested, 'Country Homes, or Green Acres, something like that.'

'Not bad, but it doesn't sound quite right. How about you, Sally? Any suggestions?'

'Have you got the plans with you?'

'Yes,' Joe said, pulling the drawings out of his briefcase and spreading them across the bed. 'As you can see, we are building the houses on the periphery of the plot. There will be five terraced houses on three sides, with a green area in the middle. The end houses will have side access, so will be priced a little higher, but all of them will have a fair sized garden with views over the meadows.'

'That's it,' Sally said. 'Call it The Meadows.'

'Yes, I like that. What do you think, Arthur?'

'Sounds good to me.'

'I've also made an appointment to see the solicitor tomorrow. It's about time we made this partnership formal.' Joe stood up. 'I'll leave you two alone now, but would you like a lift home, Sally?'

'No, but thanks for the offer.'

'Don't be daft, love,' Arthur said. 'Why get the bus when Joe can drive you?'

The two men watched the range of emotions that ran across Sally's face, and for a moment Arthur looked puzzled. 'Have you two fallen out or something?' he asked.

'No,' Joe said, finding that he and Sally spoke in unison.

Sally flushed, saying quickly, 'I didn't want to put Joe out, that's all.'

'You won't be putting me out.'

'All right, if you're sure, I'll be glad of a lift.'

'Right, that's settled and I'll wait for you outside. Bye, Arthur. I'll keep you up to date with developments.'

'Thanks, but are you sure things are all right with you and Sally? You both seem a bit tense.'

'You're imagining things, mate,' Joe told him, but as he said goodbye again and left the ward, Arthur's comments reinforced his decision to stay away from Sally. From the first time they had met, he and Arthur had hit it off, and he didn't want anything to jeopardize their friendship, more so now than ever. They were to be partners, and this could be the start of many years of working together, years that he hoped would be prosperous.

When Sally joined him half an hour later, Joe was polite but businesslike. 'Thanks for coming up with a name for the development,' he said, gunning the engine to life.

'I'm glad you both like it.'

'Have you any idea how long Arthur's going to be in hospital?'

'No, but his head injury hasn't given any cause for concern. Once he can walk on crutches I should think he'll be able to come home.'

'That's good,' Joe said, but then found he had to concentrate on the road as traffic increased. Conversation was sparse after that, and in no time he was pulling up in Candle Lane.

'Please, don't get out,' Sally said, her voice stilted.

'Right, bye then,' and hardly waiting until she had closed the passenger door, Joe sped off.

It was no good, and half an hour later Joe found his thoughts still on Sally. It had to stop, and somehow he had to put her from his mind. Maybe if he had his own girlfriend it would help, and he found himself wondering if Janet Croft, an old childhood friend, was still available. Yet why had he thought of her?

Who are you kidding? he thought, as his speed increased. Janet Croft had lovely green eyes, just like Sally.

Sally was amazed at how quick the journey home was in comparison to the buses, and cursed herself for wishing it took longer. She found that she wanted to stay by Joe's side, and hated these feelings. Somehow she *had* to fight them, and shaking her head impatiently as though to clear all thoughts of the man from her mind, she walked into the kitchen.

Her eyes narrowed when she saw Tommy Walters sitting by her mother, looking completely at home. Sally opened her mouth to protest, but something in her mother's eyes stilled her. Instead she said, 'Where's Gran?'

'She's in her room.'

'I fink I'd better go now,' Tommy said as he scrambled to his feet.

There was something different about him, Sally thought, her head cocked to one side as she looked at the boy. His clothes – that was it. Instead of his usual torn and patched trousers, the ones he had on now, though not new, looked in good condition. He also wore a nice thick jumper with a crew neck, and there were no signs of any holes. 'New clothes, Tommy?' she asked.

'She got them for me from Rosie's,' Tommy said, indicating Ruth.

So, her mother was clothing the boy now, albeit in second-hand garments. As a child she too had been dressed in clothes from Rosie's, her mother skilful at rummaging through the piles of old garments. 'Well, Mother, I suppose it makes a change for you to be sorting out boys' clothes,' she said, her voice dripping with sarcasm.

'My God, you've turned into a sanctimonious little bitch! So much for your so called spirituality when you'd begrudge this kid something a bit decent to wear.'

'Surely clothing him is his mother's responsibility. Not yours.'

'Maybe, but you've seen how he's been dressed, and *I* don't begrudge the few shillings these clothes cost. Anyway, what I do with my money is my business.'

'What has Laura Walters said about it?'

'Nothing – she's always too pissed to care about the boy, and her old man's no better.'

Tommy had been edging towards the door, his back towards it, only to find himself thrown forward as Sadie thrust it open. 'Is *he* still here?' she demanded.

'He's not an optical illusion, Mother,' Ruth said before turning to Tommy. 'I'll see you tomorrow, love. Off you go now.'

Tommy shot out of the room and, as the street door slammed behind him, Ruth's eyes narrowed into slits. 'Now pin back your lug 'oles the pair of you, 'cos I've already told my mother this but she obviously didn't listen,' and her voice rising she shouted, 'It's *my* business who comes into this house!'

'Yes, I think you've made that clear, Mother,' Sally said. 'But as I told you, I don't want Angel mixing with that boy. As soon as we hear that Arthur can come home I'm going to start looking for a flat.'

'Fine, and the sooner the better.'

Unable to believe her ears, Sally stared at her mother in amazement. It seemed that she was obsessed with the boy, so much so that she was putting him before her own family. Unusually her gran was saying nothing, and that surprised Sally too. It was almost as though she was intimidated by this new persona Ruth was presenting. Their eyes met; looking bewildered Sadie shook her head, her feet unsteady as she made for a chair by the fire.

Ruth, glaring at them both, left the room in a huff, saying she was going upstairs for a bath.

Sally waited a moment and then knelt by her grandmother's side. 'Are you all right?'

'Yeah, but I don't recognize me daughter nowadays. That boy is in here as soon as you leave most evenings. I've tried telling her to keep him out, but every time I open me mouth she turns on me.'

'Oh, Gran,' Sally whispered, heartbroken to see tears in the old lady's eyes.

'She keeps saying this is *her* house, and only yesterday said that if I don't mind me own business about Tommy she'd have me put in a home.'

'She what!'

'It's all right, I know she don't mean it, but she's changed, Sally, and I don't blame you for wanting to find your own place. Gawd, my head is aching with all this. I think I'll have an early night.'

Sally stroked her gran's hand and for a moment she studied her aura, relieved to see that it looked no worse than usual. She helped her up, gave her a kiss on the cheek, and then watched her tottering from the room. Poor Gran, she was showing her age now, the once formidable woman looking stooped and feeble as if all the fight had gone out of her.

Sally flung herself on to a chair, worried about leaving her gran, yet she had promised Arthur that she'd find a flat for them, and couldn't let him down. He, and their marriage, had to come first. And she *had* to stop thinking about Joe Somerton!

Twenty

It was drizzling with rain when Sally awoke in the morning and turning over in bed she saw that Angel was still asleep, thumb in her mouth as usual. As if aware of her mother's scrutiny her eyes opened, looking glazed for a moment until she fully awoke.

'Come on, Angel, let's get you washed and dressed.'

In no time they were on their way down to the kitchen. It was lovely and warm as they entered the room, a fire blazing in the grate, and Sally was pleased to see the table already laid for breakfast. Ruth smiled a welcome, last night's bad feelings obviously forgotten.

Angel ran up to her nanny and Ruth ruffled the top of her head. 'Morning, darlin', I expect you're ready for your breakfast so go and sit down.'

Angel did as she was asked, and then with a petulant expression she said, 'Don't want porridge.'

'Don't you, darling,' Ruth said. 'How about some nice toast then?'

Sally paused in the act of pouring milk over the oats. 'I've started making it, so she'll have to have porridge.'

'No, don't want it.'

'It won't hurt her to have some toast for a change,' Ruth said, unceremoniously shoving Sally out of the way and placing two slices of bread under the grill.

Angel smiled happily while Sally fought to control her anger. Her mother was taking over, undermining her authority, and it had to stop.

At ten thirty Sally was sitting by the fire whilst perusing the local paper. Her mother was at work, her daughter in school, and the housework could wait for a while. There were only

131

a few two bedroom flats advertised that might be suitable, one looking more promising than the others. She mentally pictured the road, close to Battersea Park, and in her mind's eye she could see the lovely tall Victorian houses. Yet with a sinking heart she realized it was too far away, a long bus ride from Candle Lane and therefore impractical.

'What's that big sigh for?' Sadie asked.

'I thought I'd start looking for a flat ready for when Arthur comes home, but the one I fancy is too far away.'

'Look, I've told you, I ain't a child and I don't need looking after,' Sadie said, her mood becoming belligerent.

'I know,' Sally placated, 'but I like being here with you.'

'Don't take me for a fool with all that claptrap, girl. Both you and your mother seem to think I'm incapable of looking after myself, but you're wrong.'

'Gran, we're just trying to care for you.'

There was a knock at the door and Sally rose to open it, pleased to see Nelly Cox on the doorstep. Perhaps seeing Nelly would cheer Gran up and put her into a better mood. With a smile she said, 'Hello, come on in.'

'Hello, ducks, and how's Arthur.'

'On the mend, Nelly.'

'That's good.'

As Nelly bustled into the kitchen, Sally was relieved to hear her gran greeting the woman pleasantly. Her mood swings were sometimes like lightning, but at other times she would remain belligerent all day.

'Do you fancy a cup of tea?' Sally asked.

'If it ain't too much trouble, I'd love one,' Nelly said, crossing to sit on the opposite side of the fire to Sadie. She saw the local paper that Sally had left on the chair. 'What's this?' she asked, seeing the page that Sally had turned to. 'Are you looking for a flat?'

'Yes, but there aren't many on offer.'

'I know of a flat going.'

'Do you?'

'Yeah, in Maple Terrace. Ted Jenson, the tobacconist, bought the house recently and has done up both the upstairs and downstairs flats.'

Sally poured boiling water into the glazed brown teapot,

her thoughts racing. Maple Terrace wasn't a bad street, in fact it was superior to Candle Lane. It wasn't too far away, only about ten minutes' walk.

'Mind you,' Nelly continued. 'From the way Ted described them, I don't reckon they'll be empty for long. He made them sound like little palaces. If you're interested it might be a good idea to see him straight away.'

'I'll pop along to see him when Mum comes home from work.'

'Why don't you go now? I'll stay with Sadie.'

'Do you mind not talking about me as if I'm not here,' Sadie snapped. 'And I don't need you to look after me, Nelly Cox.'

'Leave it out, Sadie,' Nelly protested. 'I ain't looking after you, but Sally can be there and back by the time I've had this cuppa.'

Sally didn't need telling twice. She wouldn't be long, and surely Gran would be all right with Nelly for a little while. Grabbing her coat and handbag she said, 'I'll be back soon.' And without waiting for an answer, she flew outside.

She was breathless by the time she reached the top of Long Street, and rushed into the tobacconist's gasping for air.

'My goodness, where's the fire?' Ted Jenson asked, his eyebrows raised.

Taking a deep gulp of air, Sally gasped, 'Nelly Cox told me you've got some flats to let.'

'Yes, that's right, though there's only one left. Are you interested in it?'

'Has it got two bedrooms?'

'It has, and it's on the ground floor with a little garden too.'

'How much is the rent?'

'It's eight pounds a week.'

'Eight pounds!' Sally squeaked, her eyes widening.

'It's not a lot for such a lovely property, and if you can't afford the rent there are others that can. I'll want a month down as deposit too.'

Could they run to that much rent? Biting her lower lip, Sally wished she had asked Arthur how much he and Joe were going to pay themselves.

'There's another couple looking at it tonight,' Ted Jenson said. 'So you'd better make up your mind.'

She narrowed her eyes in thought. Nelly was with Gran, so surely it wouldn't hurt if she was out a little longer. 'Can I go to see it now?'

'Yes, but I can't leave the shop so you'll have to go on your own. Do you know Maple Terrace?'

Sally nodded. Taking a set of keys out of his pocket, Mr Jenson handed them over. 'It's number seventeen, and bring those keys straight back.'

Once again Sally found herself running, but was unable to keep up the pace, and by the time she reached Maple Terrace she had slowed to a rapid walk. Panting now, she turned into the road, smiling with delight. She'd forgotten it was tree lined and, not only that, each house had a little front garden.

Most of the two-storey properties looked well cared for and, reaching number seventeen, she was impressed at how neat the house looked. The window frames were white, and she saw two street doors, one for the downstairs flat and one for upstairs, both painted dark blue with brass letter-boxes.

Heart thumping with anticipation she walked up the small path, hoping it would be as nice inside. The door was a bit stiff so Sally had to push it open, the smell of fresh paint greeting her as she stepped into the hall.

It was love at first sight, and even if eight pounds was a struggle to find, she *had* to have this flat. The front room had bay windows letting in lots of light and she even liked Ted Jenson's choice of pale blue, embossed striped wall-paper. Unlike the garish, huge patterns that were in vogue at the moment, this décor would look lovely with the almost antique furniture they had in storage.

Sally wandered to the kitchen, finding it modern with frosted glass wall cupboards, and the view from the window showed a small garden, perfect for Angel to play in.

Anxious now to get back she had a cursory look at the bedrooms. The large one had flowered wallpaper, as did the small one, and though not to her taste, they were clean and bright. Lastly she looked in the bathroom, her face again lighting up with delight. It was half tiled, with a brand new bathroom suite, and a lovely big Ascot which would supply plenty of hot water.

With a last glance over her shoulder she left the flat and hurried back to the tobacconist's. 'I'll take it,' she said without preamble.

'I thought you might,' Ted said, smiling smugly. 'As I said, I'll need a month's rent as deposit, and your first week's rent.'

Sally fumbled in her handbag. Arthur always gave her the housekeeping money in cash, and though she had a cheque-book for emergencies, it was rarely used. With relief she found it, and after writing one out she handed it to Ted Jenson.

'When are you moving in?' he asked.

'I'm not sure, but until I do I'll see that the rent is paid.'

'Right, and you'll need to sign this,' he said, handing her an official-looking document.

'What is it?'

'A tenancy agreement.'

Sally quickly scanned the document, but finding it pretty straightforward she signed it with a flourish.

Ted Jenson eyed her signature. 'As stated in the agreement, rent arrears will not be tolerated. I will expect your rent on the dot every week.'

'Of course,' Sally said, her head high, watching as the man filled in a rent book.

'I'd normally ask for references,' he said, handing it across to her. 'But I've known your family for years. I also know that your husband works for his father and it's a well established company.'

'Is there anything you don't know?' Sally asked with a smile.

'There isn't much that goes on around here that I don't hear about.'

Sally quickly lowered her eyes. Should she tell him that Arthur no longer worked for his father? No, she decided, it really wasn't any of his business, and he would get his rent on time each week. 'Thank you, Mr Jenson, and can I keep the keys now?'

'Of course, and if you have any problems, let me know.'

Sally had a few more words with the man and then left the shop, a smile plastered on her face. Oh, wait until she told Arthur. He'd be thrilled to bits.

* * *

135

'Well, how did you get on?' Sadie asked.

Sally threw off her coat saying with a grin, 'It's a lovely flat and I took it.'

'How much is the rent?'

'It's eight pounds a week.'

'My God! It's Maple Terrace, not bleedin' Buckingham Palace,' Sadie snapped.

'What's it like, Sally?' Nelly asked.

'It's got a lovely big front room with bay windows, a modern kitchen, and two bedrooms. There's also a nice bathroom and a little garden for Angel to play in.'

'Huh!' Sadie exclaimed. 'If you're paying that much for it, the bloody bathroom must have gold taps.'

Sally chuckled. 'Very funny, Gran, but don't forget it's all been completely renovated and we can move in without doing a thing.'

'He's a pretty shrewd man,' Nelly observed. 'That's the second house he's bought and converted into flats. He must be raking the money in.'

'If you ask me it's daylight robbery,' Sadie snapped. 'You shouldn't have taken it on, Sally.'

'We'll manage, Gran.'

'Huh, if you say so.'

'Now that you're back, Sally, I'd best be off,' Nelly said.

'All right, and thanks for staying with Gran.'

'She could've gone. I don't need anyone to sit with me.'

'Yeah, I know that,' Nelly said, her tone conciliatory. 'But I enjoyed your company.'

'Don't take me for a mug, Nelly Cox!'

'Nobody could ever take *you* for a mug!' she flung back, showing a display of spirit. 'I'll pop down to see you again soon . . . that's if you want me to.'

'Please yourself.'

Nelly's lips tightened, but she just shook her head with exasperation before walking out of the room. Sally followed her to the door where she laid a hand on the old lady's arm. 'Thanks for the tip about the flat, and I'm sorry that Gran was so rude.'

'You don't have to apologize for Sadie, and I'm glad you like the flat. Mind you, she's right – the rent is a bit steep.'

'I'm sure we'll manage. Bye, Nelly, I'd best get back to Gran.'

Nelly shook her head, sighing as she said, 'It ain't right. You shouldn't have to spend your life looking after Sadie. To be honest, I don't know how you put up with her moods.'

'She can't help it, Nelly.'

'Yeah, I know love, but she's hard going sometimes. When are you moving into Maple Terrace?'

'As soon as Arthur comes out of hospital, and I can't wait,' Sally said, smiling happily again at the thought as she said goodbye to Nelly and closed the door.

The rest of the day passed slowly, and at six thirty Sally was ready to leave for the hospital when Aunt Mary called round.

'How is Arthur? I know I've rung you nearly every day, but I just wanted to double check.'

'He's fine, and on the mend. In fact I've just found us a flat in Maple Terrace for when he comes home from hospital.'

'Yes, and you're paying daylight robbery for it,' Ruth snapped.

'They need a place of their own and as far as I'm concerned it's wonderful news. It means I definitely won't have to cancel my plans now.'

'Plans. What plans?' Sadie asked.

Mary took a seat, pulling off her gloves. 'I'm going away for a while.'

'Oh yeah,' Sadie said, her eyes narrowing. 'And where are you going?'

'On a world cruise.'

'What! Have you won the football pools or something? Them cruises cost a bleedin' fortune.'

'No, Mother, I haven't won the pools, but I *have* been saving for five years. I'm not getting married now, and as I've always wanted to travel, this is as good a time as any.'

'You're off yer bleedin' rocker. Who's going with you on this cruise?'

'I'm going on my own, and I'll be away for several months.'

'But what about your job?' Ruth asked.

'I can always get another job,' Mary said, her back

straightening. 'When Arthur had his accident I thought Sally may have needed me, and if that was the case I would have cancelled my trip. However, as she just said, Arthur is making a good recovery. That means I can take the cruise a week on Saturday.'

'So soon, but when was all this arranged?' Sally asked.

'I booked the cruise after breaking up with Leroy.'

There was a stunned expression on Ruth's face. Sadie looked equally dumbstruck. Angel had stopped painting, her brush poised as she listened to the conversation.

'Auntie, I think it's wonderful,' Sally said, breaking into the strange silence that had descended on the room, 'and I shall expect a postcard from every port of call.'

'Of course, my dear. That goes without saying.'

'I'm sorry, but I must go to visit Arthur now. Have a wonderful time, take lots of photographs, and I can't wait to hear all about it when you get back.'

'Thank you, and give my love to Arthur.'

Sally hugged her daughter and aunt, said goodbye to the others, and as she walked out of the room she heard Angel say, 'What's a cruise, Auntie?'

She hurried along Candle Lane, still amazed that her aunt had booked such a long trip. Yes, she had heard of people travelling abroad now, Spain being the most popular destination, but even that sounded very exotic and foreign to Sally who had never been further than Brighton on a day trip.

Arthur had his eyes on the door, smiling when he saw Sally entering the ward. She hurried to his side, her face alive with excitement. 'Hello, love, I've got some wonderful news.'

'Give me a kiss, and then let's hear it.'

'Sorry, darling, I'm just so excited.'

Arthur felt her lips on his cheek, and then she blurted out, 'I've found us a flat!'

He grinned with pleasure as Sally went on to describe the place, but when she told him about the rent he frowned. Christ, he would have to have a word with Joe about how much they were going to pay themselves. Would they be able to manage eight quid a week? But to get away from

Candle Lane it would be worth it, and anyway, as soon as the houses were sold he and Joe would be raking it in. 'That's the best news you could have given me, and I can't wait to see it,' he said, squeezing her hand.

'I'll ring the storage facility soon to make sure that our furniture is in place for when you come home. Speaking of that, do you know when that's likely to be?'

'No, but I think I'll be able to get about in a wheelchair soon.'

'Oh, that's good. I've got some other news too.'

'Have you? Let's hear it then.'

'Aunt Mary is going on a world cruise.'

'No – you're kidding!'

Sally told him she wasn't, and the rest of the visiting hour passed quickly as they discussed the flat and her aunt's trip.

Arthur took Sally's hand as the bell rang. 'Who knows, love? If Joe and I make a lot of money, we might be able to go abroad one day.'

'I'll hold you to that.'

As usual Sally was the last to leave but, seeing a nurse approaching, she gave him a quick kiss.

'Bye, love,' Arthur said, watching her with a smile on his face as she hurried out.

'Your missus is a bit of all right,' Dick Harris commented from the next bed.

'Yeah, I know.'

'They're letting me out of here tomorrow.'

'Are they?'

'Yes. I'll be on crutches for a while, but I'll be glad to go home. Not that I haven't had a few laughs since I've been in here. Fred's a right lad, isn't he?'

Arthur glanced across to the opposite bed, but Freddie Royston wasn't in it. 'He's a case all right and a bloody menace in his wheelchair. I heard that he pulled a nurse on his lap yesterday and raced her through the corridors.'

'Yes, I saw it, but by the way she was giggling I think she was enjoying herself.'

'Sounds like fun,' Arthur said. 'But if matron caught them they'd be in trouble. Still, I must admit I'll be glad to get out of this bed.'

'I expect they'll give you a wheelchair soon, and then, like me, you'll be going home in no time.'

Arthur smiled and, leaning back on his pillow, he decided that he'd miss Dick Harris. His leg was throbbing a bit, and feeling uncomfortable he shifted slightly. Yes, with any luck he'd be out of here soon, and he had so much to look forward to. He and Sally would be in their own place again, and the flat sounded great. And not only that – he'd be working with Joe.

Twenty-One

On Sunday morning, Sally went to buy a newspaper for Sadie, but then, as she turned back into Candle Lane, the sound of yelling and screaming reached her ears.

She saw a circle of women, all shouting, and as she drew nearer, Sally could see two women in the centre. She blanched. One was her mother, the other Laura Walters, both with outstretched arms and gripping each other's hair as they grappled like wrestlers.

'Mum,' she called, trying to force herself through the ring of neighbours. 'Stop it. What on earth are you doing?'

Laura Walters suddenly released Ruth's hair and with a cry of anger she raised her fist, punching her opponent full in the face.

'Ouch!' Ruth cried. 'Why . . . you . . . you,' and lunging forward she kicked out, her shoe contacting with Laura's shin.

'That's it, Ruth. You give her what for,' Nelly Cox encouraged. She then saw Sally looking at her with outrage, and smiled ruefully. 'Well, it's no more than Laura deserves. Tommy went to your mum in an awful state. He's got a black eye, and bruises all over his body.'

Sally looked around frantically, wondering where her daughter was. Her mother was supposed to be looking after the child, but instead she was fighting in the street like a fishwife. There she was, looking out of the window, Gran beside her as they watched the spectacle.

'That's enough, Mum,' Sally shouted as Laura Walters again squared up for the fight. She was wasting her breath.

Both women lunged forward. They grappled again, panting, but then with a huge shove from Ruth, Laura Walters found herself on her back, the wind knocked out of her.

She looked up as Ruth stood over her, her stance

141

threatening as she spat, 'If you lay a hand on that boy again you'll be sorry, you drunken slut.'

Gasping for breath Laura wasn't ready to give in. 'He's *my* son, not yours. Keep your nose out of my business.'

'I know full well he isn't my son. In fact I'm old enough to be his grandmother. You're a disgrace, Laura Walters, and you should think yourself lucky that I ain't reported you to the authorities. Mind you, I could still do it, so think on that.'

'I'm not scared of you, *or* the so called authorities. The boy deserved a thrashing, and I gave him one.' She scrambled to her feet, her chest heaving, and pressing a hand on her heart she made for her street door, ignoring the jeers of her neighbours.

Ruth stood looking after her, eyes still dark with anger. As the crowd began to break up, hands patted her on the back. 'Good on yer,' one said. 'She's been asking for it,' said another.

Sally turned away from the scene and with a shake of her head she went into number five, leaving her mother to her admirers.

'Nanny was fighting, Mummy,' Angel said, scrambling from her vantage point at the window.

'I know.'

'Tommy's got a bad eye.'

'Yes, I can see that.'

'Nanny said he'd be better off living with us.'

'She what?' Sally exclaimed, her eyes now shooting to Sadie. 'Do you know anything about this, Gran?'

'Your mum's just spouting hot air, love. She knows she hasn't any claim on Tommy and it's just wishful thinking. For some reason she seems overly fond of the kid,' Sadie replied in a rare burst of clear thinking.

'Yes, I know,' Sally murmured. When they moved to Maple Terrace it meant her mother would have a spare room. Would she try to move the boy in? Don't be silly, Sally berated herself. Laura Walters would never stand for it. Or would she?

'Well, that sorted her out,' Ruth said when she finally came indoors. 'Now then, Tommy, if your mother touches you again I want you to tell me.'

Tommy nodded, his eyes wide and Ruth added, 'I don't

think it's safe for you to go home yet, so you'd best stay here for a while.'

Sally opened her mouth to protest, but the look her mother gave her was ferocious. Instead she said, 'Come on, Angel. Let's get you ready for the hospital. Daddy will be looking forward to seeing you.'

Angel followed her upstairs without demur and, as Sally bathed her daughter before dressing her, she wondered what it was with her mother and Tommy Walters? She had never seen her involved in a street fight before – her mother had been like a lioness protecting her cub.

For three days there were no further incidents, and Sally had begun to relax. Laura Walters was still keeping her head down, and so far it seemed the boy hadn't been beaten again.

It was Wednesday and half day closing, but as usual her mother didn't arrive home until nearly three o'clock. She always stayed behind to fix lunch for Sid, often joining him, but with Christmas looming in a less than four weeks, Sally was anxious to shop for presents.

She sighed, it would have been nice to have the afternoon free, but now it was time to pick Angel up from school. 'Mum, when I come back with Angel I want to go out again. Is that all right?'

'Where are you off to?'

'I want to do some Christmas shopping.'

'Yeah, all right, love.'

Sally rushed to the school and on the way back Tommy tried to tag along. She hated doing it, but Angela had to come first and, and trying to say it kindly, she asked him to go away. He stared at her for a moment, but then with a scowl he ran off.

'Mummy, why did you do that? I like Tommy.'

'I don't want you mixing with him.'

'You're mean! I hate you, Mummy,' Angel shouted, yanking her hand away and running on ahead.

'Come back here!' Sally shouted, but her daughter had already reached number five where she banged on the front door.

'Nanny!' she cried as Ruth opened it. 'I don't like Mummy.'

'Now, what's brought all this on?'

143

'She made Tommy go away.'

'Did she now?' And throwing Sally a look of disgust, Ruth drew Angel inside.

The atmosphere was strained, her daughter petulant, and Sally was relieved to leave the house. The shops in the High Street were brightly lit, Christmas decorations adorning every window, and Sally was pleased to find some reasonably priced presents. Angel wanted a tricycle and, praying they could afford it, Sally ordered one.

The cold air hit her as she stepped outside the shop and, though reluctant to give up her short spell of freedom, she made her way home.

Dinner was ready when she arrived, but it was obvious that Sally was still in Angel's bad books as they sat down to eat. The child was picking at her food.

'Eat your carrots,' Sally told her.

'Don't want them.'

'There are lots of people in the world who don't get enough to eat and would be glad of the food on your plate.'

'Tommy is always hungry. I could give it to him. You like him, don't you Nanny?'

'Yes, he's a nice kid.'

Sally gritted her teeth, saying nothing, and after clearing the table she washed up before going upstairs to get ready to visit Arthur.

She relaxed for a while in the bath, lying back with the water lapping over her shoulders. It was as Sally closed her eyes that the feeling washed over her. A feeling of foreboding. Sitting up she shivered with fear, hoping that it was just her imagination.

Once again Sally was glad to leave the house, and though frozen by the time she reached the hospital, she smiled at the other patients as she entered the ward. They were a good crowd, all suffering from fractures and, unlike Arthur, most caused by motorbike accidents. They were nearly all young men too and, though suffering broken bones, they weren't ill. The ward was a lively place, with jokes flying around, and goodness knows how some of the young nurses coped.

'Hello love,' Arthur said, his usually bright greeting sounding weak.

'You look a little flushed. Are you feeling all right?'

'Not really and I'm hot.'

Sally focussed on Arthur's aura and was immediately worried by what she saw. Seeing the darkness around his leg, she gasped. Moving from his side to the bottom of the bed, her eyes were drawn to his foot where it stuck out from the plaster. Sally wasn't looking at his aura now; she was looking at the strange blisters that had formed over his toes. They were almost black, as though filled with blood, and she stared at them worriedly. 'Arthur, has anyone said anything about these blisters on your foot?'

'No, but my leg has been feeling uncomfortable since you left yesterday.'

'I'm just going to have a word with Sister Moody,' Sally said, and though Arthur called out for her to wait, she ignored him as she hurried to the office.

The woman looked a little annoyed when Sally barged in without knocking, but after listening to her blurted explanation, Sister Moody rose to her feet.

'Black blisters, you say,' she said sharply. 'I'll come and have a look.'

From the moment Sister Moody saw Arthur's foot, panic seemed to set in. She almost ran back to her office and in what seemed like seconds a doctor appeared.

'What's going on?' Sally demanded as the curtains were hurriedly drawn around Arthur's bed.

'Your husband has developed an infection,' Dr Willis said, and then immediately instructed the sister to give Arthur what, to Sally's ears, sounded like an enormous dose of penicillin. 'We'll get this plaster removed and then he'll have to be put in an isolation ward.'

'Isolation! But . . .' Sally gasped.

'If you wait outside I'll see that someone talks to you as soon as possible,' the doctor said dismissively, and at his words a nurse came to Sally's side, leading her from the ward.

Sally sat on a hard chair, but unable to settle she jumped up again, hovering by the door. After about ten minutes porters arrived to wheel Arthur out of the ward, a nurse at his side. She saw panic in his eyes and rushed forward. 'Wait, where are you taking him?'

'It's all right, Mrs Jones. We're just taking your husband to have his plaster removed,' the nurse said. 'Sister Moody is coming to have a word with you.'

Sally didn't know what to do. Should she follow Arthur? Should she wait for the sister? The decision was taken out of her hands when the woman appeared, indicating that she should follow her into the office.

'Mrs Jones, as the doctor told you, your husband has developed a very nasty infection.'

'What sort of infection?'

'He has developed what is commonly called gas gangrene.'

'No . . . Oh no!' Sally cried. So this was why she'd had that awful feeling of foreboding. Oh, God, Arthur!

'Your husband will be put in a side room, given antibiotics to treat the condition, and of course analgesics for the pain.'

'Will . . . will he be all right?'

'We've caught the condition early so the prognosis is good, but now I suggest you go home.'

'Home! But I want to see him.'

'Very well, but you will have to wear a surgical mask at all times, and I'm afraid you will be the only one allowed to visit him for the time being.'

'But his parents . . .'

'I'm sorry – I'm afraid not.'

Sally slumped in the chair, the full impact and serious-ness of Arthur's condition sinking in at the sister's words. Gangrene, Arthur had gangrene, and her stomach churned. She felt sick – she was going to be sick, and hand over her mouth she fled to the toilets.

Everything had happened so quickly that Arthur's mind refused to function. One minute he was in the ward with Sally, the next it seemed that all hell had broken lose. He'd been given an injection of penicillin, one that took ages to administer, and then he'd been rushed down here.

He lifted his head as the plaster was removed, and gagged. God, the stench! 'Doctor, just what sort of infection is this?'

'Don't worry, Mr Jones,' the doctor replied. 'We'll soon sort you out.'

Arthur was given a local anaesthetic, and soon after they began to tend the wound, the process taking a long time, but at last they finished.

'Right, Mr Jones. We'll put a new plaster on now, this time with a lift-up flap over the wound.'

Arthur raised his head, his eyes widening with horror. What had been a flesh wound now resembled a huge hole, one that he could fit his fist into, and seeing it bile rose in his throat. His anxiety heightened. He'd seen other patients in the ward with broken legs, many of whom had recovered sufficiently to go home, and until this moment he'd expected to do the same. His thoughts spun, but before he could put them into coherent order he was wheeled back to the ward, his brow creasing when this time he was put in a side room. What the bloody hell was going on?

Once settled in to his bed, Arthur was determined to ask questions, but almost immediately Sally came in, a mask covering the lower half of her face. 'How are you feeling?' she asked, her voice sounding muffled.

'What's going on, Sally? And why are you wearing a mask?'

'You've got something called gas gangrene, but don't worry, darling. I had a word with Sister Moody and she said it's been caught early so should respond to treatment.'

'Bloody hell!'

'Mr Jones, I'm Nurse Trimble and I'll be looking after you.'

Arthur turned his head to look at the nurse who had now entered the room and found he had to force a smile.

'Don't worry,' she said. 'You'll be out of here in no time.'

'Yes, but will it be in a box?'

'Arthur!' Sally exclaimed. 'Don't talk like that.'

'Sorry, just a joke,' he said, finding that his voice had grown weak.

'You look tired. Perhaps I'd better go,' Sally said, and he could see the strain in her eyes.

'Yes, that would be for the best,' Nurse Trimble agreed. 'Did Sister Moody tell you that your husband won't be able to have any other visitors?'

'No other visitors!' Arthur protested.

147

'Not for the time being. We need to get this infection under control and this room must remain as sterile as possible.'

'Blimey.'

'Yes, blimey,' Nurse Trimble repeated. 'Now, I'll leave you to say goodbye.'

'She seems nice,' Sally said as the door closed.

'Yes, she's all right,' he agreed, determined not to let Sally see how worried he was. 'I can't kiss you in that mask so perhaps you had better take it off.'

'No way! For the time being you'll have to do without kisses.'

'Huh, I'll ask Nurse Trimble to kiss me goodnight then.'

He was pleased to see a smile in Sally's eyes, and squeezed her hand as she whispered goodbye.

When Sally left the small room, exhaustion washed over Arthur. Alone now he closed his eyes, admitting to himself how terrified he was. Bloody hell! Gangrene!

Sally found herself shaking on the journey home, the dreaded word gangrene going round and around in her mind. She almost stumbled indoors and reaching for the telephone she picked up the receiver. Somehow she had to break the news to Arthur's mother; taking a deep breath to hold herself together, she dialled the number.

She braced herself as Elsie answered and, though she tried to speak calmly, her mother-in-law immediately sounded as distraught as she herself felt.

'He seemed fine when I saw him this afternoon! Oh, Sally, gangrene! Bert and I will go to see him first thing in the morning.'

'I'm afraid you can't. They've put him in isolation and I'm the only one who can visit him.'

'But I'm his mother!'

'I'm so sorry, Elsie, they were adamant.' Sally's heart went out to her mother-in-law. How would she feel if Angel were ill and she was barred from visiting her?

'I suppose I'll just have to ring the ward for news,' Elsie said, a sob in her voice.

'Yes, and I'll call you after every visit,' Sally assured her.

'What sort of treatment is he having?'

'Huge doses of penicillin, and of course painkillers.'

'Oh, poor Arthur,' Elsie cried, and then after a few more words they said goodbye, Sally finding her hands still shaking when she replaced the receiver.

'Sally, your face is like lint! What on earth's the matter?' her mother asked as she walked in to the kitchen.

It was then that she broke, all her pent up fears and anxieties rising to the surface and tears spurting from her eyes. 'Oh, Mum, Arthur's got gangrene.'

'No!' Ruth gasped.

'Stone the crows!' Sadie said. 'They'll have to take his leg off.'

'Don't say that!' Sally cried.

'Well you might as well face it now as later,' Sadie snapped. 'Lots of blokes lost their limbs to gangrene during the war. Once you get gangrene it's inevitable.'

'No it isn't. The ward sister said that Arthur should respond to treatment.'

'Huh, who's she kidding?'

'She may be right, Mum,' Ruth said.

'Poppycock! I've told you – once you get gangrene they take your leg off. It's the only way to stop it spreading.'

Sally couldn't bear it, couldn't stand the thought of Arthur losing his leg. Her gran had to be wrong . . . she just had to.

Blinded by tears she stumbled across the room and flopped on to the sofa, aware then of her mother's arm around her shoulder, her earlier bad feelings obviously forgotten as she said, 'Come on, Sally, you've got to be brave. Arthur will need you to be strong when he has the amputation.'

Sally cuffed at her face. 'Stop it! Stop talking as though it's a foregone conclusion. The doctor didn't mention amputation, and Gran isn't the font of all knowledge. Medical science has come a long way since the war, and Arthur is going to get better – I just know he is.'

'All right, love, calm down. I'll make you a nice cup of tea . . . it'll make you feel better.'

Sally laughed then, but it was hysterical laughter. As though it were a cure-all for everything, whenever there was an upset, her mother made a pot of tea. Oh, if only life was as simple as that.

Twenty-Two

'I'm sorry,' Sally told Joe as she pushed down her mask. 'You can't see Arthur while he's in isolation.'

'But why has he been isolated?'

Sally sighed, annoyed that she hadn't thought to ring Joe Somerton. Arthur had been in the side-room for three days, and now Joe had come to the hospital with papers for him to sign. Of course he hadn't been allowed to see Arthur and Nurse Trimble had called her outside to speak to him. She went on to tell Joe about Arthur's condition, watching as his face darkened with anxiety. 'Are the papers urgent?' she finally asked. 'Or can they wait?'

'They can wait. I had a solicitor draw up a partnership agreement, but there's no hurry.'

'I'm sorry, I should have rung to tell you that Arthur isn't allowed visitors and saved you a wasted journey.'

Joe's hand came out, touching her arm, his voice soft as he said, 'There's no need to apologize. I should think ringing me was the last thing on your mind and that's perfectly understandable, but tell me, how's he doing?'

'There's little change. However his nurse assures me that he's responding to treatment, even if I can't see it myself.'

'Listen, you go back in now and I'll hang about to give you a lift home.'

Sally was about to refuse, yet quickly realized she was being silly. Her whole attention was now focussed on Arthur, and her silly crush on this man – and that's all it was, a crush – had shrunk to insignificance. 'Thanks, Joe, it's good of you.'

'I'll wait in my car. Give Arthur my best and tell him not to worry about the business. It's still early days yet and I can manage without him.'

Sally smiled, thanking Joe again, and then went back into the small room. Arthur turned his head, his voice reedy, 'I

150

think you had better tell Joe to find another partner.'

'There's no need for that. He said to tell you that he can still manage without you.'

'Yes, but for how long? It's not fair on him, Sally, and let's face it; I could be stuck in this bloody hospital for ages.'

'You'll be fine once this infection has been dealt with and then you'll be home in no time.'

Arthur closed his eyes, obviously exhausted, and as he drifted off to sleep again Sally sat by his side. She had wanted to ask him about the flat, but doubted he would wake again before visiting time was over. He was on strong painkillers and rarely stayed alert for long – drifting in and out of sleep each time she came to see him.

What should she do? Arthur was right and he could be in hospital for some time, so should she continue paying rent on the flat? Without a wage coming in money was getting short in their current account, and soon she would need to break into their savings. But how much money was earmarked for this venture with Joe?

The time ticked by, and at the end of visiting hours Sally stood up and quietly left the room. She made her way to the car park; her questions unanswered, and worry about the flat and their finances heavy on her mind.

'How is he?' Joe asked as she settled beside him in the car.

'I left him asleep, but I passed on your message.' Sally bit on her lower lip and then blurted out, 'Joe, has Arthur given you any money yet?'

'No, but there's no immediate hurry. Why do you ask?'

'I've found a flat, but to keep paying the rent I'll eventually have to break into our savings. I don't want to use money earmarked for the business.'

'God, what a numbskull I am! Of course you shouldn't use your savings, earmarked or not. Joe and I agreed we'd pay ourselves a wage until the houses are sold and now that he's left his father's firm I should have realized you wouldn't have an income. Look, draw out what you need each week and I'll deduct it from the money Arthur has agreed to invest. In that way there's no need to worry him at the moment.'

Sally heaved a sigh of relief, glad that she'd raised the subject. 'Thanks, that's a load off my mind.'

151

'Where is this flat?'

'It's not far from Candle Lane, and ideal. I'll still be able to look after my gran every day, and Angel can stay at the same school.'

'Do you need any help with moving in?'

'Thanks for the offer, but I can manage. We won't be moving in until Arthur comes home. My mother looks after Angel while I visit the hospital, so I have to stay in Candle Lane for the time being.'

'Well, the offer's there if you need it.' As Joe spoke he turned briefly to look at her, and as their eyes met Sally smiled, realizing that for the first time this man hadn't touched her emotions. There was no denying his good looks, but she loved Arthur, would always love him, and now felt a deep shame that she had been attracted to his partner. She cringed in her seat, thinking how awful it would have been if Joe had known about her silly crush.

He spoke now, breaking into her thoughts. 'Try not to worry too much. I'm sure Arthur will be fine. He's strong, and he'll fight this infection.'

Sally nodded. Joe was a nice man, a good man, and from now on, like Arthur, she would welcome him as a friend.

A few days later, Sally was at Maple Terrace. The storage facility hadn't been able to deliver on a Sunday, but determined to look to the future and have the flat ready for Arthur's homecoming, she had approached her father-in-law. He had come to the rescue, sending one of the firm's lorries to pick up the furniture for her.

They had just left, and delighted she looked around the flat. Luckily their old curtains fitted the windows, and the room looked lovely. She ran a hand over the oak sideboard, remembering how excited she and Arthur had been when they found it. The second-hand shop in Northcote Road was mostly full of junk, but against the back wall, and piled with cardboard boxes containing a mishmash of books, old lampshades, crockery and china – they had seen it. It was filthy, but under the grime they could see that the doors were carved oak, and other than a few minor scratches it looked to be in good condition. It had two drawers, and they weren't sure if the handles were original, but it didn't matter, they loved it anyway. After a bit of bartering they got it for a good price, and flushed with success they spent many happy hours after that scouring second-hand shops for other choice pieces. The brown leather three piece suite had been a good find, the hide cracked and worn in places, but nevertheless they loved it too – loved the way the oak arms and legs matched the sideboard perfectly.

Not for them the latest suites in garish colours, or black vinyl. They also shunned modern coffee tables with chrome legs, along with Formica topped kitchen tables. Instead they found one in pine, with a welsh dresser for their china, but these sadly wouldn't fit into this flat.

There was a knock on the front door and, wondering who it was, Sally rushed to open it. On the step she saw a tiny, slim young woman, with short, straight blonde hair that framed her elfin face. She had blue, heavily made up eyes, amazingly long eyelashes, and an almost childlike, innocent smile. My goodness, Sally thought, she looks like a pretty porcelain doll.

'Hello,' she trilled, 'I saw your furniture arriving and thought I'd better introduce myself. I'm Patsy Laurington and I live upstairs.'

'Oh, hello,' Sally said, liking this tiny woman on sight. 'I'm Sally Jones – please, come on in.'

'Are you sure you're not too busy?'

'No, I've almost finished sorting everything out. There's just the linen and china to unpack. In fact, until that's done I can't even offer you a cup of tea.'

'That's all right, I've just had one, but if you're thirsty I can lend you some cups for now.'

'Thanks for the offer but I've got to go soon. My husband's in hospital and I'll be going to see him this afternoon.'

'Oh dear, what's wrong with him?'

Sally saw compassion in Patsy's eyes as she told her about Arthur, and then said, 'What about you? Are you married?'

Those large blue eyes now darkened with pain. 'I was,' Patsy said quietly, 'but not anymore.'

Sally bit back the questions that sprung to her lips. Not any more – what did that mean? Was Patsy a widow? Or perhaps her husband had left her? Instead she said, 'How are you finding the neighbours?'

'In the house next door to the left, there's a young couple living upstairs, and I suspect they're newlyweds. The downstairs flat is empty. In the house on our other side, a young man lives alone in the top flat, and below him an elderly couple, though I haven't seen much of them.'

'Do you work?' Sally now asked, then kicked herself. God, she sounded like a right old nosy parker.

'I work for myself. What about you?'

'I have a five-year-old daughter, and I also stay at home to look after my grandmother,' Sally told her, wondering if she dare ask what sort of work Patsy did that enabled her to be self-employed.

'Crumbs, it'll be a bit of a squeeze for you in here, especially as you've got another one on the way. Will your gran and daughter share a bedroom?'

'No, my gran won't be living with us . . .' Sally paused as something Patsy had said sunk in. 'Another one. Do you think I'm pregnant?'

'Well, you are, aren't you?'

'No, I don't think so.'

'Oh, well, I can usually tell when a woman's pregnant, there's a certain look. Still, this time I must have made a mistake.'

Sally's mind reeled as she frantically worked out dates. No, surely it wasn't possible! Had she had a period last month? There had been Arthur's accident, and then his awful infection, so much had happened in such a short time that she couldn't remember. Was she due another period? Her heart thumped wildly. She hadn't had any morning sickness and her tummy wasn't swollen. No, she couldn't be pregnant. But what if Patsy was right?

'What does your husband do for a living?'

'What? Oh, my husband,' Sally said, her mind still distracted. 'Until recently he was a partner in his father's removals company, but now he's investing in building houses.'

'Goodness, that sounds impressive!'

'It isn't really.' Sally said. She glanced at her watch, and her eyes rounded. 'Look, I'm sorry, but I really have to go now. It was nice to meet you and I hope we can get together again when I move in.'

'Yes, that would be nice. Give me a knock and I'll show you my flat.'

'Thanks, I'll do that,' Sally said, and as soon as Patsy left she grabbed her coat, rushing back to Candle Lane. Was it possible? Was she pregnant? Hardly daring to hope she decided to see the doctor in the morning.

She touched her tummy. If she *was* pregnant, that could explain why her emotions had been so up and down recently. She was sometimes irritable and knew she was being awful about Tommy, but somehow she had been unable to stop the bitchy remarks she made to her mother.

Her thoughts turned to Patsy as she hurried through the streets. She had taken to her upstairs neighbour and would like to get to know her better. Perhaps they could become friends.

'Hello I'm back,' she called as she went into the kitchen.

'About time too,' her mother complained. 'Dinner's nearly ready.'

'Sorry, but it took a while to put all our furniture in place.'

'Huh, I still think you're mad to take that flat on. Arthur's in hospital and though he may be a little better, he's not out of the woods yet. What's going to happen if this friend of his gets tired of waiting and finds another partner?'

'Joe won't do that. He's already told Arthur that he can carry on without him for some time yet.'

'And if Arthur loses his leg. What then?'

'He's *not* going to lose his leg. The gangrene is responding to treatment and he'll be back in the ward soon.'

'Yeah, that's what you've been told, but what makes you so sure? Gangrene ain't that easy to cure.'

'Why would they lie to me? And why do you have to be so pessimistic, Mum?'

'I'm just trying to prepare you for the worst, that's all.'

'Well I'd rather you didn't. I prefer to be positive, and anyway, Arthur looked a lot better yesterday.'

'All right, if you say so. Now get the plates out and I'll dish up.'

Sally did as she was told, and soon they were all tucking in to her mother's delicious Sunday roast. The pork was succulent, the crackling crisp, and the roast potatoes golden brown. Sally was pleased to see that Angel was even eating her vegetables without complaint and asked gently, 'Have you finished Daddy's painting?'

'Yes, and can I come with you to give it to him?'

'No, sorry darling, but I'm sure you'll be able to see him again soon.'

'Why won't Daddy be home for Christmas?'

'He's still not well, but if you're a good girl and he's back in the ward, you'll be able to give him your Christmas present.'

'Will he get me a present too?'

'Of course he will,' Sally said, knowing it would be her job to buy something from Arthur to put it under the tree. 'When Daddy comes home from hospital the three of us will be moving into a nice new flat.'

Angel's brow furrowed. 'Nanny come too.'

'No, Nanny will stay here with Gamma. Don't worry, the flat isn't far away and you'll still see each other every day.'

'I don't want to go.'

'Now then, darling, you'll love our new home. There's a nice garden for you to play in, and you'll have your own bedroom again.'

'Don't care. I want to stay with Nanny.'

Sally heaved a sigh, wishing now that she hadn't broached the subject, and decided to drop it for now. 'When you've finished your dinner why don't you get your painting and I'll take it to Daddy.'

As usual the journey to Putney seemed endless, the bus service sparse on a Sunday, but at last Sally arrived, hugging her secret to herself. Oh, please let Patsy be right!

'Hello, love,' she said, stepping into the side-room. 'You look a lot better.'

'I feel a lot better, but the consultant said I need to have my leg put into a splint.'

'A splint! But why?

'It needs traction to keep it straight. Apparently it isn't a huge procedure, and after it's done I can go back in the ward.'

'Oh, good, that must mean the gangrene has cleared up.'

'Yes, it has, but I must admit I was scared for a while. When they said I had gangrene I thought I'd lose my leg.'

'Well you haven't, and thank God for that. When are you having the splint fitted?'

'In the morning. I just wish I could be at home for Christmas.'

'I don't think there's any hope of that but we'll all come to visit you.'

'I'm sick of this place, Sally.'

'Once the traction is out of the way, I'm sure you'll be home in no time, and wait till you see our flat. Now that the furniture's in place it looks wonderful. I met the girl who lives upstairs and she seems really nice.'

Arthur smiled faintly, and then said, 'Will you give Joe a ring when you get home. Tell him that I'll be back in the ward and he can visit me again.'

'Yes, all right.' Arthur looked so down that Sally was tempted to tell him that there might be a baby on the way. It would make him so happy, but what if she was wrong? No, better to wait, she decided.

During the rest of the visit she did her best to cheer him up, speaking of the future, glad to see him looking a little happier when she left.

Christmas, Sally thought, as she made her way to the bus-stop, only a week away, and then soon after it would be the New Year. So much of 1966 had passed her by – not only the latest music and fashion, but world events too.

She tried to recall news items, vaguely remembering the anti-Vietnam war protest that had taken place in Grosvenor Square during July. It had turned into a riot, feelings strong, and she wondered how much longer the awful conflict between America and Vietnam would last. Yet dreadful as this war was, it had hardly touched her consciousness. She'd been so caught up with her family and so afraid Arthur was having an affair.

The year had brought changes for her too. She had come back to Candle Lane to look after Gran, Angel had started school, and her mother was now working for Sidney Jacobs.

Then in November there had been Arthur's dreadful accident. Would he be home soon? Oh she hoped so – hoped that 1967 would be a good year for them all. And a new baby would make everything just perfect.

Twenty-Three

The following morning, saying that she had to get another Christmas present, Sally took a chance and asked Nelly Cox to sit with Gran. Now, as she came out of the doctor's surgery, she was beaming with happiness. Oh, it was wonderful. After all this time they were to have another child and she couldn't wait to see Arthur's face when she told him.

It didn't take her long to get home, and she burst into the kitchen. 'Gran, Nelly, I'm having a baby!'

'Well, ain't that nice,' Nelly said, rising to her feet and giving Sally a cuddle. She winked. 'So where's this urgent Christmas present?'

'Sorry, Nelly, but I didn't want to say anything in case it was a false alarm. Mind you, I think this is the best present ever.'

'I'm pleased for you, love,' Sadie said. 'And it's about time too.'

'Angela will be thrilled, Gran. She'll have a little brother or sister.'

'Yeah, I 'spect so, but she may well be jealous. She's been an only child for over five years.'

'Oh, Gran, don't put a damper on it.'

'Sorry, love. I can see how happy you are, and as I said, I'm pleased for you.'

Sally hugged herself with delight, wishing the hours away until she could go to see Arthur. She rang the hospital, pleased to be told that the procedure had been successful and Arthur was back in the ward.

The day ticked slowly by and she did her best to keep herself busy, relieved when at last she left to pick Angel up, one of her last weeks before the school broke up for the

Christmas holidays. Things were certainly going to be different for the child. A new home, a new baby brother or sister, but oh, it was wonderful.

Sally clasped Angel's hand as they walked home, listening with half an ear to her daughter's chatter.

'Mummy, we've all got to take some food for the class-room party.'

'All right, love, I'll sort something out.'

Angel skipped on ahead as they turned into Candle Lane, but as soon as they were settled in the kitchen, Sally knelt by her daughter's side. 'How would you like a baby brother or sister?'

'But I want a bike for Christmas.'

Sally laughed as she hugged her daughter. 'The baby isn't your Christmas present, darling.'

'When am I getting it then?'

'Oh, not for a while yet.'

Angel looked puzzled, and taking a breath Sally said, 'The baby is growing in my tummy, darling, and it's not big enough to be born yet.'

Angel's eyes widened, her finger pointing. 'It's in there?'

'Yes, sweetheart.'

'Was I in there?'

'Yes, you certainly were.'

'How did I get out?'

'You've started something now, Sal,' Sadie chuckled.

'I know,' and closing her eyes momentarily, Sally struggled to find an answer for her daughter. 'There's a special place for the baby to come out when it's ready to be born.'

'Oh,' she said, her curiosity satisfied as she asked, 'Can I go out to play now?'

'Darling, it's freezing outside. Why don't you do some painting instead?'

Angel pursed her lips, her glance flicking to Sadie. 'Yeah, do some painting, love,' she advised.

Sally smiled, pleased that Gran was like her old self again. She was definitely a lot better, these periods now lasting longer and longer.

'All right, I'll paint a picture for Daddy.'

As Angel scampered off to find her paint box, Sally once

again glanced at the clock, willing the hours away. She wanted to get to the hospital, to break the news to Arthur, but oh, how slowly the time was going.

Ruth too was thrilled with the news, Sally telling her as soon as she arrived home from work. 'A boy would be nice this time,' she said.

'Yeah, I want a bruvver,' Angel agreed.

'Brother,' Sally corrected, but her heart wasn't in it.

They had dinner, and then she left to get ready, glad that at last it was time to go.

After a quick goodbye she hurried to the bus-stop, and after what felt like the usual endless journey, her heart was pounding in her chest with excitement as she entered the ward.

'Hello, love,' Arthur said, looking decidedly uncomfortable as he tried to raise himself into a sitting position.

The splint looked awkward and cumbersome, and Arthur fed up, but Sally knew that was all about to change. She leaned forward to plant a kiss on his lips, saying quietly, 'Hello, new daddy.'

His brow creased. 'New daddy?'

She smiled at his confusion, and then drawing out a chair she sat down beside the bed. 'Yes, darling, I'm having a baby.'

'What? How?'

'I should have thought that was obvious.'

'But we haven't . . .'

'Yes we have, darling. Going by the dates, it happened on that one occasion when Angel went to stay with your mother for the night.'

At last a grin spread across Arthur's face. 'God, this is wonderful.' He struggled higher in the bed, shouting down the ward, 'Here, you lot, guess what? I'm having a baby!'

'Blimey, you must be a miracle of science,' Fred Royston called. 'Either that or you're a woman in disguise. No, I take that back, being opposite I've seen what you've got down there and it ain't a pretty sight.'

'Leave it out, you cheeky sod. I mean my wife is having a baby.'

160

'Really! Well, congratulations.'

More shouts of congratulations followed and a nurse walked over, smiling widely. 'Well done, Mr Jones.'

'Thank you, and now the sooner I get out of here the better.'

'I'm sure it won't be long now,' she said, but then someone called her and she hurried away.

'Oh, Sally, this is the best news you could have given me. Wait till I tell Joe. How about having him as a godfather?'

'You're jumping the gun a bit, Arthur. There are months to go yet.'

'Yes, of course. When's it due?'

'Next year, in July.'

His hand reached out, awkwardly touching her tummy. 'I wonder if I have a son in there.'

'You'll just have to wait and see. Would another girl be so bad?'

'No, of course not, but a boy would be nice.'

For the rest of the visit Sally was delighted to see Arthur looking so much happier. They had so much to look forward to. A new flat, a new baby, and as the nurse said, Arthur was sure to be allowed home soon.

Twenty-Four

Christmas hadn't been the same with Arthur in hospital, but they had all gone to visit him. He was amazingly cheerful, still chuffed about the new baby, and though disappointed that he wasn't at home, the ward had been a happy place that day. Angel had bragged about the tricycle from Father Christmas and was thrilled with her nurse's outfit from Arthur, even more so when a group of nurses came into the ward wearing their caps and capes, their sweet voices singing Christmas carols.

And now it was New Year's Day, Sally thought, deciding that 1967 was going to be perfect. She placed her hands over her tummy, her face soft.

A ring on the doorbell broke Sally out of her reveries, and she was delighted to see her friend, Arthur's sister, on the step. 'Ann, how lovely to see you.'

'Mum's looking after the kids so I've got a couple of hours of freedom.'

'What am I thinking of, leaving you on the doorstep, come on in.'

Ann walked into the hall, smiling as she said, 'So, you're having a baby? And about time too. It's wonderful news but what a shame that Arthur's still in hospital.'

'I know, but he's dead chuffed about the baby and it's keeping him cheerful. I do feel sorry for him though. With his leg in traction, held up by a five pound weight, he keeps sliding down in the bed.'

They entered the kitchen, Ann saying, 'Hello everyone.' Her glance then fell on Angela and she held out her arms. 'How about giving your auntie a kiss?'

Angel hesitated, but only for a moment, then running up to Ann she asked, 'Where are them boys?'

'If you mean your cousins, Darren and Jason, they're with your grandmother.'

'But I want to see them.'

'You will, darling. Your granddad is coming to pick us all up at two o'clock. We'll be going see your daddy first, and after that you and Mummy will be coming back to Wimbledon with us.'

'Ann,' Sally said hesitantly.

'Don't worry, it's all arranged.'

'This is all news to me. I usually visit Arthur in the evening.'

'I know, but for once Mum is swopping with you. Didn't you tell her, Ruth?'

'I was about to when you arrived. You're earlier than I expected.'

'Yes, I know, but I wanted to spend some time with Sally. We hardly see each other these days.'

'When was all this arranged?' Sally asked.

'Elsie rang while you were visiting Arthur yesterday,' Ruth said.

'Why didn't you tell me?'

'I thought it would be a nice surprise and it'll make a change for you.'

Sally stared at her mother, amazed that she had been so thoughtful, but then Sadie spoke.

'At least Ann's bleedin' hooligans ain't coming here.'

'Gran!'

'It's all right, Sally,' Ann said. 'Yes, Sadie, they can be a handful.'

'Why don't you two go out on your own for a while?' Ruth suggested.

'If you're sure you don't mind, Mum.'

'Of course not, and you can take Ann to see your flat.'

'I want to come too,' Angel demanded.

'But I'm making cakes and need you to help me,' Ruth said.

Angel looked perplexed for a moment, but obviously the thought of baking with her grandmother won. 'All right, I'll help you, Nanny.'

'Oh, thank goodness for that. I couldn't manage without you,' Ruth said with a sly wink at Sally.

163

Taking their cue, the two young women left the room and in no time were emerging on to Candle Lane, Sally saying as soon as they began to walk, 'I'm sorry about my gran.'

'You don't have to apologize for her. And let's face it, my twins *are* a handful.'

'They aren't hooligans.'

'Don't you believe it. Now come on, let's forget about Sadie for a couple of hours.'

Sally hooked her arm through Ann's, her mood light as they made their way to Maple Terrace. 'Things are looking up,' she said. 'I'm pregnant, Arthur's getting better, and when he comes home we'll be in our own little flat. And talking about husbands, where is yours?'

'Billy's in Wimbledon with my parents and is supposed to be helping Mum with the kids. Huh, fat chance of that.'

'Isn't he good with them?'

'He's like all men, and if I asked him to change a nappy he'd run a mile.'

'Yes, Arthur used to disappear too. Mind you, I don't think I would have trusted him with a safety pin. It was bad enough for me when Angel used to wriggle when changing her nappy and I was always frightened of sticking the pin in her.'

'Me too at first, but I've had plenty of practice now. By the way, have you heard from your Aunt Mary?'

'Yes, we got a postcard a few days ago and it sounds like she's having a wonderful time.'

'You never know, she might meet a nice rich widower on board.'

'I wish she would meet someone – rich or not. She deserves a bit of happiness.'

They turned into Maple Terrace, Ann exclaiming, 'I'd forgotten what a nice road this is.'

'It's better than most, and unlike nearly everything else around here, it isn't scheduled for redevelopment.'

When they reached the flat, Sally opened the door with a flourish, leading Ann into the sitting room.

'It's lovely,' she said. 'But flipping freezing.'

'I'll light the gas fire. Blast, I haven't any matches. Oh, I know, I'll give Patsy a knock.'

'Who's Patsy?'

'The young woman who lives upstairs. I won't be a mo.' Sally hurried outside again, and as she knocked on Patsy's door she hoped the girl was in.

Footsteps sounded, and as she opened the door her neighbour smiled with delight. 'Hello, come on up,' she said, gesturing Sally inside.

'Sorry, I can't. I've just brought my friend around to see the flat, but without any matches I can't light the fire.'

'Oh, there's no need to sit in a cold flat. You can both come up to mine.'

'Well, maybe just for a little while,' Sally said, hoping that Ann wouldn't mind.

Ann had a quick look around the flat, saying it was lovely, and then they hurried up to Patsy's, finding her living room was all vibrant colour. In contrast to Sally's flat, Patsy's was totally modern. Her suite was black vinyl and scattered with bright orange, shaggy fur cushions. The wallpaper was predominantly orange too, making Sally's eyes swim with its psychedelic, swirling pattern.

'Oh, this is nice,' Ann said.

'Please, sit down,' Patsy invited, her coal-effect fire looking welcoming to the two girls.

At first conversation was a bit stilted, but gradually the ice broke, especially when Ann found out that Patsy was a mobile hairdresser.

'I used to do hairdressing before I got married,' Ann told her. 'And when my children are older I'd like to go back to it. Mobile hairdressing sounds ideal. Mind you, I'm out of practice.'

'I get mostly elderly, housebound clients, so I don't get the chance to do many modern styles. I can't see them wanting a Vidal Sassoon cut,' she said, laughing at the thought.

'I just love his geometric five point cut,' Ann enthused.

Whilst they were talking, Sally took in Patsy's striking outfit. She was wearing a black polo neck sweater under a black and white check, mini-pinafore dress, and looked great.

'Oh bugger,' Patsy said, surveying her legs. 'I've got a hole in my tights.'

'Are they comfortable?' Sally couldn't help asking.

'Yes, and a darn sight better than wearing a suspender belt and stockings. Anyway, with minidresses it would be a bit difficult to sit down without showing your stocking tops. How's your husband, Sally?'

'On the mend, and I hope he'll be home soon.'

'Oh good, that means you'll be moving in downstairs.'

'You might not say that when my brother starts playing his old records. He prefers Frank Sinatra to any of the modern stuff.'

'Your brother?' Patsy said, looking confused.

'Yes, sorry, I should have explained. Ann is my friend, but she's also my sister-in-law. By the way, you were right, I am having a baby.'

'Are you pleased?'

'Pleased is an understatement. I'm ecstatic!'

'Well, congratulations then,' and swiftly changing the subject she turned to Ann. 'Do you live around here?'

'I used to live next door to Sally in Candle Lane, but moved out of London when I married Billy. Anyway, back to hairdressing. How did you build up your clients?'

'It was easy really; I just put an ad in the local paper, and placed cards in a few newsagents' windows.'

Sally could see that Ann was impressed, but with young twins and a baby under a year old it would be some time before she could consider hairdressing again. She found her attention drifting as her eyes roamed around Patsy's sitting room, and spotting a photograph of a child on the long, low-line sideboard, she wondered who it was.

'I can't wait to see your little girl, Sally,' Patsy said.

'You might not say that when you meet her. Angel can be a proper little madam.'

'Don't take any notice of Sally,' Ann said. 'Her daughter is adorable.'

'Angel. What a lovely name.'

'It's Angela really,' and plucking up the courage Sally added, 'I see you have a photograph of a child on your sideboard.'

'Yes,' Patsy said and abruptly stood up. 'What must you think of me? I haven't even offered you a cup of coffee.'

'We'd love one,' both chorussed and, as Patsy left the

room, Ann glanced at the photograph. She obviously found
Patsy's answer abrupt too, and now looking at Sally she
raised her brows in a silent enquiry.

Sally shrugged, and both remained quiet until Patsy
returned with a pyrex cup and saucer in each hand. 'Here
you are,' she said, placing them on the coffee-table.

Ann picked hers up, took a sip, and then said, 'Are you
married, Patsy?'

'Not any more,' she said, and Sally held her breath. Would
Ann ask her what she meant?

'I'm so sorry, did you lose your husband?'

'He isn't dead, if that's what you mean. We're divorced.'

'Divorced! But you're so young!' Ann blurted out.

Patsy shrugged, but Ann's curiosity was obviously piqued.
'Is the little girl in the photograph yours?'

'Yes,' Patsy murmured.

'She looks lovely, but where is she?'

'Look, I don't usually talk about it, but if you must know
she lives with her father.'

'Goodness, it's unusual for the father to get custody and
it must be hard for you.'

There was a small silence, but then Patsy spoke again.
'It's no more than I deserve.'

'Oh, I can't believe that. No mother deserves to have her
child taken away.'

'Ann,' Sally warned, 'I don't think this is any of our business.'

'It's all right,' Patsy said. 'You might as well hear the rest.
I married young, and soon found out it was a mistake. A
year later I fell in love with another man and ran off with
him, abandoning my daughter. You'll be pleased to know,
I'm sure, that I got my come-uppance in more ways than
one. You see after only a few months he left me.'

Both Sally and Ann gawked, neither saying anything. 'Now
you can see why I don't usually talk about it, and I don't
know why I opened up to you,' Patsy said bitterly. 'By the
look on your faces you're both judging me and no doubt
finding me wanting.'

'No, of course not,' Sally said, and she meant it. Who was
she to judge Patsy? She had been attracted to another man,

lusting after Joe Somerton like a bitch on heat.

'I'm sorry for quizzing you, Patsy,' Ann said, looking shamefaced.

The atmosphere was tense, but then Ann jumped in again, obviously thinking that it was best to change the subject as she complimented Patsy on her outfit. The conversation turned to fashion, and gradually the tension eased, all three girls chatting freely.

'I'm sorry to break this up,' Sally said, rising to her feet. 'But we'd best go to Candle Lane. I want to get changed to visit Arthur and there's Angel to get ready too.'

'All right,' Ann agreed. 'It was nice to meet you, Patsy.'

'Thanks, it was nice to meet you too.' She turned to Sally. 'Will you pop up to see me again? Mind you, I'll understand if you don't want to.'

'Don't be silly, of course I'll come to see you again, and once I move in, you can pop down to see me any time you like.'

Patsy smiled widely before showing them out.

Both Ann and Sally were quiet as they walked home, until Sally said, 'Patsy's nice, isn't she?'

'Well . . . yes, I suppose so.'

'You don't sound too sure.'

'She seems nice enough and there's no denying that she's friendly, but . . .'

'But what?'

'Well, it was a bit much when she told us about abandoning her little girl.'

'I was as shocked as you, but I felt sorry for her. I can't imagine what it must be like to be stuck in a loveless marriage, and she must have been desperate to run off like that.'

'That's no excuse. She could have taken her daughter with her. Think about it, Sally, could you abandon Angela? I know I could never leave my kids.'

'No, I couldn't leave her, but I think there's more to Patsy's story. Maybe her husband wouldn't let her take the child.'

'Yeah, I suppose that could be it.'

'Anyway, enough about Patsy. I want to pick your brains about what to get your dad for his birthday.'

'Blimey, I haven't got a clue. I had enough trouble finding him something for Christmas.'

'What about cuff-links?'

'Yeah, I suppose so. It's a shame that his birthday party has been cancelled, but with all that's happened, Mum wasn't in any state to organize it.'

'I know, but Arthur is sure to be home by the end of January, and maybe we can just have a family party or something.'

Ann nodded as they turned into Candle Lane. As they went into number five, Sally went to get both herself and Angel ready.

Soon after Bert arrived, and seeing his granddaughter looking so pretty he picked her up, planting a kiss on her cheek. 'Hello, sweetheart. You look nice.'

'I don't like this dress. I want to wear my trousers.'

Bert put her back on to the floor, saying with a chuckle, 'Well, *I* think you look lovely, and I'm sure your daddy will too. Now come on, let's be off.'

When they all went into the ward, Arthur still looked uncomfortable, but smiled with pleasure when he saw them.

'I doubt if I'll get away with this many visitors around my bed, but as it's New Year's Day you never know.'

Angel fed him a slice of Ruth's freshly baked fruit cake, and whilst Arthur was distracted, Sally looked at his aura. There was darkness, but considering he'd had gangrene, she guessed it was normal. At least he seemed pain free, and bless him, he was so happy about the pregnancy.

The ward was noisy and it wasn't until the end of visiting time that Sally got a moment alone with her husband.

Arthur kissed Angel, said goodbye to Ann and his father, and as they left he said, 'Did you ring Joe?'

'Yes, and he's coming to see you tomorrow evening.'

'That's good and listen, with Joe coming, why don't you stay home tomorrow. It must be a trek coming to see me every evening and I don't want you wearing yourself out.'

'I don't mind. I'm pregnant, not ill.'

'I know, but there's no need. Anyway, it'll give me a chance to talk business with Joe.'

'Well, if you're sure.'

'I am, now give me a kiss.'

Sally bent forward, and as she kissed Arthur she felt a shiver of intuition. 'You're going to tell Joe to find another partner again.'

'Christ, you're like a witch at times. It's the only thing to do, Sally. I had a word with the doctor and he said that after this traction, I'll have to have another plaster fitted. He couldn't say for sure when I can come home, and it's not fair on Joe. He's waited long enough.'

'I doubt he'll agree.'

'I won't give him any choice. Now you'd best go before Sister Moody descends on us.'

Sally waved as she left the ward, but as she joined the others she wondered what would happen if Joe agreed to break the partnership. Would Bert take Arthur back into the business? Yes, she decided, of course he would.

When they arrived in Wimbledon, Angel's face lit up when she saw not only her cousins, but a huge spread on Elsie's dining-room table. There were sandwiches, cakes, jellies, and a large bowl of trifle. 'Blimey, are you feeding an army?' Bert asked.

'There are eight of us, and no doubt you're all hungry. How was Arthur?'

'Not too bad, but he'll be glad to have the splint removed.'

Sally saw a slight frown on Elsie's face, but it soon cleared, and then handing everyone a plate she insisted they help themselves. 'Sandwiches first,' she told the twins as their hands grabbed for cakes. 'I still can't believe I'm going to have another grandchild, Sally.'

'Yes, and isn't it great.'

'It certainly is,' she said, kissing her on the cheek, but not before Sally again saw a hint of worry in her eyes.

It was an hour later before Sally got a chance to speak to Elsie. She could still sense that something was wrong, and taking the opportunity whilst Ann was feeding the baby, she went into the kitchen to help with the washing-up. 'Is there something on your mind, Elsie?'

'What makes you say that?' Elsie asked as she plunged a pile of tea plates into the water.

'I can sense that something is worrying you.'

'I think you're imagining things.'

'Come on, you can't fool me. If you're worried about Arthur, there's no need. I know he's been through a rough time lately, but he's over the worst now.'

Elsie's hands became still, and as she turned to meet Sally's eyes, her gaze was penetrating. 'It was just something I saw in the cards that didn't make a lot of sense. I did the spread twice, and it was almost identical. I suppose that's why I'm a bit worried.'

'What did you see?'

'Are things all right with you and Arthur?'

'Yes, of course. Why do you ask?'

'Oh I don't know, but I thought I saw another man in the background.'

Sally felt her face growing hot and quickly looked away. 'Oh Elsie, surely you don't think that I'm being unfaithful.'

'No, of course not, but it was such a strange reading. Mind you, there was a warning of illness too, but as Arthur is getting better, it can't be him. How is your gran?'

'About the same and her aura looks fine.'

'Perhaps I'm losing my abilities, or it may be that I'm doing the readings for myself. I know they aren't always clear when you do that.'

'I doubt you're using your ability.'

'Sally, I hope I am,' Elsie said earnestly. 'I saw danger in the spread too, violence, and that's what worried me the most. I've never seen cards like it.'

Sally shivered. No matter what Elsie said, she knew her mother-in-law was rarely wrong with her tarot reading. Violence! Danger – and closing her eyes, Sally prayed for everyone she loved.

Twenty-Five

Over two weeks passed with no sign of Elsie's predictions, and Sally had begun to relax. Arthur's leg was now out of traction and a new plaster put on, the doctor now saying he'd be able to come home soon.

On Wednesday it was half day closing in Sidney Jacobs' shop, and Ruth arrived home at one thirty. Sally looked up in surprise. 'You're early, Mum.'

'Yeah, I know. Sid's son turned up so I left them to it.'

'Did he? That makes a change.'

'He's trying to talk the old man into retiring and if you ask me he's up to something. Mind you, Sid's looking really tired lately, despite me taking on most of the work. Christ, Sal, I hope he doesn't pack it in. I love me job.'

'I doubt he'll retire, Mum. He loves the shop.'

'Huh, he's hardly ever in it and spends most of his time upstairs.'

Sally rose to make her mother a cup of tea, pleased when she said, 'Why don't you take yourself out for the afternoon. I can collect Angel from school. You could have a look around the shops and it'll give you a break.'

'Yes, I'd like that. It would be nice to have a look at baby clothes, and I need to find something for Bert's birthday at the end of the month. I think I'll go to Clapham Junction.'

In no time Sally was ready, and wrapping herself up against the icy wind she left the house with a smile on her face.

When getting off her bus at the Junction, Sally made for Arding & Hobbs, happily going straight for the department selling baby clothes and prams. So many of the things she saw were gorgeous, and unable to resist she purchased a lovely pale lemon pram set.

172

She would need maternity wear soon, but saw nothing she fancied and meandered on, passing other departments. It was lovely and warm in the store, and in no hurry to leave she looked at some cuff-links for Bert, but saw none she thought he would like.

Eventually she left the store, tucking her scarf closer to her neck as she walked along looking in shop windows. It was already nearly five o'clock, but there was no need to rush home. Mum was collecting Angel, and she wasn't visiting Arthur that evening.

She strolled on, crossing to Northcote Road and, passing a pawnbroker's shop, she paused to look in the window. There were trays of rings, unclaimed and now for sale, causing Sally a tinge of sadness as she wondered about their history. Had they been pawned by people desperate for money? Had someone died, the ring raising a few pounds for the family?

Her eyes now moved to gaze at some gold chains, but then something else caught her eye. In a little velvet box, she saw a figure of an angel. It was silver, and though quite plain, the delicate filigree work of the wings made her gasp in wonder. There was no price tag, and on impulse she stepped into the shop.

Sally didn't know what to expect, maybe piles of junk, but instead she was confronted by a pristine room with just a large mahogany counter. A variety of clocks were displayed on shelves behind, and there were barometers hanging up, some looking antique. There was a little room off to the left and seeing her looking at it a young woman behind the counter asked, 'Do you want to pawn something?'

'Oh, no,' Sally said, noticing that the young woman's hair was almost exactly the same shade of red as hers. 'Goodness, your hair is very much like mine,' she remarked as she approached the counter.

'Yes, and we have almost the same style too. Now, how can I help you?' she asked, glancing at her watch.

'I'm interested in that little angel brooch in the window. May I see it, please?'

The girl sighed imperceptibly, but took some keys and unlocked the widow, sliding it along before reaching in to take out the little box. She then handed it to Sally, saying, 'It's very pretty.'

Sally gently removed the brooch, holding it on the palm of her hand. Someone had loved this little angel, she could sense it, and she loved it too. 'How much is it?'

'A lot of work has gone into those wings, but you can have it for fifteen bob.'

Goodness, Sally thought, it seemed a lot for such a tiny brooch, but looking at it again she just had to have it. 'I'll take it.'

'You're just in time. I was about to lock up when you came in.'

When Sally paid for the brooch she hardly had any money left in her purse and, as the girl was placing it in a bag, she glanced out of the window. Her eyes clouded. It was raining heavily and without an umbrella she took a headscarf out of her bag, flicking it over her head and tying it in a knot under her chin. Obviously impatient now, the assistant handed her the package. 'Thanks,' Sally said. 'And I'm sorry if I held you up.'

'That's all right,' but the redhead's hand was already reaching for the light switches.

Sally had barely reached the door when the lights started to go out.

'Oops, sorry,' the girl called.

With a smile over her shoulder, Sally now opened the door, all the lights going out and a wall of rain hitting her as she stepped outside. She was soon drenched, and knowing there was a small café in the next side-street, she turned down it, deciding it might be prudent to pop in for a hot drink until the rain eased off. She was only a little way along the dimly lit street when she had a strange feeling of someone close behind her.

Sally was about to turn, but before she could, something was thrown roughly over her head. She screamed in shock, her voice becoming muffled as a hand was placed over her mouth.

'Shut up,' a voice growled.

Hands grabbed her, lifting her from her feet, and she kicked out wildly. *Oh God*, her mind begged, *someone, anyone, please help me!*

'Quick, get her in the car.'

She was then thrown, landing heavily, a cry of pain escaping her lips. Doors slammed, an engine revved, and now, as sheer terror took over, she fainted.

As Sally slowly came to, she opened her eyes, but couldn't see a thing. Stifled, she struggled to remove the cloth that was over her head, but found it impossible. Movement, she was aware of the vehicle moving, and tried to lift herself up.

'Stay down,' a voice growled, and what felt like a foot pushed on her shoulders.

'We're nearly there,' another voice said.

Oh, God, what was happening? She began to shake. Was she going to be raped?

The stinking cloth was cloying and she gagged, fighting desperately to hold down the bile that rose in her throat.

The car suddenly turned sharply before stopping, and then she was being dragged from the vehicle. Her legs could hardly support her as she was shoved forward and, unable to see a thing, Sally stumbled.

She could sense they were inside now, heard a door crashing shut, and then she was shoved forward again.

'Sit,' a voice growled as though talking to a dog.

Aware of something behind her legs, she was pushed down on to a chair, and unable to control her limbs, she shook from head to toe.

'Scared are yer?' a voice said, thick with menace. 'Good. Now it's up to you. If you want to get out of here in one piece, you'd better tell us what we want to know. Give us the combination number of the safe.'

'W . . . what?'

'Don't act dumb. Now, as I said, give us the combination number.'

'I . . . I don't know what you mean. I haven't got a safe,' she said, aware that her voice sounded strange through the thick material.

'Very funny. We've been casing the pawnshop for weeks, and know that your boss is a fence. We also know that he's away until tomorrow, *and* what he's got stashed in the safe.

175

We've got the keys from your bag, so stop playing games and tell us what we want to know!'

'Please, you've got to listen to me. I don't work in the pawnshop!'

Sally was struck violently, her head snapping back, and for a moment she saw stars. Then the fist struck again, this time knocking her from the chair. She crawled into a ball, trying to protect herself and her unborn baby, but they dragged at her, yanking her up and forcing her back on to the seat.

'I'm losing patience. Now tell me the number!'

Her head was swimming, her voice a croak as she managed to gasp, 'I think you've mistaken me for someone else.'

'Games again. Christ, you're a stubborn bitch!' She was struck again and screamed with pain.

'Give me the number!'

Sally licked her lips, tasting blood. She had to convince them, somehow managing to speak. 'I . . . I really don't work in the shop.'

There was a moment of silence, then the voice growled, 'Come on, we'll cover our faces and then get that sack off.'

Her senses reeling, she drew in a great gulp of air as the cover was removed. She stared at the two men towering over her in terror. They were wearing black balaclavas, only their eyes and slits of mouths visible – hard eyes that bored into her.

'Bloody hell! We've got the wrong girl.'

'Shit! How did we make that mistake?'

'Look at her, you daft sod! She's got red hair, she's about the same build, and she was wearing that bleedin' scarf. She also left the pawnbroker's when it closed.'

'Christ, what are we gonna do now?'

'I dunno. Give me time to think,' and striding away the tallest man walked to the far end of the room.

Barely able to focus, Sally looked around. She wasn't in a room; it was more like a garage or lock-up. 'Please,' she whispered. 'Please let me go.'

'Shut up!'

The other man walked back and Sally cowered in fear as he spoke.

'We'll 'ave to get rid of her.'

'No way – if we got caught we'd go down for life. She

ain't seen our faces, she knows nothing, so what could she tell the old bill?'

'You've got a point.'

He paced for a minute, deep in thought, and then said, 'We ain't mentioned any names, and you're right, she's got nothing on us. Shove that sack over her head again and we'll dump her now.'

Sally slumped. They weren't going to kill her! Oh, thank God.

'All right but it's a bit early. We might get clocked if we dump her now.'

'Yeah, you're right. We'll have to hang about for a while.' He chuckled. 'She ain't a bad looking bint, and to kill time we could have a bit of fun.'

No! No! Sally thought, rising unsteadily. They were going to rape her! She had to get away!

The man chuckled again, 'Blimey, look, she's on her feet and can't wait.'

His hands grabbed her and she screamed in terror as he forced her to the ground. 'No, please, don't touch me. I – I'm having a baby!'

Her pleas were ignored as he tore at her clothes. She fought, writhed, the stench of his body in her nostrils. 'No! Please no!' she cried as his knee went between her legs, forcing them apart.

'Hold on. Don't do it. She said she's 'aving a baby.'

'So what!'

'How would you like it if someone raped *your* wife?'

'Bloody hell, what's the matter with you. Are you going soft?'

'No, but this ain't right.'

The man moved off her and Sally rolled away, curling up into a ball.

'Sod it,' he said, 'I've gone off the boil now. All right, I'll leave her alone. Here, help me to put her back on the chair.'

Hands dragged at Sally again, but this time she didn't resist. The man who had spoken on her behalf was smaller than the other one, his voice softer as he said, 'Are you all right?'

'Yes, but please, please let me go.'

'For Christ's sake shut her up! I can't stand whining women.'

A fist came out, connecting with Sally's jaw, knocking her senseless.

When Sally came to she could barely open her eyes. Her head was pounding and she had no idea how long she'd been unconscious. She'd hardly gained her senses when the cover was thrown over her head again. Hands, she was aware of hands, and shook with terror. She was pulled to her feet, dragged forward, and then feeling freezing air she knew they were outside. With a shove Sally was pushed into a vehicle, and then down into a cramped space. She could hardly move and gasped in pain, but guessed she was on the floor behind the front seats.

'Right,' the gruff voice said. 'Drive to the downs.'

Her head still pounding, Sally registered the words. They were going to dump her now, but at least she hadn't been raped, and she was alive!

The car sped along, seemingly for miles, Sally's muscles screaming in pain as she tried to move.

'Stay down,' a voice said and once again she felt a foot on her back.

The car turned sharply, driving over rough ground. 'Yeah, good spot. Slow down and I'll chuck her out.'

Sally was pulled up by the scruff of her neck and she gagged, but was aware then of a rush of air. She felt a mighty shove in her back, barely had time to register that she was being thrown out of the car, before landing heavily, the wind knocked out of her body on impact.

Pain shot through her – pain like a knife in her stomach. *Oh, no, not my baby!* Then she knew no more.

Ruth kept glancing at the clock, her hands wringing with anxiety. 'God. Mum, what's keeping her?'

'Perhaps she went to see Arthur.'

'No, Joe's going tonight, and even if you're right, she'd be home by now.'

The door opened, Angel knuckling her eyes as she came into the room. 'Where's Mummy?'

178

'Angel, what are you doing out of bed?'

'I want Mummy.'

Ruth crossed her fingers as she told the lie, 'She's visiting your daddy and won't be home yet. Come on, let's get you back to bed.'

'Mummy's not well.'

The child's eyes began to fill with tears, and hiding her emotions Ruth took Angel into her arms. 'I think you must have had a bad dream, darling. Mummy's not ill, she's fine. Now come on, upstairs.'

Thankfully with a little more reassurance, Angel went back to sleep and as Ruth returned to the kitchen, her stomach was churning. 'Something's wrong with Sally, I don't know what, but I'm worried sick!'

'It won't hurt to ring the hospital. As you say she may have been to visit Arthur and then somehow got held up.'

'Yes, I'll do that, but if there was a problem surely she'd have rung us. Maybe I should call the police.'

'That won't do any good. As far as they're concerned she's just late home.'

'But it's not like her, and you know that.'

Sadie pursed her lips. 'It's strange that Angel thinks Sally ain't well.'

'Strange – why strange? I think it was a bad dream.'

'Yeah, of course it was,' Sadie placated. 'Go and make your call and give Elsie a ring too. Perhaps Sally went there.'

Ruth hurried to the telephone, her hands shaking when told that Sally hadn't been to the hospital. She then dialled Elsie's number, fear making her voice wobble. 'Is . . . is Sally there?'

'Sally, here! No, of course not.' Elsie's voice rose as she added, 'What's wrong, Ruth?'

Ruth told her, her voice breaking when she came to the end. 'Oh, Elsie, where can she be?'

'I don't know, love, but like you I'm worried. Perhaps you should check all the hospitals.'

At Ruth's gasp Elsie then added, 'Look, I'll get Bert to run me down to you. We'll be as quick as we can.'

As soon as Ruth replaced the receiver she grabbed the telephone book, and going through the list she began to dial.

She was still at it when Elsie arrived, and hearing that Sally wasn't in St Thomas's she ran to answer the door. 'I've tried all the hospitals, but she's not in any of them. Oh, Elsie, where is she?'

'I don't know, love, but let's get inside.'

'I'm worried sick,' Ruth cried, leading them into the kitchen.

'Right, start at the beginning,' Bert said.

Unaware that she was wringing her hands, Ruth told them, seeing their faces darken with worry too.

'Where did she go shopping?'

'She said she was going to the Junction.'

'Did she seem worried or upset?'

'No, she was fine!'

The room was silent, Elsie flopping on to a chair, 'Look, it's getting on for eleven o'clock and I think we should ring the police.'

Sadie shook her head. 'Ruth suggested that earlier, but they won't do anything. It's too soon for her to be listed as a missing person.'

'We'll see about that!' Bert snapped. 'Sally isn't in any of the hospitals, so she hasn't had an accident. I'll take a drive to Clapham Junction to see if there's any sign of her, and I'll also go to the police station. It'll be better to see them face to face, and I'll *make* them listen to our concerns.'

'Yes, do that,' Elsie urged, watching as her husband hurried from the room.

'Oh, if only she'd ring us!' Ruth cried.

'Try not to worry. Sally is a sensible girl and I'm sure she's fine.'

'But that makes it worse, Elsie. She would never just go off somewhere without letting us know. Oh, God, what if some nutter has got hold of her?'

Ruth saw the expression on Elsie's face and knew she was thinking the same thing. Tears flooded her eyes. Oh, Sally, Sally, please be all right.

When Bert returned all three women looked at him expectantly, but his face was stiff and Ruth's heart sunk. 'What did the police say?'

'Huh, not much. They took Sally's details, but didn't take it seriously. I talked until I was blue in the face, assuring them that Sally would never go off anywhere without telling us, but I don't think they'll do anything until she's been missing for twenty-four hours.'

'Oh, Bert, that's terrible!'

'I know, but they said it's procedure. If Sally were a child it would be different, but she's an adult.'

Ruth looked at the clock again and sobbed. Despite not wanting to think the worst, all sorts of horrendous things filled her mind. Had her daughter been raped – murdered – was she lying injured somewhere? She felt an arm around her shoulders and turned, sobbing into Bert's jacket. Like Arthur, he was a great bear of a man, but instead of finding comfort she shuddered. Had a huge man like this taken her daughter?

Twenty-Six

Sally came to shivering with cold, aware of wracking pains in her abdomen. She tried to stagger to her feet, unable to see where she was in the dark. There was stickiness between her legs and she cried out in anguish, 'My baby! Oh, my baby!'

As feelings of despair washed over her, she sank down again. It was pitch black without a single light in sight, but slowly her eyes adjusted. There was hardly any moon, but when she looked up there appeared to be millions of stars. Oh God, are you up there? And if you are, how could you let this happen?

Slowly the voice of reason crept in. No, it wasn't God's fault. It was the evil men who had taken her, beaten her. She shuddered, trying to wrap her torn coat around her body. If she didn't move soon, she'd freeze, but oh, the pain in her stomach.

Finally Sally managed to stand and, staggering, she began to walk across grass, leaving icy footprints in the frost as she stumbled across the rough terrain. If she could find a path perhaps it would lead somewhere, anywhere but here.

Pain gripped her again and she fell, knowing by the sensations in her tummy that her baby had miscarried. For a while she tried to stem the flow of blood whilst hate washed over her – hate for the men who had done this. Somehow it gave her strength and once again she was able to stand. With no idea of what direction to take, she reeled forward like a drunken woman.

How long had she been walking? Sally had no idea, but it began to rain again, rain mixed with sleet that blew into her eyes and blinded her. She was freezing cold, but sweating, and fighting dizziness every step of the way.

When she was almost on the verge of collapse her feet touched solid ground, a path of some sort, or maybe even a road. Summoning the last of her strength she stumbled along it, and just when her knees buckled beneath her, she saw headlights approaching.

On her knees now she held up an arm, trying to call for help, but unable to utter a single sound. *Please stop, oh please stop*, but only her mind screamed the words.

'Charles, what's that in the road?'

He peered through the windscreen, but with rain falling heavily it was difficult to see. 'It's probably an animal, a deer or something like that.'

'What, waving an arm!'

Charles Bradshaw slowed the car, both of them now making out what looked like someone wearing a bundle of rags. 'I think it's a girl, Edwina.'

'More like a tramp I should think.'

'What, in the middle of nowhere and on a night like this?'

Charles could now make out a young woman with wet hair plastered to her face, and in the headlights she looked deathly white as she waved feebly. He got out of the car, and mindless of his dinner suit getting soaked, he ran to her side.

'Help me, please help me,' she gasped, but then her eyes closed and she slid down on to the wet road.

'Edwina, give me a hand,' he shouted as he tried to lift the girl.

'But the rain! My dress!'

'Damn your dress! This girl is in an awful state and we need to get her to hospital.'

Muttering complaints, Edwina got out of the car. 'I told you not to take this short cut,' but as she reached his side her voice came out in a gasp, 'Oh, the poor thing. Look, she's covered in blood.'

'Help me to lift her.'

Sally groaned, her eyes opening. 'No! Please don't hit me again!'

'There, there, it's all right. You're safe now,' Edwina consoled, and between them they managed to get Sally to her feet.

183

Hardly aware of anything now, Sally was half walked, half carried to a car and, as she was helped inside, she was only aware of the smell of leather before she lost consciousness again.

Voices, Sally could hear voices, and struggled against them. She didn't want to wake up. It was nice in the soft warm place she was floating in.

'Come on, my dear, try to drink this.'

No, don't bring me back. Leave me, just leave me.

'I think she's coming round, Doctor.'

Sally could fight it no longer and opened her eyes. A cup was held towards her and aware of a raging thirst, she gulped the cool liquid. In horrifying flashes it came back. 'My . . . my baby?' Yet even as the doctor spoke, she knew the answer.

'I'm sorry, my dear, I'm afraid you miscarried. Can you tell us your name?'

'Sally. Sally Jones.'

'The police are waiting to talk to you. Do you feel up to it?'

Sally moved slightly, aware that she ached in every part of her body. 'Yes, I'll talk to them.'

'Would you like us to contact anyone – your family?'

God, Sally thought, struggling to sit up. Her mother! Angel! Gran! They must be worried sick! She gasped, feeling a wave of dizziness, and sank back again.

'It's all right, you're going to be fine. You haven't sustained any serious injuries, but you're badly bruised. Do you have a telephone number to contact your family?'

Her vision cleared again and she told them the number, the nurse taking note and leaving the room. 'I'll send the policemen in now,' the doctor said, before he too left.

For a few minutes Sally lay still, now recalling vividly most of what had happened, and only unable to remember how she had ended up in hospital. Her hands moved to her stomach and she sobbed, feeling a well of emptiness at the loss of her baby.

Two policemen came into the room and as they approached the bed, one cleared his throat. 'Can you tell us what happened to you, miss?'

Sally fought her tears, and though she tried to recount what had happened, it all came out in a jumble until the last part. 'Then . . . then they threw me out of a car.'

One policeman drew out a chair and sat down, his voice soft and patient as he gently questioned her, taking her through all that had happened, step by step. Sally relived the terror, the pain, the fear, until she was emotionally drained.

'Thank you, miss. We'll liaise with our colleagues in the Met, and I'm sure they'll want to talk to you.'

Sally barely registered their words. She had been beaten, nearly raped, thrown out of a car, yet she had lived. She touched her stomach again and sobbed – but they had killed her baby.

During the early hours of the morning, Sally had cried on and off until she was drained, and now felt dead inside. She dozed, aware of the gradual increase of noise; the hum of voices, the rattle of china on a trolley. It was morning, and when a breakfast tray was put in front of her she turned her head away.

Time passed, a nurse taking her blood pressure and temperature whilst Sally watched listlessly, glad when she left.

All too soon the door opened again. Why wouldn't they just leave her alone?

'Sally. Oh God, Sally. Your poor face,' Ruth cried as she approached the bed, Bert behind her.

'I've lost my baby.'

'I know, love, they told us, but you're gonna be all right. We were going frantic and when the police knocked on the door in the early hours of the morning I nearly fainted with shock.'

'I hope they catch the bastards,' Bert growled.

So they knew, Sally thought, just glad that she didn't have to tell it all over again.

Her mother spoke again, 'You might be able to come home tomorrow and thank Gawd for that. It's miles to this flippin' hospital and took ages to get here.'

'Did it?' Sally asked dully.

'Fancy dumping you in the middle of Epsom Downs –

the bastards,' Ruth spat. 'God, if that couple hadn't found you.'

'What couple?'

'I don't know their names, but they brought you to this hospital and for that I thank them from the bottom of my heart.'

'I'll see if I can find out who they are, and thank them personally,' Bert said.

Sally nodded and then turned her head away, finding that she just couldn't be bothered to talk.

'Elsie and Bert stayed with us all night, and thank goodness Angel slept through it all. Mind you, she's gonna be upset when she sees your poor face.'

Her mother's voice was grating, getting on her nerves as she rattled on. 'Elsie stayed with your gran and Angel while Bert ran me here. We wanted to come earlier, but they said you were asleep and to wait until this morning.'

'Ruth, I think Sally needs to rest,' Bert urged.

'But we've only just got here!'

'I know, but she's been through a lot. I'll run you up again this evening, and if she can come home tomorrow, I'll pick her up.'

'Thanks, love, that's good of you. Sally, we're going now. I'll fetch you some clothes tonight, and is there anything else you need?'

She kept her eyes shut and didn't bother to answer, relieved when they left.

'Oh, Bert, she looks awful!'

'I know, but the doctor said her injuries are superficial. She was lucky, Ruth. From what the police told us, it could have been worse.'

'Worse than having her face used as a punch-bag? I hope they catch the animals that did this, and her baby, she's lost her baby. Christ, and we've still got to tell Arthur.'

'Elsie's going to the hospital this afternoon.'

'I'm going to be in a right old fix now. How can I go to work with Sally in that state?'

'You can't, Ruth. Take some time off.'

'It ain't that easy.'

'Sidney Jacobs thinks the world of Sally and he'll understand.'

'He can't manage the shop without me.'

'Maybe not, but Sally comes first, and if it's money that's worrying you, I can help out.'

'Thanks, but I'll manage.'

Bert was frowning as he opened the passenger door of his car, waiting until Ruth was settled before closing it again. Sally may be allowed home tomorrow, but from what he'd seen, he was worried about her state of mind.

He got behind the wheel, and as they drove back to Battersea, he was hardly taking in a word of what Ruth said as she prattled on. He'd like to get his hands on the men who had done this to Sally, but deep down he doubted they'd be caught. From what the police said, Sally hadn't been able to tell them much, only that they thought she was someone else – someone who worked in a pawnshop.

'It don't seem fair, Bert. First Arthur had that awful accident, and now this. Sally was thrilled about the baby and looking forward to moving into their new flat when Arthur comes home.'

'I know, but the main thing is she's alive. As I said, it could have been worse. They'll bounce back and who knows, there may be another baby.'

'Oh, I hope so,' Ruth said as they finally turned into Candle Lane.

Arthur smiled as he surveyed the ward. It was visiting time and his mum would be arriving soon, no doubt armed with a few of her home-made cakes. There she was now, but at the expression on her face, Arthur tensed.

He hardly gave her time to sit before he asked, 'What is it? What's wrong?'

She took his hand, her eyes moist as she said, 'I'm afraid I've got a bit of bad news, son. Sally has lost the baby.'

'Christ, Mum! Is she all right?'

'Yes, but I'm afraid there's more.'

Arthur reeled as his mother told him what had happened, his fists clenched in anger. 'Mum, I've got to get out of here. I've got to see Sally.'

'Oh, son, you know that's impossible. She's all right, honest, and we'll take good care of her.'

He slumped in despair, looking at his leg in disgust. Bloody hell, just when things were looking up, this had to happen.

'Listen, Arthur. I know it's dreadful, but it's not the end of the world. Sally will soon recover, then you'll be coming home, and you can always have another baby.'

He nodded, but his mood didn't lift. He should be with Sally, not stuck in this bloody ward. She'd been great the whole time he'd been in hospital, and he didn't know how he'd have got through the horror of gangrene without her support. Now, when she needed him . . .

'Ruth said Sally's injuries are only superficial. A couple of black eyes and a cut lip. She's a bit bruised where she was thrown from the car of course, but nothing was broken.'

Once again Arthur's fists clenched in anger. What sort of men were they to beat a woman? Animals, they were animals and he'd like to wring their bloody necks.

His mother was still speaking, and he did his best to answer, but when the bell rang to signal the end of visiting time he wasn't sorry to see her go. He wasn't in the mood for company – he was still full of fury.

Twenty-Seven

Sally had been home for over a week, but she was a shadow of her former self. She was still lethargic, showing little interest in anything, and even Angela was unable to arouse her interest.

There was no news of Arthur coming home, but it was bound to be soon, yet even this couldn't break through her misery. She had lost her baby, and instead of moving into their new flat with something wonderful to look forward to, she felt empty, lost.

Over and over again Sally relived what had been done to her. She had felt powerless, helpless, and shied away from a part of the horror that she wanted to forget. She still hadn't told anyone about the attempted rape, omitting it when she had spoken to the police. Why had it happened to her? Why?

When the police called again, this time plain-clothed officers from Lavender Hill Police Station, she shrank away from their questions.

'Is there anything else you can tell us, anything at all?'

'No,' Sally said listlessly.

'Why don't we start at the beginning? You had just left the pawnbroker's when the two men grabbed you.'

'Yes,' and once again she told them what had happened, but suddenly one officer interrupted.

'They said the pawnbroker is a fence? Are you sure about that?'

'Yes, I'm sure.'

They glanced at each other. 'He's not a fence, Mrs Jones. We've known the owner for a number of years and he's an honest man, quick to let us know if anyone offers him stolen goods. Those men must have got the wrong information from somewhere.'

'Wrong information – I went through all that because they had the wrong information!'

The officer hung his head, and then rose to his feet. 'We'll do our best to apprehend them.'

Sally watched them leave. They wouldn't catch them, she knew that, but to her they weren't just thieves, they were murderers who had killed her baby. Why couldn't she feel something? Why couldn't she cry? Dry eyed she rose to her feet and went back upstairs.

Ruth frowned as Sally left the room. She would have to go back to work soon or Sid was sure to replace her, but her daughter wasn't mentally fit to be left. Since coming home from hospital Sally wouldn't leave the house, and even going to the street door left her a trembling wreck.

'Christ, Mum, I don't know what to do about Sally. Maybe she should see a psychiatrist?'

'No, she'd be put on pills. Mary was given them once and she was like a zombie.'

'Huh, Sally's almost comatose now. From all the response I get I might as well be talking to a brick wall.'

'She's depressed, and after what she's been through, it ain't surprising.'

'I know, but she won't even leave the house to visit Arthur.'

'You can't blame her for that. The swelling on her face has only just begun to go down and parts of her are still black and blue.'

'It ain't just her face, Mum. Since the kidnap she seems terrified of going outside.'

'Give her time, she'll come round.'

'Yeah, but when.' Ruth glanced at the clock. 'Oh, sod it. I'd best pick Angel up from school.'

As the street door slammed behind Ruth, Sally came back downstairs, and going to the sink she poured a glass of water.

'Are you still feeling down, love?' Sadie gently asked.

'I'm all right.'

'No you're not. Talk to me, get it out of your system.

Scream, yell, cry; I don't mind, but you've got to buck yourself up.'

Sally looked up; her poor bruised face still yellow and purple. 'There's nothing to talk about, Gran.'

Sadie sighed, wishing she could do something, anything to make her granddaughter come alive again. 'Why don't you go to see Arthur tonight? Bert would run you to the hospital.'

'No, I'm not up to it yet.'

Sally then sat by the fire, gazing into space, and it was only fifteen minutes later when Angel ran into the room ahead of Ruth.

'Look, Mummy, I got a gold star for my painting.'

Sally smiled faintly, abstractedly patting her daughter on the head. Then rising, she made to leave the room.

'Where do you think you're going, Sally?'

'Upstairs, Mum.'

'No you're not. You're staying down here. I've had enough and you have a daughter to take care of. Or have you forgotten that!'

'Ruth,' Sadie said, her voice holding a warning.

Sally left the kitchen without saying a word whilst Ruth shook her head worriedly. 'I know that sounded harsh, Mum, but I'm just trying to bring her to her senses.'

'I don't think shouting at her is the answer. She needs our love and understanding.'

'Yeah, but I'm scared of losing me job, Mum.'

'Sally is more important than your job. You can always get another one.'

Angel began to cry, and Ruth pulled the child on to her lap. 'There, there, darlin',' she soothed, rocking her back and forth. Angel cried for a while longer, but then she put her thumb into her mouth as she drifted off to sleep.

'The poor mite,' Sadie whispered.

'I know, but if I let her have a nap she won't sleep tonight. It's been rough for her. She's still missing her dad, and now that Sally is wrapped up in her own pain, she's neglecting the child. Poor Angel just doesn't understand what's going on.'

'I tried to get Sally to open up while you were out, but she hardly said a word.'

'I'll give Elsie a ring later to see if there's any news about Arthur coming home. It would be wonderful for Angel, and with any luck it might be what Sally needs to snap her out of this flaming depression.'

Twenty-Eight

Another few days passed, but there was no change in Sally, and no news of Arthur coming out of hospital. Ruth had spoken to her boss, and though he understood, Sid was once again seriously considering retirement.

At four o'clock someone came to the door, and sighing Ruth went to answer, returning with Elsie behind her.

Sally didn't look up, and only raised her head when Elsie took a seat opposite her, speaking urgently. 'Sally, listen to me, I know you're still in a state, and I'm sorry, but I've got a bit of bad news.' Elsie then leaned forward to take Sally's hand, her voice now cracking. 'I've just come back from seeing Arthur and . . . and . . .'

'And what?' Ruth said as Elsie seemed unable to continue.

'Arthur's got to have another operation.'

Something stirred in Sally, her eyes widening. 'Another operation?'

'Yes, love. You see, for some time now there's been concern that Arthur's fracture hasn't mended. We didn't say anything as you haven't been yourself and we didn't want to worry you.' Elsie paused, rubbing her hand across her face before continuing. 'Oh, Sally, there's no easy way to tell you this. I'm afraid he's got a disease in the bone marrow, something called osteomyelitis. It's preventing the break from knitting together, and though they could perform a sequestrotomy, Arthur has decided against it.'

'What's a seques . . .' Sally couldn't grasp the word.

'They cut away the dying bone, and if successful, the break would heal.'

'But why has Arthur decided against it?'

'Because there's no guarantee it would work, and if that's

193

the case they'd have to perform another, leaving one leg considerably shorter than the other.'

'But you said he's having an operation. What are they going to do then?'

Elsie closed her eyes for a moment, fighting tears. 'He . . . he's going to have his leg cut off from below the knee.'

'No. Oh, no, Elsie!'

'Sally, he needs you. He needs to see you.'

Sally felt as if she was living in a nightmare. 'Why?' she shouted, jumping to her feet, eyes heavenward. 'Why is this happening? What have I done to deserve it? First my baby, now this!'

'Stop it!' Ruth cried. 'This isn't the time for self-pity. You've been through a dreadful experience, and I could kill those bastards, but you've got to buck yourself up now. Can't you imagine how Arthur is feeling? He's going to lose his leg, and as Elsie said, he needs you!'

Sally sank back on to her chair, her mother's words sinking in, hating herself and her behaviour. All she was thinking about was herself, her own pain. 'Oh, Gran, you were right all along. You said Arthur would lose his leg.'

'Yes, but I wish to God I'd been wrong. Oh, the poor lad.'

Sally's eyes were burning, but still dry as she stood up again. 'I must go to the hospital.'

Elsie put a hand on her arm. 'You can't go now, love. Visiting time is over, but you can go tonight.'

'Surely they'll let me see him now.'

'They won't, love. You know how strict the ward sister is.'

Angel started to cry, and hearing her something broke in Sally. God, Angel shouldn't have heard about Arthur like this. She knelt down, holding out her arms, and as her daughter ran into them she held her tightly, her own tears falling at last.

Sally was ready. She had applied some powder to her face, hoping to hide the bruising a little, but her lips were too sore to add lipstick.

She had rung Joe and he had insisted on taking her to the hospital. Now he nodded in approval when she came downstairs.

'You look fine, Sally. Come on, let's go.'

She said goodbye to her mother and gran, glad that Angel was in bed and asleep, the emotions of earlier wearing her daughter out.

As Joe held the street door open, Sally began to tremble. It was so dark outside and her heart began to thump wildly. Her chest tightened. She couldn't breathe! 'I . . . I can't,' she cried.

'Sally, come on, nothing is going to happen to you. I'm with you and I'll keep you safe,' Joe urged as he took her arm.

Despite the cold air, perspiration beaded Sally's face. She tried to move, but her feet were rooted.

'Come on, you've only got to take a few steps to my car.'

Sally was aware that her mother was behind her in the hall, her voice soft as she said, 'Go on, love. You can do it. Arthur needs you.'

She felt a tug on her arm, and her feet moved on to the step. Joe's car was parked in the kerb, right outside, and she kept her eyes fixed on it.

'That's it, Sally,' he said. 'Come on.'

Obeying his voice Sally took one step, then another, and as Joe unlocked the door she threw herself inside, wrenching it shut behind her.

'Well done,' Joe said as he climbed in beside her and started the engine.

She couldn't turn her head, couldn't look at him, and as they drove to Putney she didn't speak, her eyes fixed on the road ahead.

They were there, pulling into the car park. It was unlit and dark, rain falling heavily, and suddenly Sally was back in the nightmare. She was unaware that Joe had got out of the car, and as the passenger door opened, a hand reached in to grab her arm. She screamed, 'No! No, don't touch me!'

'Sally, calm down. It's me, Joe. I'm not going to hurt you.'

Tears spurted from her eyes and heaving sobs wracked her body. She didn't know how it happened, but the next thing she was in Joe's arms.

'Oh, Sally, what did they do to you?'

She blurted it out, telling him the only thing she had kept back. Her terror when she had nearly been raped. 'Oh, Joe,

I couldn't fight him, couldn't do anything. I felt so helpless . . . dirty . . . and later I was thrown out of the car as though I was worthless. A piece of junk!'

'Sally, you're not worthless. You're a wonderful woman with an adorable daughter and a husband who loves you. Don't let those bastards beat you. Don't let them ruin the rest of your life. They're the worthless ones – not you.'

Joe's words began to sink into Sally's tortured mind, and she drew in juddering breaths. She pulled herself out of his arms, but the car park was so dark that she cringed, almost flying into them again.

'Sally, come on. Be strong now. You can do it, and Arthur needs you.'

She nodded and as Joe wrapped an arm around her shoulders, they moved towards the entrance. Light hit them and looking down at her Joe paused, taking a handkerchief out of his pocket. He licked a corner, then lifted her chin with his forefinger, gently wiping under her eyes.

'Your mascara has run and we can't have you going to see Arthur looking like a panda.'

His gentleness, his kindness, brought tears to Sally's eyes again. He was such a good man, and it gave her strength. The men who had attacked her were just animals, Neanderthals, but not all men were like that. There was Arthur, Bert, Sidney Jacobs, all good men like Joe. She managed a small smile. 'You're right; I can't let those pigs beat me. Come on, let's go to the ward.'

As they walked through the corridors, Sally was still jumpy with nerves, but she took deep breaths, determined not to let this beat her. She paused, laying a hand on Joe's arm. 'Thank you for helping me to pull myself together, but there's just one thing. I haven't told anyone else about what one of those men was going to do, and I don't want Arthur to know. I don't think he could cope with it just now.'

'Sally, I won't tell a soul. It's over now, and I hope that one day you can put it all behind you.'

'I'm trying,' she said as they reached the ward.

'You go in on your own, Sally, I'll be along later.'

'Thanks, Joe,' and taking a deep breath, she went inside.

* * *

'Hello, Sally, so you've come to see me at last,' Arthur said.
'How are you feeling?'

'I'm all right. It's you I'm worried about. Oh, darling, your leg.'

'It's a bugger, Sally. I was on the mend, about to be given crutches ready to come home, but instead this has happened. Christ, it seems to be one thing after another.'

Sally hung her head. Yes, it *was* one thing after another, their lives like a see-saw, one minute up, the next down. 'We'll get through this, Arthur.'

He squeezed her hand. 'I'm sorry about the baby, love, and look at your poor face.'

Sally felt tears well and fought them. 'It's only a bit of bruising,' she said, struggling against the feelings that threatened to drag her down again. 'We can always try for another baby.'

'Yeah, I suppose so, but God knows when.'

'We still have each other, and Angel.' She felt another squeeze on her hand, and very gently she leaned forward to kiss Arthur, ignoring the pain of her lips. 'Arthur, can't you change your mind. Why don't you try the operation to cut away the dying bone?'

'No, love. If I have that done there's no guarantee it will work and that would mean another operation. I'd end up with one leg a lot shorter than the other and be stuck wearing one of those surgical boot things.'

'But surely that's better than losing your leg?'

'Sally, I can't face the thought of operation after operation. At least this way I'll still have my knee joint and it will make adapting to an artificial leg easier. It's nothing compared to Douglas Bader. He lost both legs during the war but still managed to fly a plane.'

Oh Arthur, Sally thought, he was trying so hard to be brave, but in truth he must be going through hell. She took a deep breath, forcing the words from her lips, 'All right, if you think it's for the best.'

'I just hope you'll still want me when I've only got half a leg.'

'How can you say that? I'll always love you, and even if you lost both legs like Douglas Bader, I'd still love you.'

Joe came into the ward then and as he approached the bed he grimaced. 'Bad luck, mate.'

'Yes, and you really must get another partner now. I know you refused the last time I suggested it, but surely you can see the sense of it now. The way things are going I could be stuck in here for months.'

'I don't want another partner and can manage without you until you're fit and well. We've got years of working together, so what's a few months?'

'No – get someone else!'

'I won't do that, and anyway, if this development goes to plan, we'll be starting another one.'

Arthur shook his head in exasperation. 'Look, Joe, I don't want to end up a burden to you.'

'You won't be a burden.'

Sally listened to the conversation whilst focussing her eyes on Arthur's aura, finding herself shivering with fear. For a moment a vision flashed in front of her eyes, a vision in which she saw Arthur's leg and the gory mess of the bone marrow. Once again she fought the tears that sprung to her eyes. Oh, God, how would he cope with losing his leg?

'When are you having this operation?' Joe now asked.

'Tomorrow.'

'Well, good luck, and now I'll leave you two alone again.'

'Thanks Joe. See ya, mate.'

Time ticked by, Arthur asking about the attack, his eyes darkening with anger as she described what had happened. 'God, I'd like to get my hands on the bastards.'

He became morose then, hardly speaking. Sally squeezed his hand. 'Are you worried about the op?'

'Of course I am. I'll be less of a man afterwards, and one who won't be able to protect you.'

'You'll never be less of a man.'

'Don't bother with the platitudes.' He turned his head away, but then heaved a sigh. 'I'm sorry, love.'

Sally kissed his cheek, her heart aching. He had tried so hard to be brave, and was it any wonder that the mask slipped? The bell sounded and she whispered, 'I love you, darling. I'll be up in the morning.'

'No, Sally, there's no point. I'll be in theatre.'

'I'll come anyway,' she insisted, her eyes moist as she made her way to the car park.

Joe was leaning against his car, and as Sally walked towards him she felt her knees buckle beneath her. The next moment she found herself in his arms again as tears flooded her eyes. 'Oh God, Arthur – poor Arthur.'

Joe's arms tightened around her, and then he led her, stumbling, the rest of the way to his car. 'Come on, Sally, you've got to be brave.'

'But . . . he . . . he was getting better.'

'I know, and he will again. It's not the end of the world, Sally. He'll adapt to the loss of his leg.'

Joe opened the passenger door and choking with emotion, she crawled inside.

It was only as they neared Candle Lane that Sally was able to pull herself together a little, and this time when they pulled up outside the house, Joe got out of the car too, saying gently, 'Come on, you look fit to drop. Let's get you inside. Have you got your key?'

'No, those men took my handbag and I never got it back,' and remembering the lovely pram set that she had purchased in Arding & Hobbs, Sally once again felt the pain of losing her baby. She'd lost her angel brooch too but it meant nothing to her now. Even if it had been found, she didn't want it back. It would only serve to remind her of the pawnshop and the men who had attacked her.

Joe knocked and Ruth opened the door. 'Sally, you look awful. Come on, come inside.'

'How was Arthur?' Sadie asked as they walked into the kitchen.

'He was trying to be cheerful, but he couldn't keep it up.'

'Well, that's to be expected.'

'Sally, I'd best go now. Will you ring me to let me know how Arthur is?'

'Of course I will, and . . . and thanks for everything, Joe.'

Ruth saw him out, and as Sally looked at her gran, she broke, running to kneel beside her. 'Oh, Gran.'

Sadie's rheumy eyes were moist. 'He'll be all right, love. Arthur will be all right.'

'First the accident, then gangrene, followed by traction. Now this! How much more can he take?'

'He's a strong man, just like his father.' Sadie then lifted Sally's chin. 'I'm proud of you, darlin'. You've had a terrible time, but you've pulled yourself together for Arthur's sake.'

Sally rose to her feet, drawing strength from her gran's words, and when her mother came back into the room she made them all a cup of cocoa. Exhausted, Sally decided to have an early night, and after kissing her mother and gran, she carried her drink upstairs.

An hour later she was still awake, her thoughts on Arthur and the operation he faced in the morning. *Where are you?* she whispered inwardly, her eyes roaming the room. Oh, how she wished her friend would come, the lovely angelic presence who used to bring her such comfort. No, that was selfish – it was Arthur who needed comfort more than her.

Go to him – please go to him, she begged, and as Sally whispered these words, she suddenly found that her worry eased.

Arthur too was lying awake, his stomach churning. He tried to picture what it would be like with only half a leg, but then his mind shied away. Had he made the right decision? God, he hoped so. Sally had said she would still want him, half a leg or not, and at first he'd been relieved, yet now the doubts set in again. His wife was beautiful, with a lovely figure and long shapely legs.

Legs, bloody hell, he shouldn't have thought about legs and once again his stomach flipped.

The ward was quiet, just a cough now and then or the rustle of sheets. The news of his op had soon filtered into the ward, and now the other patients avoided meeting his eyes. Was this the shape of things to come? Would people shy away from him, seeing him as a cripple? And at that thought, Arthur closed his eyes in despair.

Twenty-Nine

Sally, with Elsie and Bert, was at the hospital the following morning. She had still baulked a little at leaving the house, but remembering Joe's words she had fought her fear. She couldn't let those animals ruin the rest of her life, and with this thought held in her mind, she was finally able to walk to the car.

They were in the waiting room, Bert looking grim, not only his hate of hospitals evident, but worry for his son too. Elsie was white, hardly saying a word, but when her husband went off to find them a hot drink she suddenly spoke.

'The tarot cards were right after all. I saw illness, and awful violence. Yet what good are the cards if these things can't be prevented? I saw the warning, but you still suffered that dreadful attack, and now Arthur is losing his leg. Am I a witch, Sally? By laying out that awful spread, did I cause all this to happen?'

Sally gripped Elsie's hand. 'No, of course you didn't.'

'Even so, I don't think I'll ever use the tarot cards again.'

Bert came back carrying white plastic cups and they sat sipping their drinks. They spoke intermittently, comforting each other, but mostly they were quiet, each with their own thoughts.

Time ticked slowly by, until at last Arthur returned from theatre. They were allowed to see him for a few minutes, but he hardly knew they were there, and as they left both Sally and Elsie were fighting tears.

'We'll pick you up again this evening,' Bert said as he dropped Sally off in Candle Lane.

Sally climbed out of the car, trying to smile but managing only a grimace.

The rest of the day dragged by. Sally kept herself busy,

turned out cupboards in the kitchen, giving them a good clean, and when it was time to get Angel from school, her mother put on her coat.

'No, Mum, I'll go.'

'Are you sure, love?'

'No, not really, but I've got to try going out on my own. If I don't, I've let those bastards win.'

'Sally, it's not like you to swear!'

'Sorry, Mum.'

'No, don't apologize. It gets it out of your system and I think your gran and I can stand it,' she said with a chuckle.

Sally threw on her coat, taking a deep breath as she left the house. A few neighbours were gossiping on their doorsteps and walking down Candle Lane she was struck by how normal it seemed. All right, it was daylight, and she doubted she'd be able to go out at night on her own, but who knows, given time she might be able to face that too.

Maureen Downy was standing on her step and smiled as Sally approached. 'Hello, love, it's nice to see you out and about again. I was sorry to hear what happened to you.'

'Thanks,' Sally murmured as she walked past. So they knew, but she wasn't surprised. News soon travelled in the lane.

When Angel came running out of the playground her face lit up. 'Mummy, you've come to get me.'

'Yes, darling, and I will every day from now on.'

'You better now?'

'Yes, I'm fine.'

They were soon home, and as Angel ran inside she called, 'Nanny. My mummy's better now.'

'I know, sweetheart.'

'Play cards, Gamma?'

'Yeah, all right. Go and fetch them from my room.'

As Angel ran out, Ruth said, 'Blimey, Sal, I've just remembered something. On the night that it . . . it happened, Angel woke up. She came downstairs and seemed worried about you. She said you were ill.'

'Really?'

'I thought she must have had a bad dream, but it makes you wonder.'

Yes, Sally thought, it did. Had it been a bad dream, or was her daughter able to prophesize?

By the time they arrived at the hospital that evening, Arthur was fully awake, but his voice was lacklustre as he greeted them. 'How are you, son?' Elsie asked.

Arthur looked at the cradle over his missing lower leg. 'How do you think?'

'The worst is over now, son.'

'Yeah, if you say so.'

Sally took his hand. He was so down, his eyes pools of sadness, and she was at a loss to know what to say. 'I love you, darling,' she whispered.

He didn't respond and though they tried to talk to him he showed little interest, and if anything he seemed relieved when they left.

'Don't worry, it's early days yet,' Bert said as they once again climbed into his car.

'He seems so depressed.'

'It's hardly surprising, Sally. Not only that, he'll be feeling the after effects of the anaesthetic,' Elsie said. 'Give it a few more days and we're sure to see a difference.'

'By the way, Sally,' Bert said, 'thanks to the police giving me the information, and with their permission, I went to see the couple who took you to hospital. They were lovely people, and pleased to know you're all right.'

'Oh dear, I feel awful. I should thank them myself, but with all that's happened . . .'

'It's all right, Sally. They seemed surprised that I took the trouble to find them, and I thanked them on your behalf.'

'Thanks, Bert,' Sally murmured, and then shivered. If they hadn't found her, how long would she have waited for help? Would she have survived? She had raged at God, but now felt sickened by her behaviour. She *had* been found, she *had* survived, and now she must put it all behind her. She would send those kind people some flowers and a card, but at the moment, all that mattered was Arthur.

Thirty

During the following few days, though it was awful to see him in pain, Sally was pleased to see that Arthur was slowly taking interest in his surroundings again. The real turning point was when Joe came to visit him, grinning as he walked into the ward.

'Well mate, how are you doing?'

'Not so bad, but I still think you should get another partner.'

'Leave it out, Arthur. You'll have an artificial leg soon and can still help me to run the business.'

'Yeah, but I don't know yet if I'll be able to drive.'

'Stop putting obstacles in the way before you know the score. Take one step at a time, mate – or should I say hop?'

Sally stiffened, but Arthur laughed. 'Yeah, and you can call me Skippy.' Both men then broke into song, '*Skippy, Skippy, Skippy the bush kangaroo.*'

'That's the spirit, Arthur,' Joe chuckled. 'Look, you're young, you're strong, and I'm sure you'll adapt in no time. Our job is to sell houses, not build them, and with the show house taking shape, we'll be able to start marketing them when you get out of here.'

'Thanks, Joe, but I won't hold it against you if you find someone else.'

'No way. We're in this together.' He touched Arthur's arm. 'I can see you're tired so I'm off now. Would you like a lift home, Sally?'

'Yes, and thanks.'

'Right, I'll be in the car park. And you, Arthur, all you've got to do is get on your feet – or should I say foot,' Joe joked. 'And no shirking because there's work waiting for you.'

Arthur laughed again and then shook the man's hand, both

he and Sally watching as he left the ward. 'He's a great bloke, Sally, and a right laugh.'

'Yes, he is.'

'He's cheered me up no end, and if he can joke about my leg, then so can others. I must admit it's been lousy in the ward. All the blokes seem to avoid talking to me.' He visibly straightened. 'Well, I know what to do now. I'll make a joke of it, just like Joe, and that'll surprise them.'

'Good for you.'

'Sally, I've been meaning to tell you something, but sometimes I think it's all in my imagination.'

'Tell me anyway.'

'Don't laugh then, but something really odd happened the night before my op. I've never taken any notice of this spiritual mumbo jumbo that you and Mum get up to, even if the pair of you have unnerved me at times. But that night . . . well . . . I sort of felt something around me.'

'Did you? Can you describe it?'

'It's going to sound daft but it was like a presence, and for a while it felt as though I was wrapped in cotton wool. The feeling was so comforting, and suddenly I wasn't scared about the op anymore. I could still sense it the next morning when I went down to theatre, but then I had the anaesthetic and the next thing I remember was waking up in the ward.'

Sally smiled, and lifting her head she gave silent thanks. 'I'm glad, Arthur. Sometimes I've had that same comfort in times of trouble.'

'Have you? Was it there when those men attacked you?'

'No, unfortunately not. I think my brain was so frozen with fear that nothing could get through.'

'The bastards,' Arthur spat, his jaw clenching.

'Don't get worked up, darling. I'm fine now.'

Arthur nodded, his fists unclenching, and as the bell sounded Sally leaned over to kiss him. 'I'd better go. Your mum will be up to see you tomorrow afternoon as usual.'

'And my dad?' Arthur said, smiling wryly.

'He sat with us the whole time you had your op, and he's been to see you since.'

'Yeah, I know, and as he hates hospitals, I'm surprised.'

205

'He was worried about you – we all were.'

'Well, you can stop worrying. According to the consultant the operation went well. Now all I have to do is to get myself back on my feet, or as Joe said – my foot.'

'Yes, and get a move on. You've lounged about in here for long enough,' Sally told him, determined to adopt the same lighthearted attitude as Joe Somerton.

'All right boss. Now give me a kiss and get lost.'

Sally left the ward feeling more optimistic. It was going to be all right, she could feel it in her bones. As she climbed into Joe's car he turned to smile at her. 'He'll be fine, Sally. Arthur's a fighter and won't let this beat him.'

'I know, and thanks for making him laugh. I think he needed that.'

'It's not the end of the world, and I hope he realizes that now.'

Sally turned to meet Joe's eyes. Yes, he was handsome, and yes, she'd been attracted to him, but now she just welcomed him as a friend. A wonderful friend who had brought her to her senses.

For Arthur, Joe's visit had been the turning point, and during the next week he became very popular in the ward as he joked about his missing leg. He'd also become a favourite of the nurses, and even Sister Moody smiled every time she passed his bed.

She was approaching now and, lifting his arm, Arthur beckoned her over. 'How much longer before I can go home?'

'Once your stump has healed you'll be sent to the Roehampton Limb Fitting Centre.'

'Any idea how long that will be? I rather fancy Nurse Trimble, and when I get my leg I wouldn't mind chasing her up the ward.'

Sister Moody shook her head but was unable to help smiling. 'Now then, Mr Jones, remember you're a married man. Your wound should heal in about four or five weeks.'

'Have I got to stay in here until then?'

'You'll have to speak to the consultant about that.'

'I can't wait to go home. Not that I haven't enjoyed your company, Sister.'

'Huh, yes, I'm sure you have,' she said, but still with a smile on her face as she walked away.

Arthur wriggled in the bed, finding that he wanted to scratch his itchy foot, a foot that wasn't there anymore. How was that possible, he mused as his eyes roamed the ward. Some of the lads grinned at him, and he grinned back, glad that he had decided not to let this beat him.

Joe's visit had inspired him, making him realize that he had two choices He could sink into depression and rail at the world, or he could fight and show them all what he was made of. It was a bit embarrassing when some of the younger patients began to treat him like a hero, and he was now dying to get out of hospital.

Five weeks at the most, and then he'd be fitted with a limb. Would it hurt? Yes, probably, but he was determined that no matter how painful, he'd get used to it. No crutches. No stick. He'd walk on his own two feet as soon as possible. Joe had waited long enough for him to make a recovery, and all he wanted now was to get back to work as quickly as possible.

Thirty-One

There had been no celebration for Bert's fiftieth birthday. None of them wanted a party, albeit a family one, while Arthur was still in hospital, and now it was mid February.

'Well, love,' he said as they sat opposite each other in their favourite restaurant. 'I'm fifty now and nearly past my prime.'

'Of course you're not,' Elsie protested, eyeing him fondly.

'It's funny how things work out. I was upset about Arthur leaving the business, but realize now that it's the best thing that could have happened.'

'Why do you say that?'

'Think about it, love. He won't be able to hump furniture around now, and I doubt he'll be able to drive a removals van.'

'I think he'll adapt to driving, but anyway, you could have put him in the office.'

'Doing what? He's no fool and would resent a position being created for him. Building up a business with Joe is just what he needs now.'

'Yeah, I suppose you're right.' She shook her head, her eyes reflecting her sadness. 'Poor Arthur's been through hell and I'm still worried about him.'

'There's no need. The worst is over and I know my boy. Once he gets his artificial leg there'll be no holding him.'

'He's a brave lad,' Elsie said. 'He must take after his father.'

Bert chuckled. 'Flattery will get you everywhere,' he said, winking lewdly.

'Oh, so your bad back is up to it – is it?'

'I'll do my best,' he said, but then saw Elsie's eyes cloud over again.

'I'm worried about Sally too,' she said. 'It's her birthday

in a couple of days but, like you, I doubt she'll want to celebrate.'

'The girl had a terrible time of it, but she's on the mend. Now why don't you stop worrying and enjoy your meal.'

Elsie nodded and Bert, trying to lighten the atmosphere, winked suggestively, saying, 'And later, I shall expect a belated birthday treat.'

'Blimey, and I thought you said you were past your prime. It doesn't sound like it to me.'

'I said I was *nearly* past my prime. Now come on, woman, eat up. I want to get you home and to bed.'

To Bert's relief, Elsie smiled at last. He tucked into his steak, sure that Arthur and Sally were going to be fine, and he didn't need his wife's tarot cards to tell him that.

During the following weeks Sally slowly got back to her old self. Her mother was back at work, but was sure that Sidney Jacobs was going to retire. His son had been down to see him again, putting on the pressure, but so far Sidney hadn't said when, or if, he was going to close the shop.

Sally still mourned the loss of her baby, but Arthur was now her main concern. His release had been delayed as he had developed a small infection in his wound, but thankfully it was clearing up with antibiotics.

It was now mid March, and with Joe visiting Arthur two evenings a week, Sally stayed home. At first she felt a little guilty that she had curtailed her visits, but there was no denying that she needed the break. Arthur had been in hospital since mid November last year, and her life, other than when she had suffered a short spell of agoraphobia, had revolved around visiting time.

So much had happened in such a short time, so much unhappiness. Angel was feeling it too and Sally felt so guilty that she had neglected her daughter. She smiled at her now as she splashed in the bath, but then Angel's face straightened.

'When is Daddy coming home?'

'I don't know, darling, but soon I hope.'

'I don't like Gamma any more.'

Sally paused in the act of soaping her daughter's back. 'Why, darling?'

'She doesn't like Tommy.'

'Oh, I see, and what makes you think that?'

'She shouted at him.'

Sally chuckled. 'Gamma is sometimes cross with everyone, but she doesn't mean it. Why did she shout at Tommy?'

''Cos he went into her room.'

'He shouldn't have done that. When did this happen?'

'Yesterday, but he only went in there 'cos I told him to. I wanted to play snap and the cards were in Gamma's room.'

Sally's suspicions were aroused, but she would have to wait until Angel was asleep before she spoke to her mother. 'It was your fault that Gamma was cross with Tommy. You should tell her the truth.'

'I did, but she still shouted. She made him go home and it's not fair. I like playing with Tommy.'

'And what did Nanny say?'

'I don't know. When Tommy went home she put me to bed.'

'I see,' Sally murmured. So her suspicions were right. Her mother *was* allowing Angel to stay up to play with Tommy whilst she was visiting Arthur, despite her assurances that the child was in bed at seven thirty. She pulled the plug out, the water draining away, and lifting Angel out of the bath she wrapped her in a large towel. 'Come on, let's get you dry, into bed, and then I'll tell you a story.'

It was half an hour later when Sally returned to the kitchen, finding her mother and gran in front of the television glued to *Coronation Street*. She knew it was one of her gran's favourite programmes so decided to wait until it had finished before speaking to her mother.

Both women were engrossed in the programme, watching the characters Ena Sharples and Elsie Tanner having a slanging match. They made an incongruous pair, Elsie Tanner dolled up and glamorous, but Ena in her usual old coat and hairnet.

There was a knock on the door and it was Sally who rose to answer it, her eyes widening when she saw Laura Walters.

'Where is he?' the woman spat.

210

'Where's who?'

'Don't play games with me. Where's my son?'

'I don't know.'

'Don't give me that. The little bugger is always in your place.'

'Well, he's not in here now.'

To Sally's amazement, Laura barged past her and lurched into the kitchen, snarling as she said to Ruth, 'Oy you, where's my boy?'

'Get out of my house!' Ruth cried.

'Not until Tommy's with me!'

'He ain't in here.'

'You're lying! Where is he!' she shouted, her eyes flying wildly around the room.

'You heard my daughter,' Sadie said, joining in the affray. 'She told you to get out!'

'Shut up, you old witch,' Laura spat.

'Now that's enough,' Sally said and, determined never to be intimidated by anyone again, she grasped the woman's arm, pulling her from the room. 'I won't have you upsetting my gran, and if you don't go I'll call the police.'

'All right, miss high and mighty, I'll go, but I'm not finished with your mother yet. I've told my boy to stay away from her, and if he comes in here again I'll flay him alive.' On that note Laura stumbled outside again, shouting as she did, 'Tommy! Where are you, you little sod!'

Sally slammed the door, and back stiff she marched into the kitchen. 'See! This is what happens when you keep bringing Tommy Walters in here. And not only that, Mum, you've been lying to me. From what Angela has told me, she's allowed up to play with him.'

'Once! That was all, and that was because she was upset over her father. You seem to forget that she's missing him, and last night she just wouldn't settle. Tommy took her mind off it for a while, and they only played cards for Gawd's sake.'

Sally took in her mother's words. Yes, of course Angel was missing her father. There was no denying that she'd been difficult lately, but she still didn't want her mixing with the boy. 'Look, Mum, I'm sorry for losing my temper, but can you please keep her away from Tommy Walters.'

'I'm sick of hearing you saying that. Even if he didn't come in here, she still sees him at school, and I'll have you know that he sticks up for her too.'

'Sticks up for her! What do you mean?'

'When you wouldn't go out of the house for a while I collected Angel from school, and on one occasion when I got there, she was being bullied in the playground. A crowd of kids were taking the micky, pulling her hair and calling her a ginger-nut. Tommy stepped in, and there was a fight. His coat got torn in the process, but thanks to him they leave Angel alone now.'

Oh God, Sally thought as she stared at her mother. She too had suffered bullying at school, and knew how awful it was. 'She didn't tell me.'

'I know that! It was me who told her to keep quiet about it. You were in a right state and I didn't want you more upset. Anyway, thanks to Tommy, it's been sorted out.'

Sally closed her eyes, taking a good look at herself, and not liking what she saw. If it wasn't for Tommy her daughter might have suffered bullying for a long time, just as she had as a child. Yet she had judged the lad and found him wanting. When had she turned into a snob? A snob who'd decided that the boy wasn't good enough to associate with Angel. 'Oh, Mum, I'm sorry. I've been awful to Tommy, and now I realize that he doesn't deserve it.'

'I've been telling you that all along, yet you wouldn't listen. He may swear, but that isn't his fault. He really is a good kid when you get to know him.'

'Yes, I see that now, and in future, if Angel wants to play with him, that's fine with me.'

'Good, I'm glad to hear it, and I *am* trying to do something about his language.'

'Well I ain't happy about the bleedin' kid being in here. He's a little bugger,' Sadie said, her face stretching with amazement when both Sally and her mother dissolved into tears of laughter. Laughter that for was, for Sally, the final step in her recovery.

Thirty-Two

The following morning as Sally walked her daughter to school, she kept her eyes peeled for Tommy Walters, but there was no sign of the boy. She wanted to thank him for looking after Angel, but even when they reached the school entrance and she scanned the playground, he was nowhere to be seen.

A familiar shiver of intuition ran up her spine and she tensed. Was the boy all right? Leaning forward she kissed her daughter, watching as she ran into the playground, joining a group of little girls. There was no sign of any trouble, and with a small smile of relief Sally began the walk home.

Her feelings of foreboding increased as she turned into Candle Lane, and reaching Tommy's house she stopped to gaze at the door. Should she knock? Unbidden her hand rose to rattle the letter-box whilst her heart beat rapidly. Something was wrong, she was sure of it – but what?

The door opened a crack, a small voice saying, 'Yeah, what do you want?'

'Tommy – is that you?'

'Yeah.'

'Why aren't you at school?'

'My mum ain't well.'

'What's wrong with her?'

'I dunno, but I'm staying home to look after her.'

'Where is your father, Tommy?'

'I dunno.'

Sally crossed her fingers, hoping Gran would be all right for a few more minutes. 'Perhaps I can help. Can I come in to see your mother?'

'No, she'll kill me if I let anyone in.'

'Tommy, if your mum's ill she may need to see a doctor.'

213

There was a pause, but then the door opened a few more inches. 'All right, come in.'

As Sally walked inside she gagged at the smell and for a moment wanted to run out again, but then Tommy led her upstairs. In the bedroom she saw what looked like a bundle of rags on the bed and, amongst them, Laura Walters. The woman's eyes were closed and she looked awful, her lips tinged blue. 'How long has she been like this, Tommy?'

'She was all right last night, but she won't get up this morning.'

'Laura – Mrs Walters,' Sally said loudly.

There was no response, and though frantic with worry, Sally tried to keep her voice calm. 'Listen, Tommy, I'm going home to call the doctor. I can't leave my gran for long, so I'm going to find someone else to stay with your mum until he arrives.'

Tommy stared up at her, his eyes round with fear, and Sally's heart went out to the boy. 'Don't worry, everything will be all right. Wait here, and after I've rung the doctor I'll go and get Nelly Cox.'

Sally shot out of the house and as soon as she got indoors she called the surgery. She then rattled off a quick explanation to her gran before hurrying down the lane to fetch Nelly.

Thankfully the old lady took in the situation straight away, and in no time they were standing by Laura's bed. 'Blimey, she looks rough,' Nelly said as she gazed down at the woman.

'I told the receptionist that it's an emergency, so the doctor should be here shortly.'

'The sooner the better,' Nelly said as she endeavoured to straighten the bed covers. 'What about the boy?'

'I'll take him home with me.'

'No, I want to stay wiv me mum.'

'All right, don't get upset, love. You can wait with me if you want to,' Nelly said, adding, 'Go on, Sally, you'd best get back to Sadie. I'll give you a knock after the doctor's been.'

Sally reluctantly left, but once indoors she hovered at the window, looking out for the doctor's car. 'Laura Walters looked awful, Gran.'

'Are you sure it isn't just a hangover?'

'It's more serious than that.'

'Did you look at her aura?'

'Yes, briefly, and I think it's her heart. Oh good, there's the doctor.'

Sally turned away from the window, but only minutes later there was a knock at the door. She hurried to answer it and, finding the doctor on the step, her face registered surprise as he said, 'I need to ring an ambulance for your neighbour. Mrs Cox said you have a telephone.'

'Yes, come in,' Sally said, stepping to one side.

She hovered whilst he rang for an ambulance – knew by his words that it was Laura Walters' heart, and then the doctor turned to speak to her again, 'I need to get in touch with Mrs Walters' husband. Do you by any chance know where he works?'

'No, I'm afraid not. In fact, I'm not sure if he has a job.'

The doctor sighed. 'The child can't be left alone in the house, and he's too young to go to the hospital with his mother.'

'It's all right. I'll look after him until his father comes home.'

'Good, well, I'd better get back to my patient.'

Things happened quickly after that. The ambulance came, and with many neighbours watching, Laura Walters was carried out. Tommy was yelling, trying to get into the ambulance too, and it took the doctor and Nelly Cox to restrain him. He was finally led sobbing into number five, where he fell into Sally's arms.

The doctor left, Nelly sat opposite Sadie, both saying nothing as Sally did her best to soothe the boy. When Tommy finally stopped crying his eyes closed, and Sally saw he'd escaped into sleep. She gently laid him on the sofa, wondering as she did so when the boy's father would turn up.

'Blimey, with the way Laura Walters treats the boy, I'm surprised he's so upset,' Nelly said softly.

'I've seen it before,' Sadie said. 'The bond is strong. Kids can be beaten, abused, half starved, but they still cling to their mothers.'

'I've never had kids so I wouldn't know, but then again my old mother was a strict and taciturn woman, yet I still loved her.'

'It's the only life Tommy knows, and so he's clinging to it.'

'The poor kid,' Nelly said. 'I hope for his sake that Laura recovers.'

'I've got a feeling she's going to be all right,' Sally murmured.

'Have you, love?' Sadie said. 'That's good. Now I don't know about you two, but I'm spitting feathers.'

Sally rose to put the kettle on. Yes, something was telling her that Laura Walters was going to be all right, but if she didn't keep off the booze – for how long?

Tommy's father rolled home drunk at eleven o'clock that evening, and when both Ruth and Sally went round to see him, he could barely take in what they were telling him.

'You wanna see my wife? What for?'

Ruth sighed with exasperation. 'We don't want to see her. We're telling you she's in hospital.'

His body was swaying, eyes unfocussed and he was clutching the back of a chair for support. He said, 'Hospital? She ain't in hospital.'

'Oh, this is hopeless. Let's leave him to sleep it off and we'll come round in the morning.'

'All right,' Sally agreed and, talking as though to a child, she enunciated her words, 'Tommy's in our house, Mr Walters.'

'Wh . . . what?'

'This is a waste of time. Come on, Sally, let's go.'

'Oy, jush . . . jusht a minute,' Denis Walters slurred. 'What was you shaying about an 'ospital?'

'For Gawd's sake go to bed,' Ruth shouted and taking Sally's arm she ushered her out of the door.

When they walked back into their own kitchen, Tommy was fast asleep on the sofa. Sally spoke quietly, 'What are we going to do, Mum? Denis Walters doesn't seem fit to look after the boy, and we have no idea how long his mother will be in hospital.'

'They may have family in the area he can go to. If not, he'll just have to stay with us for the time being,' and seeing the expression on her daughter's face, she added, 'It won't be so bad. He'll be at school all day.'

'Yes, but what about when he *isn't* in school. I won't have Angel running wild with him on the streets.'

'I'm sure he won't mind staying in. The boy craves love and a bit of attention. He'll do as you say, Sally.'

'But what about Gran? She won't be happy about this.'

'Until Laura Walters comes home – she'll just have to put up with it.'

'Have you forgotten that we aren't supposed to upset her?'

'It ain't my fault if she's set her mind against the boy. You've come round now, and she can do the same.'

'Oh, Mum, I don't know about this. Yes, I feel sorry for Tommy, and I've said he can play with Angel, but having him living with us is a different matter.'

'It won't be for long, love. Have a heart.'

Sally looked down, her thoughts racing. She would have to look after the boy before and after school. Would she be able to control him? There was only one way to find out, and that was to give it a try, but would Denis Walters allow the boy to stay with them? 'All right, Mum. If there's nobody else and the boy's father agrees, we'll look after him.'

'Thanks, love, and I'll give the lad a good talking to. He'll behave, you wait and see.'

'That remains to be seen, but I'm off to bed now. Let's hope we can get more sense out of Mr Walters in the morning.'

'All right – night, love.'

Sally kissed her mother on the cheek before going upstairs. The bathroom was freezing and she shivered as she washed, glad to jump into bed. Oh, how she wished she could cuddle up to Arthur, still missing the warmth of his body.

Her mind turned. He'd be home soon and they could move into their flat. It would make things a bit difficult if Laura Walters was still in hospital, but as long as her mum got the boy ready for school before she left for work, it should be all right. She only had to make sure she was at Candle Lane for eight thirty, leaving her mother plenty of time to get to Wandsworth.

She glanced across at her daughter, her eyes softening. Angel was an only child, as was Tommy, and perhaps that was why they were drawn to each other. Yet there would

217

have been another child, Sally thought, eyes darkening with pain. *Stop it – stop thinking about it. It's in the past . . . let it go.*

Pulling up the blankets Sally closed her eyes. She *must* look to the future, a time when she, Arthur, and Angel were in their own home again and, God willing, there might be another baby one day.

She snuggled deeper into the bed. Perhaps when she saw Arthur tomorrow there would be some news. He might have been told when he could come home, and she smiled at the thought.

Thirty-Three

At eight o'clock in the morning, with Tommy hovering
behind her, Ruth was thumping on Denis Walters' front
door.

'Wassa matter,' he said, eyes fuddled with tiredness as he
opened the door.

'Mum's in 'ospital,' Tommy said as he darted forward.

Denis Walters shook his head in bewilderment, but
managed to focus on his son. 'What are you talking about?'

'Mum was ill and she went in an amlance.'

'Ambulance, Tommy,' Ruth corrected. 'I did try to tell
you last night, Mr Walters, but you obviously don't
remember.'

'Did you? Look, you had better come in.'

Ruth followed the man inside, appalled again at the state
of the place, but at least he sounded sober now. The sink
was piled high with dirty dishes, the table strewn with a
variety of rubbish; old newspapers, an empty jam-jar, crushed
cigarette packets, and an overflowing ashtray. The hearth
was as bad with old ashes thick under the grate, and care-
lessly thrown fag-ends.

'Why was my wife taken to hospital?'

'She had a heart attack.'

'No! Where did they take her?'

'I don't know. You'll have to ask the doctor. Anyway, it's
Tommy I've come to see you about. Have you got anyone
who can look after him?'

'There's only my wife's brother, but he lives in the
North of England. I suppose I could send Tommy to stay
with him.'

'No, Dad, I wanna stay here.'

Ruth watched as the man sank on to a chair. Placing both

hands over his face, he groaned softly. 'I can't seem to think straight.'

Deciding to take him in hand, Ruth said, 'Tommy can stay with me. It hardly seems worth sending the boy away until you know how long Laura's going to be in hospital. Why don't you find out where she was taken to, and in the meantime my daughter will see that Tommy goes to school.'

'Yes . . . yes, good idea.'

Ruth studied the man's face, realizing that if it wasn't for the effects of alcohol, he could be good-looking. Now though his cheeks were sunken and his eyes bloodshot. She could see his hands trembling, a sure sign of a heavy drinker, and said briskly, 'Say goodbye to your father, Tommy. He'll come round later to tell you how your mum is. That's right isn't it, Mr Walters?'

'Yes, I'll do that, and thanks.'

'Dad, can I come with you to see Mum?'

'No . . . you get yourself off to school.'

'But . . .'

'You'll be able to see her soon,' Ruth consoled, taking the boy's hand. 'Perhaps this evening if you're a good boy.'

'Will you take me later, Dad?'

'I dunno, maybe.'

Before Tommy could protest, Ruth said, 'We're off, Mr Walters, and if there's anything else I can do, let me know.'

'Yes, thanks, and you'd better behave yourself, Tommy, or else.'

Tommy nodded, reluctantly following Ruth outside, where out of his father's hearing he said, 'He won't take me to see her – he'll be too pissed.'

'Tommy! What have I told you about your language?'

'But he won't!' he cried, and Ruth saw tears welling in his eyes.

'Listen, darling, I know you're worried about your mum, but if your dad doesn't take you to see her, I will. That's a promise. Now come on, you don't want Angel to see you crying, do you?'

The boy cuffed his face with his sleeve and, sniffing loudly, he shook his head. Smiling gently and ruffling his hair, Ruth led him back to her house.

'What did he say?' Sally asked as soon as they walked in.

'He said there's only a brother up North somewhere and agreed that Tommy should stay with us for the time being. Right now he's going to find out what hospital Laura was taken to.'

'So we're stuck with him,' Sadie commented.

'Yes, Mum, we are, and try to be nice for a change. The boy won't be any trouble.'

'Huh!'

Ruth shook her head, but said nothing further and, anyway, if she didn't get a move on she'd be late for work. Crouching down she pulled Tommy into her arms. 'Sally will take to school, and bring you back here afterwards. I've got to go now, but I'll see you later.'

She felt Tommy's arms snaking around her neck, and felt tears forming in her own eyes when he said, 'I don't want you to go.'

'You'll be all right with Sally. She'll look after you.'

'I . . . I want me mum.'

'I know you do, love, and I'm sure she'll be home soon. Now be a good boy and I'll see you later.'

'Kiss me too, Nanny!'

'Oh, Angel, of course I will. Come here, pet.'

Angel ran across and, as she disengaged Tommy's arms, Ruth cuddled her granddaughter. 'I'll see you later too,' she said, giving her a hug.

'You're *my* nanny, not his,' Angel said petulantly.

'Of course I am, and I'll always be your nanny. Now let me go or I'll be late for work.'

'See – she's *my* nanny, not yours!' Angel said, scowling at Tommy.

Ruth was surprised at Angel's behaviour. This was the first time she had shown jealousy towards Tommy, and hoped it wouldn't be a problem. She glanced up at Sally, saw the worried expression on her face and, then letting go of Angel, she rose to her feet. 'It'll be all right, don't worry,' she told her daughter.

'If you say so,' Sally replied doubtfully.

'I must go, but Denis Walters may call round after he's

been to see his wife. If he does, ask him to take Tommy with him to the hospital this evening.'

'Yes, all right. Bye, Mum.'

When her mother left, Sally piled the breakfast dishes in the sink, all the while keeping an eye on Angel and Tommy. Her daughter seemed to be in a sulk, and Sally could understand why. She had been the centre of attention for so long, and was now seeing Tommy as a usurper. It would make matters worse if she made a fuss of him too, and though she felt sorry for the boy, it would be better to keep her distance. 'Right, you two, it's time for school,' she said briskly.

'I don't want *him* to come with us,' Angel said.

'Now then, that's enough of that. Have you forgotten who stood up for you in the playground? Tommy stopped you being bullied.'

For a moment Angel hung her head, looking thoughtful. She then looked at the boy from under her lashes. 'Sorry, Tommy. You can share my nanny if you want to.'

'Fanks,' Tommy said, a smile lighting his face at last.

Sally buttoned her daughter's coat, saying gently, 'Good girl. Now say goodbye to Gamma.'

Angel ran across the room, gave Sadie a quick hug, and then said, 'Tommy, you can cuddle my gamma too if you like.'

Tommy looked momentarily panic stricken as he stammered, 'No . . . no, I don't fink so.'

'And why not, young man?' Sadie asked.

'Er . . . er . . .'

Sadie held out her arms. 'Come on, I don't bite.'

'Go on, Tommy. I don't mind,' Angel urged.

Looking decidedly reluctant, the boy walked towards Sadie, his little body stiff as he gave her the briefest of hugs.

'See, I told you I don't bite. Here, have a Fox's Glacier Mint,' she said, pulling one out of her apron pocket. 'Here's one for you too, Angela.'

'Fanks, missus,' Tommy said, his little eyes wide.

Angel kissed Sadie on the cheek, and then Sally broke up the little tableau by saying they had to leave or they'd be late for school.

They hurried out. On reaching the school gates both children ran inside. Sally watched them for a minute before making her way home again, thinking about her gran's change of heart towards the boy. Would it last? She had been nice to him that morning, but there could be a complete change around by this afternoon. Angel seemed used to her great-grandmother's mood swings and took them in her stride, but she doubted that Tommy would understand.

When Sally arrived home, Sadie greeted her with a smile. 'That Tommy isn't a bad kid really.'

'I know, but we'll have to be careful. Angel was really jealous for a while.'

'She's an only child, so it's to be expected.'

'Anyway, Gran, what brought on your change of heart? I thought you couldn't stand the boy.'

'I think it was seeing Angel's jealousy this morning. The boy looked stricken and I suddenly felt sorry for him.'

'I wonder how long he'll be with us.'

'We'll find out when Denis Walters comes back from the hospital.'

'Yes, and in the meantime I'd best get on with the house-work.'

'Wait a minute, Sally. You've been through a lot lately. Are you sure that looking after Tommy won't be too much for you?'

'I'll be fine, Gran, and anyway, I don't think I have much choice.'

'Your mum thinks a lot of Tommy, but she should have given you some consideration before offering to take him on. She can be thoughtless at times, but then again, who's perfect? Anyway, come here, love.'

Sally went to her gran's side, and as she did so Sadie took her hand. 'Listen, Sal, life's been cruel to you, but somehow you've managed to bounce back. You're a brave girl, and though I don't always say it, I feel it every day. I love you, darling.'

'Oh Gran,' Sally said, her eyes filling with tears.

'Gawd blimey, don't cry. You've shed enough tears lately.'

'They aren't tears of sadness, Gran, and I love you too.'

'Sally, I hate being a burden to you.'

'You'll never be a burden to me. Never!'

'If you say so, but surely you can see that I'm a lot better now.'

'Yes, I know you are, but I still don't think you're up to being left on your own.'

'Will you ever listen?'

'I will when I know that you're a hundred per cent OK. Now I'd better get on with the housework.'

'Yeah, all right. Mind you, I wouldn't mind another cuppa first.'

'You and your tea, Gran,' Sally said, laughing as she put the kettle on.

'That's it, girl. Laughter is the best medicine and we ain't had many doses lately.'

Thirty-Four

It was nearly three in the afternoon before Denis turned up, and when she opened the door, Sally found him swaying on the step.

He grinned crookedly, his voice slurred. 'I've been to see me wife and she's gonna be all right. She's in Bolingbroke Hospital.'

'Did they tell you when she can come home?'

He swayed again, but then seemed to gather his thoughts. 'They're doing tests, but I think in a few days.'

'Are you taking Tommy to see her?'

'Nah, he doesn't need to go. She'll be home soon.'

'He's upset and I think it would help if he could see that his mother is all right.'

'Jusht tell him she . . . she's fine.'

Sally glared at him. 'It wouldn't hurt to take him with you this evening.'

'I'm not going again 'cos I've got to meet a mate in the Kings Arms.'

She could see it would be pointless to argue with the man. He could hardly stand, let alone take in what she was saying. Her temper flared at his selfishness. 'Go to the flaming pub then, and *we'll* look after your son.'

'What's up, love?' Sadie asked as Sally slammed the door and returned to the kitchen.

'That was Denis Walters. Apparently Laura is all right, but he's not taking Tommy to see her tonight. He isn't even going himself.'

'Why ever not?'

'It seems he has to meet a friend in the pub.'

'The man's a bloody disgrace.'

'Perhaps Mum will take him. Oh, look at the time, I must pick the kids up from school.'

'Now that Tommy's dad is home, there's no need to bring Tommy back here.'

'Denis was drunk, Gran, and in no fit state to look after the boy.'

Sadie sighed. 'I suppose we haven't got much choice then, but if you ask me, Denis Walters is taking the micky.'

'You may be right, but I've got to go,' Sally said as she rushed out.

When Ruth arrived home there was a flurry of activity as Tommy ran across the room, throwing himself into her arms. 'Me mum's all right, but can you take me to see her?'

'Er . . . yes . . . maybe . . .' she floundered.

'You promised.'

'Won't your dad be taking you?'

'No, Sally said he ain't going to see her again today.'

'What's all this?' Ruth asked, turning to look at her daughter.

As Sally drew her to one side, quietly relating what had happened, Ruth's lips tightened. 'The pig,' she hissed, and then moved across the room to pat Tommy on the head. 'All right, love. I'll take you.'

'Cor, fanks, can we go now?'

'I think we should have dinner first, and anyway, we'll have to wait until visiting time.'

Sally piled the food on to their plates, but Ruth noticed that unusually, Tommy hardly ate. She finished her own dinner and then rose to her feet. 'Come on, Tommy, let's get you spruced up to see your mum.'

The boy scrambled from his chair and in another half an hour they were ready to go, Angel saying, 'I want to come too.'

'I'm sorry, pet, I'm afraid you can't come with us.'

'Why not,' Angel demanded.

'Er . . . well . . .'

Thankfully Sally intervened. 'Tommy's mum is only allowed two visitors, just like when I take you to see your daddy.'

Angel still looked peevish as Ruth clutched Tommy's hand, murmuring a hasty goodbye as they hurried out.

* * *

226

Ruth was thankful that they didn't have a long wait for a bus, and in no time they were walking into the old Victorian hospital. She had to ask what ward Laura was in and, as they walked along dismal corridors, she wondered how Sally stood the months of going to see Arthur in Putney. She had been to see him herself a few times, but always found visiting times difficult. Once you asked them how they were, and chatted for a bit, conversation dried up and it was a relief to leave.

Laura saw them almost immediately. As Tommy ran up to her, she said, 'Hello, love, so you've come to see me.'

'You all right, Mum?'

'I'm fine,' and smiling pleasantly at Ruth she added, 'Thanks for bringing him.'

Ruth could scarcely believe her eyes. Sober, Laura Walters was like a different woman, and cleaned up she looked almost attractive. Her hair was the same dark auburn shade as her son's, and if she weren't so gaunt from the ravages of alcohol she could be beautiful.

'Denis told me that Tommy is staying with you, and I'm very grateful.'

'That's all right. He's a good kid and we don't mind having him.'

'When are you coming home, Mum?'

'Soon, love. But until I do, you be a good boy.'

Ruth took a seat at the side of the bed. 'Is there anything you need?'

'No, but it's kind of you to ask.'

'Here, Mum,' Tommy said, obviously anxious to get her attention, 'Angel's dad's had his leg cut off.'

'Is this true, Mrs Marchant?'

'Please, call me Ruth, and yes, I'm afraid it is.'

'How awful – did he have an accident?'

Obviously events in Candle Lane had passed Laura Walters by and, knowing that the young woman was usually drunk, this didn't surprise Ruth. She went on to tell her about the car crash, and they chatted amicably, Tommy happy to have his mother's attention until the bell sounded to signal the end of visiting time.

They were just about to leave when Laura took Ruth's

hand, pulling her forward until their faces were almost touching as she whispered, 'This heart attack has made me take stock of myself. I'll stay off the booze from now on.'

'For Tommy's sake, as well as your own, I hope you mean that.'

'I do. I wasn't always like this you know but, after losing my little girl to polio, the pain was so bad that I turned to drink.'

Ruth saw the agony in the woman's eyes and kicked herself. She had judged the woman, found her wanting, but now understood. She couldn't imagine how awful it must be to lose a child and no wonder the woman had turned to alcohol to dull the pain. 'Oh, I didn't know, Laura, and I'm so sorry. When did it happen?'

'How could you know? It was over a year ago, just before we moved to Battersea. Bessie was a beautiful little girl, and the youngest. When . . . when we lost her, I just didn't want to go on.' She smiled wanly at her son. 'Poor Tommy, he's had it rough since then, and when I think about my behaviour . . .' Pausing she held out her arms, adding, 'Come here, son, and give me a hug.'

Tommy for a moment looked bewildered, but then he scrambled on to the side of the bed, wrapping his arms around his mother's neck. She buried her face in his hair, saying, 'I haven't been much of a mother to you lately, but that's all going to change now.'

Ruth watched the scene, saw the love of Laura's face, and hoped to God that this was the start of a new chapter in the woman's life. She'd had no idea that Tommy had once had a little sister and now, for his sake, she hoped that Laura really would stay off the booze.

Thirty-Five

Five days passed and Denis Walters had only called to see his son once. On Wednesday, when Ruth arrived home early from work, he knocked on the door.

'My wife's coming home in the morning,' he said.

Ruth saw that his eyes were glazed with booze, but chose to ignore it. 'Blimey, it seems a bit quick.'

'She's gone against the doctor's advice and won't stay in hospital any longer.'

Yeah, but what was she coming home to? Ruth thought as she recalled the state of their house. 'If you give me a key to your place I can tidy it up a bit before she arrives.'

He swayed, but fumbled in his pocket. 'All right, I don't suppose it will do any harm.'

Ruth said nothing as she took the key, and was relieved to close the door. Christ, the man was a bloody disgrace, and she dreaded Tommy returning to live next door. Still, she consoled herself, Laura had promised she was going to turn over a new leaf, so maybe the lad would be all right. She grabbed her coat. 'I won't be a minute, Sally. I'm just popping along to see Nelly.'

'Hello, love,' Nelly said as she opened her door. 'Come on in.'

Ruth followed Nelly into her kitchen, saying without preamble, 'I've come to ask if you'll do me a favour.'

'Of course I will.'

'I want to give Laura's place a clean up before she comes home. It's in a right old state and I don't think I can manage on my own. If you'll sit with Sadie this evening I can rope Sally in to give me a hand.'

'I'll come along now if you like.'

'Thanks, Nelly, but I'd rather do it this evening. The kids

229

will be home soon and I could do without trying to clean the place with them under my feet. We'll start once they're in bed and asleep.'

'All right, I'll be down later.'

Ruth thanked her. Sally would be picking the kids up from school soon, and no doubt chaos would reign for a while. She smiled. Despite that she would miss Tommy when he returned to his own home.

That evening Ruth, with Sally in tow carrying a mountain of cleaning materials, went next door.

Denis Walters was out and, as they stepped inside, both almost baulked at the task before them. 'God, Mum, this is awful,' Sally said, her nose wrinkling.

'I know, but we can't let Laura come home to this.'

They tackled the kitchen first, Ruth saying as they worked, 'It's just as well you aren't going to see Arthur this evening. I wouldn't have been able to do this lot on my own.'

'Joe's gone to see him and no doubt the two will be discussing business again.'

'What will Arthur's role be in this new firm?'

'He and Joe will be project managers, and they'll be marketing the houses. As soon as they've got a good return on their investment, they'll plough it back into another development. That means looking for more land, and starting all over again.'

'It all sounds a bit risky to me, but I suppose they know what they're doing. I still think it's amazing how well Arthur is coping.'

'Yes, I know, and I realize now that having the amputation was probably the best thing. If the osteomyelitis had spread any further, he could have ended up losing the whole leg.'

'Talking about work again – I still don't know what Denis Walters does. I did try to pump Tommy, but the kid doesn't know. The man's always drunk, and what sort of employer would put up with that?'

'Perhaps he's unemployed.'

'If that's the case, where does the money come from for booze?'

Sally didn't answer the question, her hand covering her mouth as she heaved. 'Christ, Mum, look at this.'

Ruth went to her daughter's side, her stomach revolting too when she saw the contents of the cupboard. There was a part loaf of bread, thick with green mould, along with a dish of dripping, also covered in a layer of fur. She saw what looked like a remnant of cheese, hard and cracked with age and, as Sally lifted the lid of another dish, she stood back in horror.

'I don't know what this is – ' Sally gasped – 'but it's crawling.'

'Chuck the lot out, dishes and all. I'm sure I've got some old ones I can replace them with.'

Sally gingerly cleared the cupboard and then, with a bucket of soapy water and bleach, she cleaned the inside. It took another hour to finish the kitchen, and then they went upstairs.

Tommy's bedroom looked a pitiful sight, his bed coverings no more than a thin blanket and a couple of old coats. Laura's room wasn't much better and, sighing heavily, Ruth said, 'It's just as well I'm a hoarder, Sally. You strip the beds and I'll pop home and sort out some sheets and blankets. I'll find a few other bits and pieces while I'm at it.'

Sally began the task whilst Ruth hurriedly went next door, finding Nelly and her mother glued to the television set. 'Are the kids all right?' she asked.

'Yeah, there ain't been a peep outta them,' Nelly said, her eyes going straight back to the screen, and just in time to see *The Saint*, played by Roger Moore, lifting one eyebrow as a halo appeared over his head. 'Cor, he's a bit of all right, Sadie.'

'Nelly Cox, you're old enough to be his grandmother.'

'I know, but if I was a bit younger . . .'

Ruth left them to it, and going upstairs she delved in the hall cupboard, pulling out some old linen. *Blankets, where did I put those old blankets*, she asked herself. At last she found them, and then back downstairs she rooted out a couple of bowls, some spare china and a nice clean tablecloth. She threw some tea, sugar and a pint of sterilized milk into a shopping-bag, adding at the last minute a fresh loaf of bread, some margarine and a jar of jam.

Sadie, despite being engrossed in the telly, turned to see what she was doing, but thankfully made no comment. Ruth called a quick goodbye, getting only a murmur of response in reply.

She hurried back to the Walters' to find Sally with a sheen of perspiration on her forehead. The beds had been stripped, and Sally had made a start on the dusting, but she frowned saying, 'I daren't touch the curtains, Mum. They're so old they'll fall apart if I try to take them down.'

'I've got some spare ones somewhere, but we can't do everything tonight. As long as the beds are made up and the place is clean and tidy, that's the best we can do for now.'

'We won't get it all done, not unless we work through the night, and to be honest, I don't fancy being here when Denis Walters comes home.'

'You and me both, love. Let's get the beds made up and we'll leave it at that.'

'The bathroom's a mess too.'

'As I said, we can't do everything. We'll just chuck some bleach down the toilet for now.'

They put in a last burst of effort and, going downstairs, added the finishing touch, Ruth's nice clean cloth on the table. With a final look around Ruth said, 'Well, it ain't perfect but it looks presentable. Let's hope that drunken sot doesn't muck it up again before Laura comes home.'

'I wouldn't bank on it, Mum,' Sally replied as they thankfully made their way home.

Joe Somerton sat by Arthur's side, pleased to see him looking so chirpy. 'Any idea when you're going to get out of here?' he asked.

'Well, the infection I had in my stump has almost cleared up, so it shouldn't be much longer.'

'Well, that's good news.'

'Yeah, and thanks for being so patient, Joe. I still think you should have found another partner.'

'Not that old record again.'

Arthur smiled. 'I've been in this place for about four months now and can't wait to go home. Sally seems dead chuffed with the flat she's found and once we're in, no doubt she'll soon be inviting you for dinner.'

'I'll look forward to it.'

'Apparently there's a rather nice looking girl living upstairs

and, knowing my Sally, I wouldn't be surprised if she tried
a bit of matchmaking.'

'If she's nice-looking, lead me to her,' Joe joked.

'Oh, I don't know about that. If you hit it off you might
just move in with her, then I'd have your clodhopping boots
over my head.'

'Bloody cheek. I'll have you know I'm light on my toes.
Anyway, joking apart, I'm in no hurry to settle down, good-
looking girl or not.'

'You don't know what you're missing.'

'Huh, from what I've heard, as soon as you marry a girl
she changes and becomes more like her mother. It's curlers
in her hair at bedtime, nagging if you go out with your mates,
and apparently it's a capital crime to leave the toilet seat up.'

'My Sally isn't like that.'

'Well, you must be one of the lucky ones,' Joe told him.

'Yes, I am, and it's good that you and Sally get on so
well. She really likes you and has said what a good friend
you are.'

Joe hung his head. A friend, yes that was how Sally saw
him, but no matter how hard he tried, he couldn't deny his
feelings. He was in love with Arthur's wife, a love he knew
was impossible. Her feelings for Arthur were plain to see,
and though at one time he thought he'd seen something in
her eyes, he knew now that he must have imagined it. He
remembered how it had felt to hold her in his arms, to
comfort her, and how he had almost burst with anger at what
those bastards had done to her. He sighed. He'd have to
settle for friendship, but he'd stay as close as possible to
watch over her, and if anyone ever hurt her again, they'd
have *him* to deal with.

'You've gone a bit quiet, mate.'

Joe snapped out of his reverie, plastering a smile on his
face. 'Sorry, and anyway it's your fault. You've got me
thinking about that girl upstairs.'

'You'll meet her soon, and I hope you won't be disappointed.'

Oh, I will be, Joe thought. There could never be another
Sally, but once again for the sake of their partnership, and
their friendship, he was determined to fight his feelings.

Thirty-Six

It was a fight to get Tommy to school. Excited that his mother was coming home he wanted to be there when she arrived. Saying firmly that he would see her later, Sally dragged the boy along Candle Lane, depositing him with relief in the playground. She kissed Angel goodbye, hugged a still scowling Tommy, and then hurried home again.

As she turned into Candle Lane, Jessie Stone was on her doorstep, and she said as Sally approached, 'I've heard on the grapevine that Laura Walters is coming home today. We've had a bit of a whip-round and got her these.'

Sally stared in amazement at the proffered bunch of spring flowers, including early daffodils and tulips, her jaw dropping even further when Jessie spoke again.

'You needn't look at me like that. I've heard that Laura Walters intends to turn over a new leaf, and none of us had any idea that she'd lost a child. It explains a lot. If there's anything I can do, just ask.'

'How did you hear about it?'

'Nelly Cox told old Mrs Driver, and she told her neighbour, who passed it on to Maureen Downy. You should know that it doesn't take long for news to spread in the lane, and we still rally round to look after our own. I'm sorry to hear about your husband too. How's he doing?'

Sally realized that for the first time she was having a pleasant conversation with the woman. She told her about Arthur, accepted her good wishes, and after a few more words, said goodbye.

'They're nice, love,' Sadie said as she stepped into the kitchen. 'Are they for me?'

'No, sorry, Gran. The neighbours had a whip round for Laura Walters.'

234

'Blimey, I thought those days had long gone.'

'Me too, but it was nice of them. If you're all right for a minute, I'll put them in a vase and take them next door. They'll be a welcome sight for Laura when she arrives.'

'Of course I'll be all right. How many times have I got to tell you that I'm fine?'

'Yes, I know you are,' Sally placated, and had to admit that Gran did seem a little better lately. She arranged the flowers and, carefully carrying the vase, she went next door.

Lifting the letter-box she rattled it loudly, but there was no response so, taking the keys out of her pocket, she let herself in, calling as she stepped into the hall, 'Mr Walters! Are you there?'

The house was quiet and, walking into the kitchen, Sally saw that it was exactly as they had left it. She placed the vase in the centre of the kitchen table, pleased to see that it added a cheerful spark to the room, and then left, her brow furrowed. Had Tommy's father come home last night? And if not – where was he?

When the hospital transport arrived with Laura inside, Sally went into the lane. Jessie Stone was on her step too, along with a few other neighbours and, as Laura stepped out, Nelly Cox bustled up to her side. 'Welcome home, love,' she said.

Laura looked stunned. 'Thanks,' she murmured.

Sally surreptitiously looked at Laura's aura and frowned. It looked awful! Surely she shouldn't be home? She too went to her side. 'Tommy's in school, but I know he can't wait to see you.'

'I can't wait to see him too and thanks for looking after him. I'd invite you in, but I dread to think what my place looks like.'

'Don't worry about that. I think you'll be pleasantly surprised,' and turning Sally added, 'Nelly, will you sit with my gran for a while?'

'Yeah, of course I will.'

'So, I'm going to be surprised,' Laura said. 'Don't tell me that my husband has pulled his socks up?'

'Well, no,' and seeing that Laura appeared to sag, she urged, 'Come on, let's get you inside.'

'Are you all right, missus?' the driver asked.

'Yes, I'll be fine, and thank you. I didn't expect to get transport home.'

They went into the kitchen, Laura's eyes immediately alighting on the flowers. Sally led her to a chair which she sank in to and, breathing heavily, she indicated the vase of flowers again. 'Where did they come from?'

'The neighbours.'

'Really! And who smartened the place up?'

'My mother and I came round to tidy up last night.'

Laura lowered her eyes, but when she raised them again, Sally saw they were moist with tears. 'You've been so good and I don't deserve it. I've got vague memories of attacking your mother on the street, yet you've done all this.'

'That's all in the past,' Sally said dismissively. 'Now, would you like me to make you a cup of tea?'

'I don't think there'll be anything in the cupboards, but thanks for the offer.'

Sally picked up a battered kettle, filling it with water before taking out the cups and saucers her mother had provided.

'Where did they come from?' Laura asked. 'Don't tell me – your mother again.'

'Yes, but don't worry, she doesn't need them. My mother is a hoarder, and never throws anything away. These haven't been used in years and I'm just glad there'll be a bit more room in our cupboards now.'

The moisture in Laura's eyes now turned to tears, but Sally decided to pretend she hadn't noticed as she made a pot of tea. By the time it had brewed and she carried a cup over to Laura, the woman had managed to pull herself together.

'I must thank your mother and the neighbours for the flowers, but must admit I'm fair worn out.'

'It can wait, and after you've had your tea, why don't you go for a lie down?'

'Yes, I think I will.'

Sally waited until Laura had finished the last dregs of her tea and then said, 'Come on, I'll help you upstairs.'

When Laura saw her bedroom, there were fresh tears. 'I just don't know what to say,' she sobbed.

'There's no need to say anything. Just rest until Tommy

comes home. Now, are you sure you can manage, or would you like him to stay with us for another night or two?'

'No, but thanks anyway. I can't wait to see him, and to show him that things are going to be different from now on. I was lucky that the heart attack didn't do too much damage and, as long as I take it slowly, I'll be fine.'

There was something in Laura's eyes, and Sally had a feeling she wasn't telling the truth. Yet why would she lie about her health? Maybe she was imagining things, and maybe her aura looked dark because she was tired.

'Oh, by the way, Sally, have you seen my husband? He was supposed to visit me last night, but didn't turn up. Not that I'm surprised, of course, but I expected him to be here when I came home.'

'No, I haven't seen him. What time does he finish work?'

'He's a casual labourer and works when the mood takes him, or when he's sober enough. If he's at work today I doubt he'll show up until after six. If he isn't working, well, your guess is as good as mine.'

'If he doesn't come home during the day and you need anything, just bang on the wall and I'll hear you.'

'Thanks, I will.'

Sally smiled at the woman before making her way back downstairs. She'd noticed that the bed hadn't been slept in, and once again wondered where Denis Walters was.

For a moment she paused, an awful thought crossing her mind. Somehow she had a feeling that Denis Walters wasn't going to show his face again, at least not for some time, and prayed she was wrong.

Thirty-Seven

Ruth sat gazing into space. She had just read Mary's letter, feeling a twinge of envy. Her sister had travelled the world, having a wonderful time. She had written to say that on her way home she had found a job in a hotel in Spain, and was now in no hurry to return home.

Her thoughts turned to Tommy. She sighed heavily, but then her mother spoke.

'What's up? You sound like a lovesick cow.'

'I was just thinking about Tommy. I hardly see him now.'

'He's with his mother – she's keeping her promise to stay sober, and the boy's happy.'

'Yeah, I know, but I still miss the little tyke. When I popped in last night to see Laura he was already in bed. Tommy in bed before eight! Who'd have thought it when only a short while ago he was running the streets all hours.'

'Has she reported her husband missing yet?'

'No, and as she said, what's the point? His wardrobe is empty so he must have planned to leave.'

'How's she coping for money?'

'She's getting national assistance, and though it ain't a lot, she manages. Like me, Laura can make a nice stew out of scrag end of lamb, and she does wonders with minced meat. Last night she roasted a belly of pork and though it was nearly all fat, she said it was tasty.'

'With all the stuff you've sorted out, her place must look nice.'

'There wasn't that much, Mum. I found some old lamp-shades, and that's an improvement on bare bulbs. The curtains were old ones, too, though they look nice.'

'Not much you say. What about the cutlery, saucepans, baking dishes and china?'

'Yeah, well, they weren't being used, and some of it was stashed in the yard.'

'That yard looks like something out of Steptoe and Son. It's about time you sorted it out.'

'It ain't that bad, and now I've passed that old sideboard on to Laura, there's a lot more room. It's lucky I covered it with an old tarpaulin or it would've been ruined. I also found lots of stuff in the drawers and cupboards that I'd forgotten about.'

'Well, what a surprise,' Sadie said sarcastically. 'Ain't it strange that Laura and Jessie Stone are becoming friendly? There's a huge age gap between them and, if anything, Jessie Stone is old enough to be Laura's grandmother.'

'Perhaps that's what Laura needs. Someone older to keep her in hand.'

'You may be right. Jessie has taken to popping in every day to see her, and if Laura isn't up to it, she gets her shopping,' and with another sigh Ruth added, 'I still miss Tommy though.'

Sadie glanced at the clock. 'Sally should be at the hospital by now.'

'It's a shame that she's still too nervous to go out on her own at night.'

'I know, and it must be costing a fortune in cabs.'

As the theme music for *The Avengers* rang out, both women turned to watch the television. 'I ain't keen on this programme,' Sadie said.

'I think it's good.'

'I don't know what's good about watching a woman prancing about in tight, black leather and fighting like a man.'

'Diana Rigg looks great, and why shouldn't women be strong?'

'All right, don't go on about it or we'll miss the plot.'

Ruth sighed in exasperation. If her mother didn't like the programme, why was she watching it? However, not wanting to miss the action, she said no more.

'Hello, darling, how are you?' Sally said as she walked up to Arthur's bed.

'I'm fine.'

She leaned forward and, as their lips touched, wolf

239

whistles rang out. 'Shut up, you lot!' Arthur called, laughing as he looked along the ward. 'You're just jealous.'

'Can't we have kisses too?'

'No chance.'

Sally grinned at the usual camaraderie. 'What have you been up to today?'

'I've been practising on my crutches.'

'How did you manage?'

'It was a doddle and in another week I'm having my leg fitted.'

'Are you? That's great. Any news about coming home?'

'Missing me are you?'

'Of course I am.'

'Well, the news is that I'm to be let out of here on Monday.'

'Oh . . . Oh that's wonderful!' Sally cried.

'Yes, it's great, and I can't wait to see our flat.'

'We won't be able to move in until you're back at work.'

'Of course we will. What's to stop us?'

'Arthur, think about it. I still need to be with Gran until Mum comes home from work, yet I can't leave you on your own. How can I be in two places at once?'

'I'm *not* coming back to Candle Lane, and anyway, I don't think I could cope with the stairs.'

'Oh, Arthur, what are we going to do?'

'Look, don't get upset. I'll be fine on my own while you're with Sadie, and anyway, once I get my artificial leg, I'll be going to work.'

'You make it sound simple, but it isn't. What about your meals?'

'For goodness' sake, stop making mountains out of mole-hills. I'll have breakfast before you leave in the mornings, and you can leave me a sandwich or something for lunch. Don't treat me like a cripple, Sally.'

'I'm not, but it just doesn't seem right to leave you.'

'It's only for a couple of weeks at most – that's all, so give it a rest will you.'

'All right, if you're sure you can manage, I'll get the flat aired and ready.'

'Good, I'm glad that's sorted out. Have you arranged to have a telephone installed?'

'Yes, it's already in, and despite having been in storage the television is OK.' Sally frowned. 'I wonder if I can persuade Mum to have Monday off. Sid should be able to manage for one day.'

'Why should she have the day off?'

'I should have thought that was obvious. I want to be at the flat waiting for when you come home.'

'Home! Sally, you don't know how good that word sounds.'

When Sally arrived at Candle Lane, she was smiling with happiness. She would have to leave Arthur during the day, but he was adamant that he could cope, and thinking about it whilst sitting on the bus, she was sure that Elsie would pop down regularly to see him. He was coming home! Arthur was coming home, and it was wonderful.

'Hello, love, you look happy. Have you got some good news?' Ruth asked.

'Yes, Arthur's coming out of hospital on Monday.'

'That's good, but I've been wondering how he's going to manage the stairs.'

'He isn't coming here, Mum. We're moving into our flat, and talking about that, can you get Wednesday off?'

'Take the day off. What on earth for?'

'I want to be at the flat when Arthur arrives. Surely you can understand that.'

'I don't see why he can't come here first. You can go to the flat when I come home from work.'

'As you mentioned, how is he supposed to get upstairs to use the toilet? Please, Mum, it's only one day.'

'Bloody hell. I've had so much time off lately and I can't see Sid putting up with it for much longer. Oh, all right, don't look at me like that. I suppose I can ask for one more day.' Ruth paused, then added, 'Angel may not be too happy about leaving here, Sally.'

'She'll be all right, Mum, especially when she sees her daddy.'

'I hope you're right, but I can see feathers flying when you move out.'

'No, she'll be fine,' Sally insisted, crossing her fingers that she was right.

* * *

As soon as her mother arrived home the next day, Sally left Angel with her and rushed to Maple Terrace. She wanted to get the flat aired and ready for Arthur's arrival. As she went in it smelled a bit musty and Sally quickly lit the gas fire. She then put sheets on the bed, dusted, but then heard a knock on the door.

'Oh, hello, Patsy. Come on in.'

'Are you sure?'

'Of course I am. Why shouldn't I be?'

'After the things I told you, I wasn't sure that you'd want to see me again.'

'Don't be silly,' Sally said, urging Patsy inside. 'I'm afraid I can't offer you a drink until I get some shopping tomorrow.'

'That's all right. Does this mean you're moving in at last?'

'Yes, on Monday.'

'That's good. I was beginning to think you'd given the flat up.'

'Sit down,' Sally invited. 'It's a long story,' and as she related all that had happened, she saw disbelief on Patsy's face.

'My God, it's like something you'd read in a book. It's bad enough that your husband lost his leg, but for you to be virtually kidnapped, beaten and then abandoned, well, it almost beggars belief.'

'It gets worse, Patsy. I lost my baby too.'

'Oh, you poor thing.'

'It's all right, I'm fine now, and we can always try again for another one.'

'Yeah, and have fun while you're at it,' Patsy said, her eyes now dancing with mischief. 'Now then, is there anything I can do to help? I don't mind housework.'

'No, I've finished now, but thanks for the offer.'

They chatted for a while longer, but then Sally glanced out of the window. 'Patsy, I must go now. It's getting dark and I still don't like being out at night on my own.'

'All right, love, and I'll see you on Monday.'

Sally saw her out, and then throwing on her coat she left to go back to Candle Lane, smiling as she made the journey. Two more days, that was all, and then Arthur would be home.

Thirty-Eight

On Monday morning, Sally was hopping with excitement as she waited in anticipation for Arthur's arrival. She had insisted that Angel shouldn't be told that her father was coming home, resulting in heated discussions with her mother and gran. There were two reasons, she told them. One – there was always the last minute chance of Arthur's release being delayed. She didn't want to think about that, but with so many setbacks in the past, she was nervous of counting her chickens. And two, she had decided that the easiest way for Angel to accept the move, was by taking her straight to the flat after school. When she saw her daddy waiting for her, there was little chance she would want to leave him, making the transition easier.

Sally had packed their clothes, hiding the cases until Bert had picked them up, and now everything was ready.

There was a toot of a horn and, rushing to the window, Sally saw Bert's car. With a smile of delight she ran to open the door but, remembering how Arthur was adamant that he didn't want to be treated like a cripple, she stood on the step as he carefully climbed out of the passenger seat.

Elsie clambered out of the back and, with a little assistance from his father, Arthur adjusted his crutches, tucking them under his armpits as he now stood gazing at her. There was an air of expectancy about him, as if gauging her reactions, and Sally, seeing one trouser leg pinned up, found that she had to fight tears.

Now, clenching her fists with determination, she forced her eyes away from his leg, saying flippantly, 'Well – are you going to stand there all day, or are you coming in?'

'I'm coming in of course,' Arthur said, carefully moving forward on his crutches.

'I hope you've got the kettle on,' Bert said, his voice equally light. 'I could do with a cup of coffee before I go back to the office.'

'This is nice,' Elsie said as she walked into the sitting room.

'You've seen it before,' Sally answered, watching for Arthur's reaction.

'Yes, but I don't think you had the curtains up then. Well, son, what do you think of it?'

'From what I've seen so far it looks great,' and, turning a little clumsily on his clutches, he added, 'I'll have a look at the rest of the place.'

'We'll just have a quick cuppa and then we'll go,' Elsie said. 'I'm sure you two want to be alone.'

Sally, though silently agreeing with Elsie, shook her head. 'There's no need to rush off.'

'Bert has to get back to work, but I'll pop down to see Arthur tomorrow. I know you'll be with Sadie, so is there anything I can do while I'm here?'

'Just make sure he has something to eat, and at other times I'll leave him some lunch. I just wish I could stay with him.'

'He's a grown man, love, and he needs to feel that he's capable of taking care of himself.'

'Talking about me, I hear,' Arthur said as he returned to the room. 'The flat is great, Sally.'

'I'm glad you like it. Now, I'd best see about making us a drink.'

Bert and Elsie stayed for another half an hour, and then rose to leave. 'Don't get up, son. We can see ourselves out,' Bert said.

'I won't argue with you, Dad, and have to admit that I feel a bit whacked.'

'That's understandable, but you'll feel stronger as each day passes. Bye, Sally.'

'I'll walk with you to the door.'

Sally accompanied her in-laws out. As Elsie gently patted her arm, she said, 'Don't worry, he'll be fine.'

'Yes, I know he will, and thanks for picking him up.'

'He's our son, love. There's no need for thanks. We'll see you soon.'

Sally waved as they drove off, and then returned to the sitting room to find Arthur slumped in the chair with his eyes closed. 'Are you all right?' she asked worriedly.

He opened his eyes and for a moment they hardened. 'I'm fine, and don't mollycoddle me. Save that for Angel.'

'Yes, sorry.'

'Oh, love, it's me that should be sorry. I've got a horror of being treated differently and I'm being oversensitive. After being in hospital for such a long time, I feel a bit disorientated, but it's wonderful to be in our own place again Come here and give me a proper kiss.'

Sally ran to his side and, kneeling by his chair, she threw her arms around him, her kiss passionate. Yes, he was being a bit snappy, but knowing that he still suffered from phantom pain in the missing limb, it was understandable. And now, despite her feelings to the contrary, she would be careful not to make a fuss of him.

Later that afternoon, Sally left to pick Angel up from school and, as her daughter ran out of the gates, she said, 'Come on, I've got a lovely surprise for you.'

'Where are we going?' Angel asked as they turned in the opposite direction from Candle Lane.

'You'll see,' Sally said, gently squeezing her daughter's hand.

As they turned into Maple Terrace, Angel looked puzzled. 'I don't want to see that place again. I want to go home.'

'I think you'll change your mind, darling,' Sally said as she opened the street door. 'Go into the sitting room and see who's waiting for you.'

'Daddy!' Angel screamed, dashing across the room.

'Hello, princess,' he said, holding out his arms.

Arthur pulled his daughter up on to his good leg, and Sally held her breath, worried that Angel might knock his stump. Angel gazed up at her father for a moment, and then looked down at his missing limb. 'Daddy, when will your leg grow again?'

With a chuckle, Arthur said, 'It won't grow again, darling, but I'm getting a new one made for me. In the meantime I'll have to get about on those things.'

Angel looked at his crutches, her eyes alight with interest. 'Can I have a go on them?'

'They'll be too big for you. Now come on, tell me how you're getting on at school?'

'It's all right, but Tommy doesn't play with me now.'

'When I was a little boy, I didn't want to play with girls, and I expect Tommy feels the same. Surely you've made other friends?'

'Yes, and they're nice. Rita is my bested friend.'

'Best friend, not bested,' Arthur said.

'Can we go home now, Daddy?'

'We're going to live here. You, me, and Mummy.'

'I want to go back to Nanny's house.'

'What – and leave me on my own?'

'You can come too.'

'No, Angel, this is our home now. Anyway, I need my princess to look after me. I thought you were going to be my special nurse?'

'But . . .'

'You'll see Nanny every day – Gamma too.'

Angel sat quietly for a moment, her head cocked to one side and, for a moment, Sally thought her daughter was going to cry. But then she placed her hand on Arthur's cheek saying haughtily, 'Have you had your medicine today?'

'No, nurse, I think you'd better get it for me.'

'Mummy, where's Daddy's medicine?'

'In the kitchen. I'll go and get it for you.'

Sally quickly emptied a bottle of cough syrup down the sink and then rinsing out the bottle she filled it with cold tea. Returning to the sitting room and winking at Arthur, she said, 'Here you are, Angel, give him a spoonful of this.'

'I'll have to put my nurse's uniform on first,' she said importantly, and then frowned. 'Oh, no, it's at Nanny's house.'

'No it isn't, pet. It's in your new bedroom.'

'Wait there, Daddy,' Angel said as she scrambled off his lap, and running from the room, Sally followed behind.

The play outfit had been a Christmas present, but for some reason Angel had refused to wear it until her daddy came home. Now, with Sally's assistance, she eagerly put it on, adding the white cap as the final touch. There was a little case to go with it, containing plastic instruments, including a pair of scissors, thermometer, stethoscope, and tweezers. A few bandages completed the kit, and now Angel grabbed it before running back to the living room.

'Hello, nurse,' Arthur said.

Angel picked up the bottle of medicine, and Sally forced herself not to intervene as she poured the liquid into a teaspoon, spilling some in the process. 'Open wide,' she said.

When Arthur swallowed the cold tea he pulled a face of disgust. 'Yuk, nurse! That's awful.'

'I know, but it's to make you better.' Angel then took out the plastic thermometer, and asking Arthur to open his mouth again, she popped it inside. Obviously this was an impatient nurse, as seconds later she pulled it out again, her little face screwed up with importance as she read the gauge. 'You have a temture,' she said, now putting the stethoscope around her neck.

Arthur hid a smile, this time not correcting his daughter's mispronunciation of *temperature*.

She placed the stethoscope on his chest, and after listening to her daddy's heart, she adopted a haughty pose. 'I can't hear anything so I think you should lie down and have a rest.'

It was too much for Arthur, and for a while he fought valiantly to hold in his mirth, but Angel's expression was the final straw and he roared with laughter.

Sally found it infectious and joined in, her heart swelling with happiness. Arthur was home at last, they were in their new home, and as their laughter subsided, their eyes met.

'I love you,' Arthur murmured.

'I love you too,' she replied.

'What about me?' Angel asked.

'And we *both* love you,' Arthur said, dragging Angel on to his lap again.

There was a knock on the door, and when Sally saw Patsy on the step she invited her in.

'Are you sure?'

'Not that again. Yes, I'm sure, so come in and meet my family.'

'Hello,' Patsy said as she walked into the living room.

'Blimey, Sal,' Arthur said. 'You're right, I think Joe's eyes will be knocked out. Oh, sorry, love. Pleased to meet you and my name's Arthur.'

'I know, and this, I presume, is Angel.'

'Yes, but don't let her name fool you.'

'She's adorable,' Patsy said. 'But what's this about knocking someone's eye out?'

'Ask my wife.'

'Arthur, you and your big mouth. Oh Patsy, it's just that I told Arthur how pretty you are and we thought you might like to meet his partner, Joe Somerton.'

'We . . . this has got nothing to do with me. It's you who wants to do a bit of matchmaking,' Arthur protested.

'Really,' Patsy said. 'What's this Joe like?'

'He's tall, very good-looking and single.'

'Lead me to him,' Patsy said.

'Blimey,' Arthur spluttered. 'Joe said the same thing when I told him about you. Somehow I think the pair of you might just click.'

'See, I told you,' Sally said, adding, 'I tell you what, Patsy. Would you like to come down for dinner tomorrow night? I'll invite Joe so the two of you can meet.'

'Yes, I'd like that.'

'How about seven thirty?'

'Fine, but I must go. I only popped down to say hello.'

Patsy said goodbye to Arthur, ruffled Angel's hair, and then Sally showed her out. 'I envy you, Sally,' she said. 'You've got a lovely daughter and your husband's a bit of all right too.'

'Thanks,' Sally said. 'See you tomorrow.' And when she walked into the living room again it was to see Arthur cuddling Angel.

She smiled at the scene, glad that the transition to Maple Terrace hadn't been too difficult for them. Arthur was stroking Angel's hair and her heart surged with love as she looked at him. So many awful things had befallen them, but they faded into insignificance now. Nothing could ever be as bad again, and as the future stretched ahead of them, Sally welcomed it with joy.